THE
LEVI GENES

A SIMPLE, FACTUALIZED TALE OF EVOLUTION AND THE GENE POOL

O.E. **Vey**

Outskirts Press, Inc.
Denver, Colorado

THE LEVI GENES
A Simple, Factualized Tale of Evolution and the Gene Pool
All Rights Reserved.
Copyright © 2010 O.E. Vey
v3.0 r1.1

Cover Photo © 2010 D.E. Franck. All rights reserved - used with permission.

Outskirts Press, Inc.
http://www.outskirtspress.com

ISBN: 978-1-4327-2607-2

Outskirts Press and the "OP" logo are trademarks belonging to Outskirts Press, Inc.

PRINTED IN THE UNITED STATES OF AMERICA

Dedication

This book is dedicated to Levi, the luckiest person in the history of mankind; for Levi has **THE LEVI GENES**. Without Levi, there is no hope for God, for the gene pool or for humanity …

Table of Contents

Preface

How did we get here?

Was it God, aliens, accident or something else? The controversy continues to rage after many thousands of years of argument, speculation, wonder ... and murder.

Was Darwin right? Did we really evolve from apes?

Is the Bible right? Were we really created by God, POOF, just as we are today ... only naked?

Is it possible that we resulted from a miraculous accident, possibly involving a meteorite and some one-celled animals?

Or, were we planted here by aliens who check up on us every so often? Are the UFOs real?

Where does the truth lie?

For reasons that are peculiarly human, we really want to know. No, more than that ... we NEED to know! Where did we come from? How did we get here? Who's our daddy?

The truth in controversial matters like these is often hard to come by ... and harder to accept. Our social and religious training teaches us to disbelieve and ignore alternate ideas.

Over the centuries, searchers of the truth have been branded as heretics, witches and worse. How do we answer the questions burning in our minds and our souls if we fear searching for the truth?

In a daring and fearless expose`, *The Levi Genes* exposes the truth of how we got here and how we've developed over the millions of years. *The Levi Genes* holds nothing back and spares no one to find, expose and explain the truth in a manner everyone can understand.

At last, the truth is told ... the truth about our creation, evolution, the gene pool, the role of man and the fingers of God.

If you can't handle the truth, pretend it's all just a made up story. You'll sleep better that way.

Chapter 1 – Darwin and the Gene Pool

Welcome to the gene pool! The gene pool is the greatest artificial intelligence, genetic development and programming endeavor ever attempted in the history of mankind. It is the core of all that lives, or has lived, on our little planet earth. It is also the nucleus of what makes each and every one of us who we are, how we got to be who we are, and what our children will be like.

The gene pool is a special place created by God to help guide and evolve human life throughout our existence. The gene pool is a marvelous creation that will be explained in simple terms and in depth throughout this book. Don't worry about this being a complex topic or too hard to understand. *The Levi Genes* is written specifically to be easily understood and enjoyed by all ... even you.

Because you're reading this and are human (put the book down if you are not human), you are a select member of this very special world, first recognized by our ancestors many millions of years ago and popularized by Charles Darwin. Just by being born, you became a member of this special genetic collection. You are a vital and valuable member of the human gene pool.

Your membership was assured at your conception. Your birth was not guaranteed. Your long life is not guaranteed. Your happiness is not guaranteed. The only guarantee is that you, like all who came before you, will die and, hopefully, pass on your genetic history, experience and proclivities to the next generation of gene pool inhabitants ... your children, then on to their children.

The human gene pool is the summation of all that has happened and learned since the earliest form of bi-pods first stood on the earth. It also includes much learning from far away times and galaxies from the beginnings of the universe. You don't believe me? Read on and you will come to understand the reality of the gene pool.

The gene pool is a terrific place and your presence in it makes it that much more wondrous. Now, having said that let me be a bit more brutally honest. There are those of you that I really don't want in the gene pool with me, for the future of the human species. Nothing personal, but if humans are to survive, to thrive, to grow, to adapt and become better, there are some of you that just do not contribute to this goal.

In fact, many of you are just too embarrassing to be included in the same gene pool with the rest of us. Unfortunately, you like yourselves too much to see what a genetic embarrassment you really are. You will get help with that later in the book. Nothing personal, but you're just, what is the right word, let's say ... undesirable.

Who am I to say such a thing? I'm just someone observing and reporting this information to you. But, you don't have to take my word for it. You don't have to trust me, either. Read this book. Then look around you. Observe others. Observe yourself. You will discover for yourself that what I report here is true.

I would like to caution you as you read this book. Don't get too serious about it and keep your sense of humor handy. If you cannot find the humorous parts, have your friends point them out or explain them to you. If you don't have any friends, buy more copies of this book and hand them out. You'll make lots of friends.

Also, it will help your enjoyment immensely if you get over yourself. If you don't understand something, ask someone for help. If all this fails, get a towel and sit on the shore of the gene pool and pretend to read this book and *act* like you belong.

Charles Darwin gets general credit for first exploring and enlightening the populous about the gene pool. I use his name for its familiarity and for what it represents. Darwin did not invent evolution or the gene pool. He did observe and make note of his observations. He brought them to the light of public review and acclaim, and also public condemnation.

Darwin dared to bring into scrutiny ideas that were the core and foundation of religions around the world. People back in his day were taught that God was the center of everything. The people were taught this by the religious leaders who claimed that they, and they alone, were the direct representatives of God on earth. Some religions still believe this.

It was declared by these same "representatives of God" that we are exactly the same as we were in the Garden of Eden – that there is no such thing as evolution. Some religions still believe this.

Of course, this is just poppycock. Maybe you don't realize it or stop to think about it, but we live in a world of genetic change every day. Our problems, turmoil and angst over evolution appear whenever we include deities, gods, prophets, etc. in our genetic lives. We get really nervous when we challenge that which we do not understand. Our instinctual reaction is denial and to attack the messenger.

Our next reaction is to just nod knowingly and say nothing. Some of the best and most successful relationships are based on this coping method.

Are we special? Well, yes and no.

NO, in the sense that we are merely like a grain of sand on the beaches of the universe and of all time. We are not alone or unique. We are insignificant by comparison to everything else that exists. As you will discover, this is ok, because we are protected by our insignificance from forces that could destroy us all in a heartbeat and protected from things we don't understand by our ignorance.

YES, in that we tend to like ourselves a lot, as individuals and as a species, and *we* think we're pretty special. I do, don't you? We all think we're fairly important. Actually, some of us think we are more important than others. In fact, some of us *know* we are.

Some people are smarter than others, or taller, bigger, faster, or better looking than others … and so on. The differences are the things that make the gene pool so remarkable and so resilient. They are what make us special and needed in the gene pool today and in the future. And this is not new! Remember your biology classes? Remember your history classes? Remember the saying that history repeats itself? That what has happened in the past will happen again in the future? Trust me, you can count on it.

One thing needs to be answered before we go any further. Is genetic manipulation, engineering or change even possible? If it isn't possible, then the whole question of evolution and the gene pool is moot. The only two alternatives left would be; it must be God doing it all by divine perspiration or it's all purely by accident.

So let's ask, is genetic manipulation even achievable? Well, duh, of course it is! Humans have been doing it for many millenniums. Early civilizations bred horses, cows, oxen, sheep, etc. to make them docile, stronger, faster or better producers. The best of the animals were kept alive and bred together to reproduce the finest traits of each. The others were food.

The Egyptians were the first to domesticate cats (as domesticated as cats can be), which resulted in the genetically altered and emotionally stunted house cats we know and love today.

Scientists create mice of different colors and genetic make-ups to use in scientific testing. Breeders of racing stock use genetic engineering to breed better and faster race-horses, while breeding out other undesirable characteristics. Farmers breed cows for better milk and use seeds genetically altered for better crop yields.

The development of clones that are, essentially, man-made, is another dramatic step in genetic manipulation and engineering. Genetic changes to counter or cure diseases are starting to come into their own. And, of course, we all know what happens when cousins marry.

There can be no doubt that genetic manipulation can and does happen. Genetic evolution happens. Are we clear on this now? Good. I'm glad we were able to resolve that.

Now, let's move on to a more difficult question. Has evolution been occurring all through the ages without our intervention? Some people don't believe this has been happening, whether naturally, or divinely managed, or intelligently manipulated or otherwise. They believe that we remain *exactly* the same as Adam and Eve were. Of course, that is just silly. For one thing, we have belly buttons and they didn't!

O.E. VEY

Some people even believe that we came from monkeys! If this is true, perhaps it started like this: once there was a very unusual, obviously defective monkey born. This baby monkey did not have much fur and had a weird shaped head. The father disavowed all parentage. After all, what self-respecting monkey would admit that he fathered such an ugly baby?

This baby was ostracized from day one of its life because it looked different, it made strange noises, and had a hard time learning monkey-speak. It didn't like climbing trees and kept falling out of them. It kept walking upright instead of on all fours, like the others.

Eventually, this baby grew up and was kicked out of the monkey clan to fend for itself because it just did not belong. And there you have the first humanoid … a genetic aberration. Poof, just like that, man was born – a defective monkey.

Not really, it didn't happen that way. There was a lot more to becoming human than a deformed monkey.

Throughout this book, I'll tell you how it really happened. For now, just accept that there is abundant evidence that evolution is real. Some of this evidence is listed here, just to tug at those of you who refuse to believe or aren't convinced.

- Some animals self-procreate when their environmental and group dynamic conditions threaten the survival of their species. They put a whole different twist on the question – who's your daddy?
- Some animals change their sex when their environment or group dynamics result in an over or under abundance of one sex. They are the original transsexuals.
- There are no one-legged or three-legged animals!
- There are no trees in the Antarctic, because they could not tolerate the weather.

- Human noses point down ... otherwise we would drown in the rain and it would be very messy blowing our noses.
- Every time the earth cooled, animals that could not adapt to the cold died off. When it warmed back up, new species developed.

We are very familiar with Darwin, and his theory of evolution, in our daily lives when we don't think of it involving humans. Let's explore a few examples, which should leave no doubt that genetic "engineering" is a historical fact and is still alive and well today.

Have you ever thought of buying a dog? If so, you probably asked yourself ... what kind of dog do I want? Small, large or in-between? Aggressive or timid? Smart and focused or dumb? Short hair or long? A lap dog or a guard dog. Good with kids or aggressive? A Labrador retriever or a Dachshund? A champion or a mutt?

We think about it, we talk about it and we argue about it. Why? Because we know that the dog's parentage and lineage have a direct influence on the puppies. We know what we want and we look to the dog's past, his gene pool, to figure out the dog's likely future traits.

We also know and accept that breeders have purposely bred dogs for certain features and we are ok with that. In fact, we celebrate this in dog shows all around the world. There is a reason that a particular dog wins "Best in Breed" and others don't. Different breeds have different characteristics.

So, did this all happen by accident? Of course not. In the later centuries, yes, man was breeding dogs for particular characteristics. But, for millions of years before we started screwing around in the K–9 gene pool, the laws of gene pool survival were well entrenched and working.

In the old days, bread was made by hand, every day. Wheat was important. Farmers worked to cultivate wheat that had better yields so they would not have to work so hard (or starve to death). They also crossbred different varieties of wheat to create crops with improved nutrition and better resistance to bugs. This is another example of gene pool manipulation that helped mankind.

As a result, today, bread lasts for days before turning green or blue. Wheat is wholesome, easy to grow and resistant to bugs and disease. Can you really deny the fact that the wheat gene pool is real and has changed? Of course you can't.

Is it a good thing? Does it help the big picture of the world and the gene pool? Maybe. We'll see as we explore this more.

Another obvious example of man stirring things up in the gene pool can be seen in horses. Who cares about horses? If you spend any time at the race-track, you care a lot. Do you think race-horses just happen by accident? Of course not! They are bred for racing. They aren't good for much else.

For example, you couldn't hook them up to a farm wagon and expect to get much work out of them. But, we have genetically selected them and engineered them for a different single, specific purpose. The same goes for draft horses, like the Belgians and Morgans, or the quarter horse (famed for being very fast for a quarter mile, but not for long distances), and Shetland ponies. You get the point?

This process didn't start with man sticking his fingers into the gene pool and start stirring things around. Oh, no. If you look at horses throughout history and in different parts of the world, you will see the gene pool at work quite clearly. The American Indians rode horses that were much smaller because of their environment where great strength was traded off for stamina.

The same goes for the ponies in Siberia and Mongolia, which developed long matted hair to protect them from the bitter cold. They were also small. Why? Well, there wasn't an abundance of food up there and it took more food and energy to feed a larger horse than a smaller one. Larger horses died off because they couldn't maintain their health and warmth as well as the smaller horses.

Let's take another look at the farm, starting with pigs ... the other white meat. Pigs were bred to produce more good tasting meat and to be more domesticated. Wild boars just do not make good farm animals and are likely to kill the farmer. They don't taste all that good, either. This, in itself, is a good example of natural selection.

Pigs (hogs) were captured and bred to improve them and used to support humans, who were purportedly higher on the food chain. We found ways to use everything from the pig for ribs, bacon, and ham sandwiches. We wear the skin in shoes. We eat the skin as diet snacks.

We eat the meat six ways from Sunday. We even use the brain to make headcheese. We grind up all the rest for sausage and other less delectable uses. There is no doubt the role humans have played to develop the best pig.

Cows are another example of man's probing dips into the gene pool. Today's cows give more milk per day than ever before in history. This is because of genetic manipulation of the species and not just because the cows like us more. Today's cattle give us more and better meat than ever before, for the same reason. Consequently, we now have better ice cream, sour cream dip, filet mignon, hamburgers, T-bone steaks, milk shakes, and so on, than ever before in history.

One last example, not because I'm running out of them, but it's getting repetitive and I'm getting hungry. We all like to have our yards looking nice. We plant different flowers and trees around the house to have specific effects. How many of those plants have *not* been genetically manipulated by man? Answer? Zero.

Blue roses with red stripes are not naturally occurring. Disease resistant trees and flowers did not just happen. Yes, if we'd given them a few thousand years, some of those developments might have happened on their own, but we are a notoriously impatient species.

We've created some beautiful plants. On the other hand, we have Kudzu. It grows everywhere, thanks to the meddling of humans, and it just won't die. There is also poison ivy … if we are going to fool around with plant genetics, why haven't we found ways to eradicate poison ivy?

I digress. We can go to the local garden store and have our pick of all sorts of plants, flowers, shrubs, seeds, grasses and bulbs. All watered with the love of the gene pool and the human hand.

Now, if we put humans back into the equation … we have a plethora of examples of the gene pool at work and man at his worst, trying against hope to manipulate it. We humans like to play God. We feel we have a divine right, a duty in fact, to do so.

But we are fickle. Some species we manipulate very carefully and others we ignore into extinction.

We think we are at the top of the food chain until we go into Grizzly bear country or surf in shark infested waters.

I cannot resist one last small item. When a child is born, what do people say? "He has your nose", or "She has your hair" or "Where did the red hair come from?" Remember, there's a reason first cousins cannot marry.

Like it or not, we are all part of the gene pool. Survive or die. Sink or swim. We are the result of those who have gone before us. For the good and the bad. Deal with it and move on.

As you read on, I'll introduce you to the inner workings of the gene pool and explore examples of its impact on where we are today. We will also take a careful look at the human gene pool, consider how to improve it, and how to protect our future as a species. In fact, I'll show you how to save the gene pool from ourselves.

Chapter 2 – Gene Pool – In the Beginning

So what is a gene pool you may be asking? What does this Darwin guy have to do with it? And why is it such a big deal? Well, second things first. Charles Darwin is the historical figurehead for evolution and for getting the whole thought process on this topic started in the scientifically enlightened days of his time.

His studies were controversial and continue to cause arguments to this very day. In addition to his study at the Galapagos Islands, Darwin is commonly remembered for the saying: "survival of the fittest". Interesting thing about that saying is ... what is the definition of "the fittest"? I'm sure it is different for a shrimp than it is for a pecan tree.

Why is it such a big deal? It's a big deal because the gene pool is the genetic DNA history and makeup of all life on earth. The gene pool is what makes each and every species, and every individual in it, what they are. The gene pool gives them their pretty feathers, attractive smells, keen hunters' eyes, speed, instincts, and more.

It also passes on genetic history to help them adapt and survive, to be resistant to certain diseases, to swim or fly to the same home every year, and much, much more. Life as we know it could not exist without the gene pool. That's why it is such a big deal.

Just who created this gene pool and who manages it? A great question, one that has puzzled humans as long as there have been humans.

There have been many theories about this topic over the ages. Was it the Gods of our forefathers? The Gods of ancient Greece or Rome? The Gods of the Egyptians or Incas? The God of modern Judaic-Christian religions? The Gods of Islam or Buddhism? Space men? Martians? Meteorites? Lightening, lava, and some enzyme acid as the planet was being born?

For the first time ever, finally, you are going to have the truth revealed to you right here. Right now.

The truth is: the entity we know as God is actually a student at Universe University (Universe U) studying to be something we can't begin to fathom. The degree he is pursuing is also something we can't imagine.

The earth and our solar system are his lab space at Universe U. God created the gene pool to create and evolve life in his lab, our earth, and to guide life's development as he progresses through his schooling. In order to receive his final undergraduate level degree, he has to create intelligent life in his laboratory. He still hasn't made that happen and we have lots of evidence to support this assertion.

Now you know the truth. The *real* truth.

The Gods of ancient Egypt and Greece? They can be better understood as God's instructors checking on the progress of our young Universe U student and offering advice.

By the way, the word God, as we know him, is really an acronym for his real name: Giuseppe O'Neil Djiboutti. We just call him God … or Sir, for short.

Universe University

Universe University is THE place to go for all up and coming students who aspire to control worlds and galaxies and general physics. At Universe U, students learn how to actually *create* stars, galaxies and many forms of life. They also learn the secrets that make it all happen. I've had a brief glimpse of their curriculum and a few of the more interesting tidbits of their studies. I can definitely testify about how advanced they are and how pitifully backwards humans are.

For example, the universe is actually a lot older than our human scientists think. The best minds on earth calculate the universe's age at somewhere around 13 or 14 billion years old. Silly humans. It is actually more than 354 billion years old.

We think we have all the answers, yet we have so little data available and such small minds to process it. We are truly the big fish in a very small pond, especially in our own minds.

The event we point to as the beginning of the universe we call "the Big Bang". It actually did happen, about 14.7 billion years ago, but it was not the beginning of the universe. What really happened was a lab prank by some advanced Universe U students that went wrong.

They were playing with multiple galaxies and trying to do something that was still beyond them when the prank exceeded the capacity of their process to control it. They are like us, or we are like them, in this regard. The young ones want to flaunt the rules and see what happens when they try new things in their pre-mature phases.

As pranks go, it was a doozie. Certainly one for the year-book. The students involved got suspended for a while and had to pay for the damages, but in the end, things were put right and all ended well.

How does all this Universe U stuff work? It's similar to our own higher education system, but on a totally different scale. Early in their curriculum, students in God's area of study learn the simple elements of the universe ... stars, planets, gravity, dark matter, anti-matter, and other such "stuff".

One of their early tasks is to create a star system. They are given some parameters for their assignment, given a lab space, and left to their work.

As we know from our observations from earth, there are many different types of star systems of varying ages. What we are actually seeing is a small part of the Universe U lab spaces and the students' works. Earth is part of God's star system lab.

Once they pull together the materials for their assigned star system experiment, they have to create and ignite the star. This is the hard part for early students. It really is not as easy as it looks to ignite a star. It takes a lot of study, concentration, a steady hand and following the proper procedure *very* carefully. One tiny little misstep can easily ruin the star and cause the student to start over or continue on with the defective star they have.

Sometimes they end up with a fizzle star that looks pretty, but isn't good for anything, except holiday celebrations.

Or they could make a red dwarf star, which is tiny and hot, but not hot enough to actually ignite, and does not put out any useful light or have the energy a real star needs. It just sits there like a galactic lump of glowing coal.

Igniting a star is a critical skill and test that Universe U students must master before moving on. If they can't ignite a simple star, they obviously can't handle all the other challenges yet to come.

Once they get their star ignited and operating properly, making sure it is under control, they progress to dealing with the rest of their star system. This involves forming planets of different types while making sure that one of them can support the type of life specified in their lab assignment.

In the early years of their lab work, their star system is protected from interaction effects from other stars and nearby galaxies in the neighboring laboratories. These include such irritants as solar winds, galaxy gravitational effects, black holes, etc. The protective measures are removed later in the curriculum, once the students learn more about the intricacies and complexities of their assigned star system and, eventually, the universe.

Students also have to deal with the effects of interference "escapes" from other student experiments. These commonly come in forms of "Oops!" and "Oh shit!" events that we know as asteroids, nova stars, comets, wandering planets, colliding galaxies and energy bursts.

The Hubble telescope has taken many great pictures of some of the lab results of Universe U grad students. As we've seen in those pictures, some results have been more successful than others.

Such is the reality in a crowded lab. Stuff happens, students are not perfect and sometimes things spill over from one lab to another. With all the room in the universe, the lab space set aside for the Universe U students is still a crowded place.

Once a student has formed his star system and has had it checked off by the teacher, they are allowed to move on in their studies to another course of study: creating life. Using the star system they created and the lab goals assign them, the students now have to create intelligent life.

Intelligent life is not always what we would think it is. It can take on many forms, most of which we cannot fathom. But take my word for it … they are there. They are not here, but they could be if they wanted to stop by. Remember to always check under your bed, just in case.

Creating life is not a simple thing and it doesn't start with some trees and a naked dude in a garden. It starts small, as the Universe U students learn. It's all about the basics. They create small and simple life forms of many types and learn to care for them and to evolve them.

Along the way, the students learn about chemistry, thermodynamics, strength, hydraulics, biology, biologic computational theory, general genetics, micro-nano genetic design, environmental management, husbandry, and life form design. The learning process continues with more learning, more complexity and more variety as the students advance.

As I said, the ultimate goal is the development of intelligent life. But here is the kicker. The so-called intelligent life must operate, without intervention, according to a set of rules. These rules provide for its continued development as the lab evolves and changes throughout the remaining curriculum. These rules cannot allow the life forms die off. If they die off, the student flunks and starts over.

The student can help a little along the way with a tweak here and a nudge there. But the goal is for the student to develop a self-sustaining, intelligent life form that grows and evolves in accordance with a set of rules that guides its evolution.

Anyone can create life. That's freshmen stuff. The key is to develop life that sustains itself and evolves as conditions change.

We on earth know this rule-based process as the gene pool, or evolution or Darwinism. Universe U students learn early on that, for most life forms, genes are the starting and ending point for creating, changing and fixing life forms. They carry the basic building codes and the basic operating system of knowledge. This genetic operating system is coded into and implemented by what we call DNA. It shapes who we are, how we think, and how we grow, as individuals, as a species and as a life form group.

Sometimes the students fail dramatically, like with the so-called Nativity Star of Jesus fame. Nothing dramatic ... just a star that didn't work right.

Other times, they develop strange life forms that do weird things, like eat themselves. Fun as a prank or to scare your sister, but not so good for perpetuating the species is it?

Sometimes students play pranks on other students or they decide to try things they shouldn't, like mixing genetic material together to see what happens. Think of the duckbill platypus on this one.

Once a student has achieved the assigned intelligent life-form level in his lab, he graduates and can choose to go home and work in his family business or move on to grad school. In grad school, students continue their education, advancing to creating and managing multiple star systems, advanced life forms, more physics (such as faster than light travel), and management of multiple galaxies.

People often ask: what about black holes? What are they? Good question with a simple answer. They are the method used at Universe U for cleaning up a student's lab space so that another student can use it. It is the ultimate form of recycling with a super high-tech vacuum cleaner. New students come in and they start all over with a brand new, clean lab. Simple, straight forward, clean, effective ... and 100% recycled.

Back on Earth

The gene pool is the only rational and reasonable explanation for such things as birds developing feathers, instead of the original skin or fur that was too heavy for long duration flying. Or the variety of big and small dinosaurs our student God (at that time, probably in his second year of classes) experimented with. Some ate meat and some ate vegetation.

This coincides with the Universe U curriculum of learning about digestion theory, tooth types (meat versus vegetation), power and thermal management in animals of different sizes, hunting resource management, and the brainpower required to make these things happen.

It's obvious from our own study of these animals that their genetic compositions were fairly rudimentary, which is exactly what one would expect from a student in the early years of his education.

The dinosaur days all ended one day in a sudden event, commonly, and incorrectly, attributed to an asteroid that wiped the earth clean of dinosaurs, and most other life. In actuality, this event coincides with the end of a course and a mediocre grade for God. He got pissed and destroyed his class life-lab project by wiping it out and cleaning house with a big rock. He had to clean it up to start the next semester anyway, but took such a messy way to do it.

Oh well, whoever said God was not human? It wasn't an asteroid. It was an angry Universe U student with a grade he didn't like. Thinking about it, I don't think I would be proud of the dinosaurs, either. They just lacked a certain, I don't know, a certain something extra to be really extra special. Maybe a few more colors, or opposing thumbs, or a brain bigger than a walnut, or the ability to draw pictures. Something was definitely missing.

This is also the only rational explanation for the existence of the duckbill platypus mentioned earlier. Consider this. Mammals do not lay eggs, or have duckbills or webbed feet.

Things that lay eggs do not have fur and nurse their young.

The duckbill platypus is a mix of all these traits and is the only example of it. It lays eggs, nurses its young, has webbed feet (with claws!), and has fur – and it swims. It also has a poison spear in its hind legs and sensors in its duckbill to electrically sense food. It is totally unnatural! It's like putting fur on an alligator to keep it warm! It's just plain wrong!

What gives with the duckbill platypus? Funny you should ask. The duckbill platypus came about as the result of a drunken experiment late one night at Universe U when a bunch of genetic materials were stirred together to see what would happen. It is the only remaining example of such an unnatural mixing of genetics.

Knowing college students as we do, there had to be other times this kind of lab play happened when the results were not as, shall we say, "successful". But this one stands out in our world and still lives. Yes, a tipsy student playing mixologist with his chemistry set and Petri dishes.

I can just see it. "Let's mix a little mammal with some laying of eggs, a touch of nursing the young, a duck's bill, and throw in some webbed feet and some protective poison. Gee, I wonder what this would look like?"

It was not pretty, but it worked and survived. Even we humans know that some things are just not meant to be genetically mixed. Elephants and hippos? Not. Cats and dogs? I cannot imagine. Humans and horses? Only in Tijuana!

The gene pool is more than we can imagine or care to think about. It is just too complex. The results from playing with it are too great for our little brains to deal with. Maybe we should just close our eyes and let it be. Naw! What fun would that be?

Alright, back to the question ... what is the gene pool? It is the secret stuff in our DNA that makes us what we are, what the elephant is, and the fish and the plants. All species have had chances to change over the thousands and millions of years. Chances to adapt to changes in weather, food sources, competition for food and shelter, disease, etc.

Not all adapted too well and some did not make it at all. Others, like the cockroach and alligator, haven't changed all that much. What does that say about their design and ability to adapt just as they are?

The gene pool is the genetic makeup and heritage of all things living. The basis of the concept is that genetic directions and guidance, strengths and weaknesses are coded in the DNA of all living things.

A cucumber "knows" through its genetic operating system how to be a cucumber and not a fruit fly or a beanstalk. It knows how tall to grow, when to grow, what cells to make, what to do with the soil and air around it, how to defend itself, and how to make more cucumbers. Without this programming, it would not know how to reproduce and there would be no more cucumbers ... or horses, or birds or people for that matter. The gene pool is the way to pass on the recipe to re-create self, otherwise the species dies right there.

Just such a thing happened long, long ago with the first attempt to make kangaroos. A mammal that stood on two feet was the goal. With a big tail for stability and to counterbalance the tendency to rock forward and fall down, it looked like a success. It hopped, it wobbled, but it didn't fall over.

Because it stood on the back two feet, the top/front two had to be changed to be more useful for food gathering. It was also fast, helping its survival. Just one problem ... the babies kept falling off. In the excitement of success, someone (guess who) forgot a pouch, or an egg basket, or Velcro or something to help keep the babies from falling off.

We know that salmon lay thousands of eggs and immediately abandon them, hoping that a few hundred will live. That would not work for these kangaroos. Eggs were not the answer. Mostly because kangaroos are mammals and the rules stated that mammals did not lay eggs. (Yes, I know, I already explained the duck-billed platypus.)

So it had to be a live birth. And not thousands of tiny kangaroos. That was just not physically possible in the space available. One baby only, or maybe two in rare situations. But they kept falling off and dying, causing God to reboot the entire species over and over again.

In researching a solution to this dilemma, it occurred to God that the opossum might be a great example of how to solve the kangaroo problem. The opossum was originally from Ireland, hence the O'Possum. The Irish spelling was dropped when it migrated around the world and just became known as the opossum, or just possum.

The possum has a pouch and crawls all through the trees without losing its babies, usually. That's where God got the idea. What if the kangaroo had a pouch like the possum? The baby could be kept in there! What a terrific idea? So he tried it.

He experimented with different sizes and placements of a pouch. Not too big, not too small, not in the back, not underneath. Finally, success was declared. After many thousands of years, the basic baby-basket kangaroo was introduced to the world and remains essentially unchanged today. It not only reproduces, it no longer loses the offspring.

The gene pool seems to have worked well for the kangaroo. It has not always been so successful for others. The ability to adapt to changing conditions is one of the main constants for the gene pool successes. Those who cannot change, or who fail to change, will die off. If you don't follow the rules, the gene pool eventually will win out.

From time to time, we humans try and tempt the rules of evolution, but in the end, the gene pool always wins.

The gene pool is extremely complex. All aspects of the gene pool are interconnected to each other, directly or indirectly. It is the ultimate chemical equivalent of a spider web where a tug on any single strand affects all the others.

The programming that went into creating the gene pool is far beyond our current limited human comprehension. In fact, it applies a form of programming unknown on earth, called "spider-web code". Humans have a primitive form of this often seen in complex software programs. We call it "spaghetti code".

Let's look at the gene pool in less than full, scientific detail and seriousness to see if we can get a better understanding of it. After all, it *is* the center of all we are and will ever become.

The goals for the gene pool are deceptively simple:

- Survival of life is the ultimate goal.
- Survival of individual species is a secondary goal, but is NOT guaranteed.
- Interspecies rules are catch and kill, eat as desired.
- New species can be developed at any time.
- Old species can die off at any time.
- Life can be anywhere and in any form.

The gene pool includes a bunch of smaller pools for different species, many of which share genetic elements. Whether you like to hear it or not, monkeys and humans *do* have a lot of genetic makeup in common. We both even have opposable thumbs. Naturally there are differences. But all living things have some core genetic features in common.

The little differences are what give us the tremendous outward differences. If you look at life on earth in a wide, wide view, such as a Universe U student might, we are all part of the same genetic pool that includes *all* life on earth. We may even be related to life elsewhere in the universe.

We know the goals of the gene pool, which are pretty simple and straightforward. But, what are the rules that govern the gene pool? How does it work?

It isn't like I have the magic lab notes from God himself. No one on earth could decipher them if I did. I will not tell you how I know that these are the real rules, but as you read on, you'll see that I really do know. And so will you. The rules of the gene pool are deceptively simple.

Since survival of life is the primary goal of the gene pool. The species, and the individuals, which best follow the rules (the "fittest") will survive. If you mess with these rules, things will go badly very quickly.

Here are the rules for the gene pool, in no particular order, other than what I liked.

1. The smart ones get extra points and do well.
2. Those who make good decisions get extra points.
3. The lucky ones live.
4. Lazy loses.
5. The healthy ones win over the sickly ones.
6. The adaptable ones survive changing times.
7. Good looks win over bad looks.

The individual rules of the gene pool are not absolutes. They are all weighted against each other and the gene pool's goals. It's similar to some of the new-fangled fuzzy math that is popular. They are set, but not absolute, and no one single rule stands on its own. In their original forms, they are very complex and beyond our comprehension. So I summarized them here for better human understanding.

While I've had some limited insight into the genesis of these rules, I don't have any special direct broadband connection with Universe U to validate what I am telling you. If I did, would I still be here or would I be at Universe U?

I do have a lot of observations, a healthy curiosity, a little imagination and lots of scientific research added to my special Universe U access. I put these to good use validating the rules of the gene pool. Silly of me to think I could validate God's gene pool rules, but someone had to do it. You'll have to judge for yourself the truth in them as I explain them. We'll review each of these rules in depth later.

We first have to stop and actually think about the rules of the gene pool for a minute. I know thinking means you have to do some work, but come on, the fun is just beginning!

As I said, the gene pool's rules are not absolutes and are not independent of each other. All life has a mix of these characteristics. Some have more of one or two than others. I swear that some people I've met have all of one and none of the others.

A couple of examples may help you understand what I mean. Some people and animals are very smart, but if they keep making bad decisions, do we really want them in the gene pool? Do we really want them propagating and creating even more little bad deciders? Bad decisions are wrong for the gene pool and for survival.

For example, it may have been smart for the buffalo to run away from hunters trying to kill them, but running off a cliff in the process was not a good decision. The decision to follow the leader making that bad decision was also not the greatest.

If they had stayed where they were, a few would have been killed by hunters. Instead, because of a couple of bad decisions, thousands died following the leader off the cliff.

One other example, a person is walking with a couple of friends and lightning hits one of the others. Who do you want in the gene pool? The one who got hit by the lightning or the lucky one who did *not* get hit? Luck is important to survival and I'll take the lucky one any time.

At the end of the day, it is the best combination of characteristics that defines the "fittest" for survival, whether we're talking about the shrimp, the pecan tree, the mighty oak or humans.

From time to time, the gene pool needs a good cleaning out with a healthy dose of genetic bleach, if you will. Sometimes things get a bit out of balance and the rules need to be tweaked a smidgen.

Excessive bad genetic characteristics are the normal reason necessitating such cleansings. Too many negative characteristics build up for normal evolutionary action to deal with. From time to time, the gene pool reaches its limit of bad genes and needs to be purged and cleansed of all things that hinder success and continuation of life.

Think of it as genetic bulimia. But instead of vomit, a huge genetic flushing sound can be heard as the gene pool self-cleanses. It could be from an asteroid, the Black Plague, AIDS, locusts, ice ages or a killer flu. The genetic purges have been around as long as the gene pool.

Are they from the imaginative student at Universe U trying to stop some experiment he started? Cleaning up the Petri dish and lab gear before the next experiment? Correcting some ideas that didn't work all that well? Having a false start and starting over? Yes, yes, yes and yes. Just be glad that we're in

God's Petri dish he's bleaching and not in his commode. That leaves a really bad, bad visual.

How do these rules for the gene pool work? Those of you who did not sleep through biology class in high school, read on. Those who did, refer back a few pages to the fourth gene pool rule. We have learned that the gene pool makes changes on its own in response to stimuli and changes it doesn't like. Animals adjusted to the environment, people lost their hairy bodies (well, most of them did) and the appendix lost its use centuries ago. We are taller than generations back and humans have adapted to many climate changes (including ice ages).

Geese figured out how to survive winter by flying south to keep from freezing when they failed miserably at making igloos and parkas. And if anyone doubts the genetic element to preserve the species, try taking a baby away from its mother. Or try cornering a docile animal who thinks it is going to die (except domesticated cows). The genetic trigger is there to survive. Find a nice warm place for the winter. Do not do dumb things.

With each new generation, the gene pool makes small, subtle changes in our DNA that reinforce or reduce characteristics to help it achieve its goal: survival of life. As the earth changed over the millennia, life on earth changed. Species came and went. Some lasted a long time, some a short time.

But, every change followed a rule-based path towards the ultimate goal. We don't need the dumb, the unlucky, the unhealthy, those who cannot adapt or make good decisions, the ugly, or the lazy in our gene pool. Get out now! Leave! Be gone! No longer dilute, pollute and diminish the gene pool and our chances for survival!

Animals seem to have a clear sense that the gene pool is at work and they don't mess with it. They accept it and try to live by the rules. There is a natural order to things and they deal with it.

Check it out for yourself. Try catching a chicken. What does this have to do with anything but dinner? Just try it. The chicken will run all over the place, flap its wings, jump around, squawk, scurry around, and will be quicker than a 2–year old on a sugar high.

But, once it's caught, what does it do? The chicken just sits there all relaxed. It did its genetic part, it tried to defend itself and survive. The chicken knows the game is up and gives in to fate. It tried and failed, so now it waits for the gene pool to do its thing.

I once watched a frog in a similar situation. A snake was stalking it. So the frog, following its genetic survival manual, just sat there, frozen and camouflaged. Of course, the snake was not fooled and crawled up to the frog and grabbed its hind leg. The frog never fought back, evidently believing that the snake still couldn't see it.

Slowly, the snake got the frog completely into its mouth without the frog ever fighting back. It followed its genetic manual on frog defense and it didn't work too well. Next step … dinner!

Other frogs developed a poison that would have killed the snake. Kind of a moot point to the frog, but it stops repeat offenders. In addition, that snake would never get the chance to pass on anything to its children about how some frogs are killers. The gene pool is at work. The animals understand and accept this.

Mankind is the only species on earth that messes around with the gene pool on purpose. Why is that? Did we evolve to be smart enough to think about it? Do we have something the other species don't have? Did the others figure it out millions of years ago and are just keeping quiet about some secret we have yet to discover? Or are they trying to tell us to leave things alone and we can't understand them? Perhaps our ego prevents us from listening?

Either way, they live their lives and the world turns. No drama. Life happens. Death happens. Species come and species go. For them, it is as it should be, as the gene pool dictates. For man … who knows?

Will man ever learn? The short answer is − no. We have to try to fool around with things we don't understand. Maybe it started in the Garden of Eden when God told his human prototypes that things were all cool and everything would be provided for them. "Just don't eat my lunch that grows on that tree over there." He told them.

Life was soooo simple. All they had to do was sit back and enjoy the situation. But, they had to screw up a good thing. Here is how it really went the first time God told us to chill out, relax, enjoy the goodies and love each other.

God (by now a beginning Junior at Universe U): "Alpha and Beta, welcome to my experiment. Things are going well, so far. You will be well cared for. I have the atmosphere controls set to be very comfortable, so there should be no drama from bad climate or colds. You are safe here with nothing to harm you. You are in my fifth mini-lab or den, as we call it here − more commonly referred to as the E-den." (Notice how God has such a great imagination for names?)

Alpha (a male and NOT some lame Judaic-Christian name like Adam … duh!): "Who is that? It sounds like Bill Cosby. Who's there?" To Beta "Hey, who are you?"

Beta (of course a female and NOT some lame Judaic-Christian name like Eve … duh!) "You talking to me? Are YOU talking to me? Are YOU talking to ME?! Who are you?

What do you want? And why are you talking to me?"

Alpha: "Of course I'm talking to you. Who else would I talk to? The grass? Christ, what an attitude. Chill out a little. Did you hear that other voice?"

God: "Alright, knock it off. There's plenty of time to act like you're married later. I have some important things to talk to you about. You two are the start of great things to come. I'm going to get a great grade and a fellowship in some really neat institute from this. So don't mess things up for me. I went through a lot of effort and study to give you everything you'll need. There's plenty to eat, no danger, plenty of shelter and good weather, so relax and chill out for a while. Ok?"

Alpha to Beta: "Do you hear that voice? It DOES sound like Bill Cosby? Where is it coming from? What's he talking about?"

Beta to anyone who would listen: "Great, I get created and look at what I have for company, a dude who is hearing things from the future. All I want is some peace and quiet. And maybe a beer."

God: "Look, this is God, your creator. I made you and everything around here. I've been working around the clock for the past 6 days. It took a while, but it's all done now. I'm taking a little nap and then we get to the real work. For the time being, you have everything you need and should be very comfortable. There's just one thing ..."

Alpha: "There's always 'just one thing'."

God: "Fine, but this one is important. Don't eat anything from that tree over there. It's my lunch and specially grown just for me. Other than that, eat anything else you want and do whatever you want. I'm trusting you while I take a day off. Ok?"

Beta: "I heard him that time. You're right, it does sound

like Bill Cosby. Where's Noah when you need him? What's he talking about: resting and lunch? What's a tree?"

Alpha to God: "What tree? What's lunch?"

God: "That tree over there with the red fruit. That's the one. Do whatever you want, but leave that tree alone. It's mine. Why don't you go play with the other animals and name a few or something? They've all had their shots. Go ahead."

Alpha: "That tree? You call that a tree? It's more like a poorly cared for bush? You call that a tree when it's really a sad excuse for a bush? Is that how you take care of things around here? You going to treat us like that, too?"

Beta: "What tree?"

Alpha: "That big bush over there. He says not to eat the things hanging from it. It's his lunch, whatever that is."

Beta: "Why?"

Alpha: "How should I know? You ask him. I just got here for crying out loud."

Beta: "Why didn't YOU ask him while you were talking to him? Why do I have to do it? Do I have to think of everything?"

God: "Look, just do as I said. Geesh, maybe I made a mistake with you two. You guys are a mess."

Beta: "This tree?"

God: "Just get away and leave it alone. Go play or get a tan or something. Go make babies, maybe."

Beta: "Oh yeah, right, you would think of that! You men are all alike! Don't play with the fruit, but go fool around with Alpha. Yuck! Then what? Tell him how great he is and cook some dinner? Is that why I'm here?"

Alpha: "What do you mean – we're all alike? I'm the only one you've ever met. And fool around? I don't even know how! And I'm not sure I would if you were the only woman on earth."

Beta: "Hating men is genetic. God made me do it. And don't give me that crap about not knowing how. I saw you behind the bushes over there before."

God: "Oh crap. What have I done? Is this what the professor meant by unexpected consequences? Look, you two, just forget about it. Do whatever you want. Just leave my lunch tree alone! Got it?"

Beta: "Right. Leave your tree alone. Like it's such a special tree. An overgrown bush is what it is. Silly red things on it don't look all that special, either. Didn't you water it?"

Alpha: "Hey, I'm hungry. What's there to eat?"

Beta: "Why are you talking to me about that? Am I supposed to feed you? What do I look like, your mother? Go try a berry."

Alpha: "Well, you know, now that you mention it, I never really did get to know my mother. I wonder what she was like."

Beta: "Probably long with a round bottom and full of genetic material. Get over it. Here eat this."

Alpha: "What's that?"

Beta: "I found it on the ground – kinda. Go on. Eat it and let me know how it is."

Alpha: "Hmmm, nice and juicy, kinda sweet. You try."

Beta: "You're right – it is pretty good. No wonder God wanted to keep it all to himself. Just like a man, he didn't want to share the good stuff."

Alpha: "Beta! You didn't take this from HIS tree, did you?"

Beta: "His tree, our tree. A tree is a tree. Anyway, it looks more like a bush than a tree. Maybe he should be more careful with where he puts his food. Besides, it didn't have his name on it."

Following a short rest after six days of hard work, God returns to his lab, E-den, and sees Alpha and Beta lolling around getting rid of their tan lines with big smiles on their faces. He knew immediately.

"You ate from my lunch tree, didn't you!" he yelled. "I told you not to eat that. Now you've ruined everything and I don't have time left this term to start over. Oh, this is terrible."

Alpha looked up at God and said "What tree?" and smiled at Beta who winked back at him.

And so it began.

Lessons learned? Did anyone learn anything from this experiment in the human gene pool? Who made the good decisions? Who was lucky? Who was adaptable? Who was lazy? Who was good-looking? Who was healthy? Any guesses? My answer is – we don't know yet. The gene pool is still figuring it out.

You see, the gene pool, and its Darwinistic nature, moves slowly. We know what it wants, but it is not all that easy to achieve. If it was, God would have gotten it right the first time.

Did we evolve for the better or for the worse? Have eons of eating apples, loosing body hair, naming animals, begetting, slaying each other, learning to wash our hands, inventing electricity and curing polio…was it for the better or the worse?

As I said, humans are the only life forms on earth that try to screw around with nature. To try and control it, to change it, to understand it, to make it better, to make it theirs instead of God's.

Animals just leave well enough alone. But humans, now that is another story all together. As just seen, we can't be trusted with a simple tree (or bush). We can screw up perfection without trying. Just give us half a chance and stand back.

We've tried playing God for as far back as there is written history. Take ancient Egypt for example. Remember all those stories about locusts, bad crops, the Red Sea parting, no rain, etc.? Maybe the gene pool (or God) was trying to purge something that didn't fit the big plan (or God's class objective)? Maybe the Pharos couldn't take a hint? Maybe someone thought they were too smart or too good for such things.

More likely, they were just too damned stubborn. They had plenty of warnings. You would think they would take a hint. But, noooo. They were too "smart" to take a hint. A blind man would have seen those hints.

It wasn't like they were dumb. They had to have something going for them to build all those pyramids and buildings. But they just didn't get it. Sometimes we humans just get full of ourselves and can't see the forest for the trees.

Actually this is a genetic condition passed on by God when he made Alpha and Beta using some of his own genetic material. God had a terrific ego and an insecurity complex. The shrinks would have a field day with him.

Rome and ancient Greece also forgot these things. Both of them, among others, were interfered with by God's instructors. They interacted with the human development project to get a first hand understanding of just what God created. Kind of like a mid-term check on a long-running class project. But, the instructors interfered with humans and affected their natural responses, instilled in them by God.

This skewed the Roman and Greek view of things. Remember how they had a lot of "gods" visit them and they had "special relationships" with them. Keep in mind, the ego humans inherited?

The Greeks and Romans must really have thought they were something special if the "Gods" were talking with them and they could call on them for special intercession. A storm here, lightning there. Some riches for me. Some death for him.

Still, their great societies died off, as all of them have. The gene pool wins in the end. It just matters whose end it's in when it wins.

Our own egos keep getting in the way and we forget just how frail we really are. It doesn't take much to kill us or put us in extremis. But, forget we do, over and over and over again.

Are we to follow the Greeks and Romans? Have we learned enough to not repeat the errors of the past? Has humanity matured? Can we stand on our own? Can we beat the gene pool? Let us read on and find out.

Chapter 3 – The Rules of the Gene Pool

In this chapter, we'll take a closer look at each of gene pool's rules for what it calls the "fittest". The gene pool and its rules ARE real. Understanding them is important to getting a notion of where we are in the big scheme of life and where we are headed. How can we survive them? What can we do? What do the rules mean to us?

Are we destined to fall as other great societies (like the ancient Greeks, Romans, Incas and Egyptians) fell? They had the scholastic "Gods" of Universe U on their side and they didn't last. They were smart, decent looking, hard working. What was their problem? Why did they not survive?

Why should we be any different? Have we had any Universe U instructors visiting us of late? Are they in UFOs? Anyone notice any special intercessions to cleanse the gene pool? Things like the Black Plague, AIDS, asteroids, a flood, earthquakes, flu epidemics, polio or tsunamis?

In the golden years of the gene pool (no, I don't know when they were or if they've even happened yet), the rules of the gene pool reigned supreme. Survival of the fittest. Simple as that.

If you did not feel well, there was nothing to come along and make you better. You had the right genes to survive or you didn't get the chance to pass on your bad genes to others. If you were a plant, you grew, you were eaten or you died. If your parents had good genes, they passed them along to you and whatever siblings lived.

Survival of the healthy was not just a concern at birth or for the very young. Oh no, this trait continued throughout a species lifetime. Catch a cold, a flu bug, a germ from somewhere, eat someone or something that made you sick and you had to have good genes to survive it. If you were hurt from battle, or falling, or rolling into a fire, or getting gored or kicked by an animal, or got stepped on or had a toothache ... you survived or you didn't.

As medical advances slowly crept beyond the eye of a newt, the root of a bush and three Hail Mary's, the odds of living improved. But to this day, doctors universally know that some patients are going to live or die ... just because. It has nothing to do with the level of care or medicines given them. This is the gene pool at work.

Remember the 7 elements of the gene pool? They all work together to support the gene pool's prime directive, which is survival of life.

1. The smart ones get extra points and do well.
2. Those who make good decisions get extra points.
3. The lucky ones live.
4. Lazy loses.
5. The healthy ones win over the sickly ones.
6. The adaptable ones survive changing times.
7. Good looks win over bad looks.

Let's take a closer look at each of them.

1 – The smart ones get extra points and do well

It makes sense that the gene pool would reward smart individuals and would want each generation to be as smart, or smarter, than the previous ones. The gene pool certainly does not want dummies swimming around in it, or floating in it or playing along its shores. The "smart" gene helps a species and its individuals make better decisions, to be adaptable, to discover new things. It helps, but does not guarantee, avoiding stupid decisions that kill off life.

It also includes some limited memory. Smart animals find food and water and remember where they are, so they can find them again when they are hungry or thirsty. Dumb animals, and those with little memory, forget where the food and water are and die from starvation. Bad for them, good for the rest of us.

Smart animals do not just run off a cliff because the others are doing it. They stop and look, see how dumb it is, and turn around. Of course, sometimes they forget that there was a good reason for running in the first place. That's when they turn around and get eaten. Just like running off a good cliff, some kids jump off a good bridge just because everyone else is doing it. We know how that excuse turns out.

Smart animals learn to stay away from predators and things that will hurt them. They don't eat the poisonous berries because good ol' Terrill died when he ate them. They store nuts for the winter and eat plenty of food for hibernation.

Smart means the invention of medicines that heal, and clothes that protect us from the elements, and weapons to defend ourselves and catch other, less smart, animals.

It means inventing language to pass on knowledge from generation to generation. Smart ones learn from others, without having to start over with each generation. Can you imagine if each generation of babies had to figure out how to grow up and feed themselves and survive without some inborn knowledge or instinct?

Without some natural core database to start with: who would tell us what others around have already figured out? Such things as, which berries are deadly and which animals will eat you? Just ponder this for a minute. What if each generation started over from scratch? It would not be a pretty picture.

The smart ones see danger coming and tell the others to run away from the danger. The dumb ones do not listen and become dinner. The smart ones get away.

If people are not smart enough to follow the crowd when they should, or have no memory of why they are running in the first place, they loose and the gene pool wins!

The gene pool needs the smart ones to survive. No rushing off cliffs just because it seemed like a good idea at the time. Generally, one has to have a damned fine reason for running off a cliff without something soft to land on. Otherwise, it is not smart decision.

Maybe some individuals were smart, or lucky, enough to let a few hundred others jump off first and had something soft (them) to land on.

Other examples of smart, you say? Ok.

Mankind is starting to get smarter. We developed medicines that heal diseases and we learned how to fix broken parts. If we were not smart, the gene pool would have dramatically reduced our numbers. Of course, we still haven't gotten smart enough to figure out how to get along with each other.

Deer somehow know to hide during the hunting season. If they don't, it is their last hunting season.

Smart zebras let others go first when drinking at the river. Polite? No, just letting the stupid zebras find out if there are crocodiles in the water.

Geese fly south for the winter, no dummies there. When flying in formation, the lead goose only flies in the lead for a short while, and then falls back and another takes his place. Flying up front is harder than flying back in the formation, so they take turns. Smart, right?

Humans learned to live in caves, then tents, and so on. Smart people moved away from the glaciers and survived. Those that didn't move became popsicles.

Sometimes we're too smart for our own good. Like when a man brought two armadillos into Florida from Texas because he thought they would do well. And they did! Now they are all over the damned place. They are slow and not good eating. You can't cook them in the shell like a turtle and they add nothing to the system there.

I would say they are as dumb as a brick, but that would be an insult to bricks. They are everywhere. How did they survive? Are they smart enough to act like they are dumb and fool the gene pool? Naw.

What do they have that the gene pool wants? No one knows.

There are so many of them killed on the Florida highways that they've been named the unofficial Florida State Memorial Animal. They dig and waddle around, but don't climb. Also, they are known to only be found in one of four natural positions:

- with all four feet on the ground;
- on one side, after getting hit by a car;
- on its back with all four feet in the air, after getting hit by a car;
- flat as a pancake, after getting hit by a car.

No one knows why they survive or what they add to the gene pool, but they thrive. Dumb as dirt, but they must have something going for them. Remember, in the gene pool, no single genetic factor ensures survival. It is a matter of special combinations of factors.

The armadillo is an excellent example of this rule in application. If smarts, or the lack of it, were a single deciding factor, there would be no armadillos left ... they would be extinct. Maybe one day, someone will figure out just what that combination is for the armadillo. Till then, it remains a ponderment.

Let's look at a more recent example of how being smart is important, but can backfire on us, if we are not careful. Take the African killer bees, please, take them.

They were imported into South America to help beef up the strength and survival of the local honey bee species that already thrived there. Good was not good enough, so we had to be smart and make things better.

Now, these killer bees, which have literally killed scores of people and hundreds of animals, have moved all the way up into the southern US. Yup! They were so good at being aggressive that they moved all the other bees out, ruined the honey business and killed people.

We still have not found a way to selectively kill them off and we can't kill all the other bees just to get to the killer bees. One wonders what the smart humans will come up with next for this problem. Stand by for more comedy brought to you by humans trying to be smart.

Will we ever learn that sometimes it is best to leave things as they are? Probably not, if the past is any predictor of the future, which it is.

2 – Those who make good decisions get extra points

As I demonstrated with the armadillo, being smart is not good enough. We all know smart people who make bad decisions. From little things, like that tie just doesn't go with that shirt; to big things, like let's start a war right about…let's see, right about … here. We all have examples of things we've done that seemed to be the right thing to do at the time, but that history proved otherwise.

For the general welfare of life on earth, and the gene pool, good decision-making is important. You better be very good with that "seemed like the right thing at the time" excuse if you plan on surviving in the same gene pool that I'm in.

Good decision-making is one of those traits that works well with smarts, but does not necessarily require smarts. In the history of survival, the gene pool needs survivors who make good decisions.

Take, for example, how the American Indians used to sometimes hunt buffalo by getting the herd running and head them running towards a cliff. The lead buffalo, seeing the cliff coming, would panic and try to stop, but the thousands of buffalo behind him just pushed him forward and over the cliff.

Sometimes, there would be a lucky buffalo, let's call him Shep, who decided to wander off to see what kind of grass grew on the other side of the hill. Shep was having a fine time dining on the greens over the hill when the ruckus started that got the others stirred up and running hell bent for the cliff.

Shep missed all the excitement because he decided to wander off and explore a little, to see if the grass was greener on the other side of the hill.

When the herd was attacked, good 'ol Shep was not there, so he didn't go over the cliff. Shep also had the good sense to not run to the herd and see what was going on. He lived to pass his trait of good decision-making on to his children.

Of course, he also passed on his tendency to not follow the heard and to wander off. I sometimes wonder how that worked out for Shep and all the little Sheps that came after him.

Good luck? Good decision-making? Some of each? Only God knows. What we know is that good decision-making plays a part in the gene pool's rules and Shep lived a while longer, in part, at least, because of his decision-making.

As we've seen, the gene pool looks favorably upon individuals who make good decisions, but haven't a clue as to why or how, as in Shep's case. Decisions just happen. How can you ignore that? Making good decisions means survival, usually.

Suppose you're lost in the woods. Making good decisions would be critical to survival.

If something were trying to eat you, some good decisions would certainly come in handy.

For the cross-dresser on the Titanic, cross dressing meant survival, since only women and children went on the lifeboats.

Other smart decisions are not so time critical and one can take some time to think about the choices. Should I take that new job? Should I marry him? Did I take my pill today? Should I have an abortion? Should I be driving this fast?

Yes, good decisions are definitely important to the gene pool. However they happen, we want good decision makers in the gene pool.

There are two things, however, that are deadly for decision makers in the gene pool. One is taking too long to make a decision. For example, while you are trying to decide whether or not to run, something else eats you. Or your mind wanders and you hit the ground while trying to figure out if 'now' is a good time to open your parachute. Or wondering if that high wave really is a tsunami and how fast you can swim.

Making a timely decision is important in the gene pool. If you can't decide, or you take too long, we don't want you. Imagine an airline pilot who can't make a decision when things get dicey: "Maybe I should turn off the engines. Or maybe not. Maybe just one of them. Right. Which one? The left one. No, the right one. No, the ..." *crash*.

The second deadly error for decision-making is making the wrong decision. Everyone knows someone else we think of as smart who makes some dumb decisions. We've all watched baseball games when the batter swung at a pitch that was waaay out of the strike zone. What was he thinking about – golf? A blind man could see that ball was way low!

How can people who are so smart bankrupt an entire automobile industry? Don't ask them, they don't know either.

Nothing surprising here, but generally, bad decisions bring bad results. That is why they are called *bad* decisions. (Duh!) No one would argue that General Custer was a smart man. But, a bad decision on his part to attack a huge collection of Indian tribes killed him and all his troopers. The decision of individual troopers to stay and fight, in spite of the odds screaming "Get the hell out of there now!!", contributed to their deaths. But, one bad decision and that was it.

Nuclear weapons and nuclear power are also on this list. We just HAD to go and find a way to kill more people with less damage to ourselves. Everyone else was doing it. We just had to have it first. And we did. And we scared ourselves silly by the massive destructive forces involved. This led to MAD, Mutually Assured Destruction, which became the basic policy of the Cold War that was supposed to keep things in check and prevent nuclear war.

The concept of MAD was that nuclear weapons were so powerful (scary) and there were so many of them, whoever used them first would be assured of massive retaliation and complete devastation by the other guys. The other side effects, like the winner would also be destroyed along with half the world's population, were downplayed, as long as we won. This was brought to us by some very smart people.

Eventually, we learned to turn nuclear energy towards more peaceful purposes, namely power generation. Thankfully, the smart ones who wanted to use nuclear bombs to create a big sea-level canal across the Isthmus of Panama didn't make the final decision on that one. (True story.)

But look at what we have instead. Massive amounts of un-usable nuclear waste and no place to safely store it. The waste from all these nuclear power sources, not to mention all the other nuclear sources, remains radioactive for thousands of years. We didn't have any good plans for keeping this waste safe (and not killing everyone within a hundred miles of it) when we started this journey.

We still don't! Thousands of tons of this waste are created each year. This particular item really could use a good decision before really bad things happen. Maybe some smart person will figure out a way to send it into the sun and help the sun last a little longer. Until then, don't go near the storage areas unless you want to glow in the dark.

One more bad decision example. Pickett's charge across the corn fields of Gettysburg, PA during the civil war. General Picket was a smart dude. There's no doubt about that. But why in the world would he order tens of thousands of his men to charge across a mile of open corn fields facing tens of thou-sands of Union soldiers and cannons?

Do you know how many places there are to hide in that corn field in July? None! How long does it take to cross a mile of corn field? About an hour in a good war! And in broad daylight! They didn't have a chance. This was a really dumb decision that had to have a huge impact on the gene pool of the United States.

Decisions, good and bad, have consequences. Some small, others very large. The gene pool is well aware of this. It tries to reward the good decision makers and eliminate the bad ones. We need good decision makers in the gene pool. But, good decisions, by themselves, just are not good enough.

3 – The lucky ones live

Luck can't be explained. Some have it and some don't. Some have it now and then not later. Some have it when it counts and don't when it doesn't count. Luck happens. Good luck. Bad luck. It happens to everyone and everything.

Naturally, the gene pool wants to keep those around who have good luck. Bad luck can do nothing but bring bad things upon the gene pool. We need the good luck.

Like the person who just happens to buy a winning lottery ticket when they normally don't buy one. The golfer whose partner gets hit by lightning leaving the golfer unhurt. Or Shep, the buffalo, who happened to wander off from the herd at just the right time to avoid getting chased off a cliff.

When skill, and smarts and everything else fail me, I'll take luck anytime. At the roulette wheel in Las Vegas, I'll take good luck and rejoice. When the tree falls and misses the house by 2 feet – I'll take it. When an out of control car just misses someone walking along the sidewalk – I'm sure they'll take it.

The deer that is hunted by a bad hunter and lives for another day, will take it. The seal that doesn't get eaten by a great white shark, but his buddy does, will take it. Good luck is good for us all and for the gene pool.

Good luck isn't a discriminator all on its own, of course. All living things have some measure of good luck. Like lucky flowers growing in the right place and not getting watered by the local dogs. All living things have it.

The *real* discriminating and deciding factor in this matter is the amount of BAD luck one has. Good luck is given to all to help survival. The development of bad luck, indeed, the perpetuation of bad luck, is used to weed out the ones we don't want to keep around.

You see, it is not the person who is NOT hit by lightning we pay genetic attention to. It's the one who IS hit by lightning. We don't want more lightning rods walking around with the rest of us, spreading the bad luck.

Was he able to pass on this bad genetic trait before the lightning struck? Hopefully, not. We sure don't want more little lightning rods walking around. We want good luck to continue, of course. But that isn't enough, we have to get rid those with bad luck.

Speaking of lightning, the gene pool was surely working overtime, a few years back, when a lady's car was hit by lightning *while she was driving* down a highway in Florida. This is most rare. Almost unheard of. Cars are supposed to be one of the safest places to be during lightning.

Not for this poor woman. It killed the car and her. For some reason, the gene pool really had it in for her. Tough luck. Wrong place at the wrong time. The gene pool wins another one.

Quiz time. Which one option from each of the following statements do we want to keep in the gene pool?

- The person who gets hit on the head with a part dropped from a building under construction or the person who dropped it?
- The person sitting at a red light in their car who gets hit by an out of control driver or the out of control driver?

- The person accidently shot during a robbery gone badly or the robber who did the shooting?
- The hunter who was killed wearing a turkey outfit or the misguided hunter who shot him?
- The whale that was impaled on the bow of a cruise ship or the one that was missed?
- The idiot savant or the idiot?
- The duck Vice-President Cheney was shooting at or the fellow hunter who got shot instead?
- In a plane crash, the survivor in seat 28a or the passenger in 28b who didn't make it?

It's clearly the bad luck that decides matters of selections of the gene pool, not the good luck. If you live near an extinct volcano that decides to no longer be extinct, you die. Bad luck on you.

A deer jumps out of the woods and gets hit by a car – bad luck on the deer and the driver.

Bad luck is all around us. Lightning, tornados, hurricanes, volcanoes, tsunamis, bingo, ice patches, roulette, cars, bullets, earthquakes, parts dropping off airplanes, floods, disease, falling pianos, bad food, and much more. Sources of bad luck are everywhere. And the gene pool is focused on ridding itself of bad luck genetic traits. We will not survive with bad luck.

4 – Lazy loses

Luck and lazy seem to go well together in the gene pool and in life. Have you ever known someone who just floated through life without a care in the world and nothing bad seemed to come to them? Isn't it disgusting and unfair? Others, including you, work hard for what you have, try to do the right thing, follow most of the rules and still bad things happen to you.

Like, when the water heater went up just after you left the house for work and flooded the house. If that happened to the lucky guy, he'd just happen have his plumber friend over for a beer and a ball game. He wouldn't have to send in the warranty card or pay overtime. Yes, luck and lazy do seem to be symbiotically connected.

But, things are not always as they seem in the gene pool. If you are too lazy to get your own food, you will starve to death. Simple and straight forward. Get off your lazy butt or die. Run from the predators or be someone else's lunch. Yum, yum.

The animal that just can't bring itself to build a shelter freezes to death in the cold nights of winter. We don't want their genes mucking up the gene pool. That would result in more and more life forms that would get more and more lazy. Too lazy to eat, too lazy to protect themselves from predators, too lazy to procreate. This could be a disaster for the gene pool.

Let's look at one example of lazy in today's wild world – the manatee. This creature has more blubber on it than a whale. Yet, for some strange reason, it can't stand it if the water temperature goes below 75 degrees. Get real! Blubber protects you from the cold.

Compare this to the manatee's blubber cousins; the whale, the sea lion, the walrus, the penguin and the seal. They all have less blubber and they live where the water freezes, for crying out loud. They swim long distances, look for water holes, duck away from polar bears and hunters and, in general, live a fairly active, cold life.

So what is it with the manatee? Poor old manatee – the water is too cold. Boo-hoo. Every year, the manatee migrate (not very far, to be sure) to the warm water springs and canals to get away from the cold waters and give birth to more little blubber bodies. This is the height of natural laziness, yet somehow they get away with it.

What are the natural predators of the manatee? There is one – motor boats. That's it. Somehow they are smart enough to stay big and fat, scaring off predators, and they stay in water other predators don't like. Smart like a fox? I won't go that far.

Their lobbyists have been successful in getting humans to bend to their plight and make rules to protect these big, lazy hunks of swimming blubber. They are too lazy to even do their own PR work or get out of the way of boats!

So now, if a boat hits a manatee, it's the fault of the boat driver! Like a boat driver can see under water to where the manatees are floating a foot below the surface. Some areas have even outlawed boating altogether, because the manatees are too lazy to get the hell out of the way. This is ludicrous.

Don't the manatees have some responsibility for their own safety and survival? Don't other species teach their young to run away from danger that would hurt or eat them? Don't we humans tell our children not to play with the electric outlet or to make sure there are no cars coming before going into the street?

Why can't the manatee teach it's young to stay away from those boats or float just a little bit deeper? I mean, even a deaf manatee can hear them coming! The motors are loud, even when the boats are going slow. Of course they can hear them! They're just too damn lazy to get out of the way.

It is hard to blame them with the great lobby efforts they have going for them. But come on, people and motor boats versus manatees? And the manatee wins? Something is really out of whack.

Maybe the manatee provides something special for the

environment? Let's see – what do they do, exactly. I mean, what do they contribute? Oh yeah – NOTHING! They float along, munching on the grasses under water, and then they shit it out after getting all the fat calories from it. They also make more little blubber bodies that look cute while floating around getting in the way. What are they good for? You got it – nothing!

They evidently aren't good to eat, though I can't find anyone who has ever tried to eat one. That's against the law, too, as is touching them or bothering them!

They don't eat any special plants that need to be eradicated. They just munch on green stuff at the bottom of the water.

Other than motor boats, they don't have to fear any natural predator, like alligators. They just float along, lazy as all get out, and do nothing. They eat when they are hungry and shit in the water when they feel like it, polluting the water so people can't swim in it.

They're living speed bumps and they are the height of lazy!

Where did today's lazy manatees come from? Is it possible that they are smart enough to genetically pass on to their young lessons learned from past survival escapades? Did they teach their young that being a manatee means getting others to do their work for them and to get everything they want without having to work for it (like liberals)?

Consider the possibility. Early manatees taught their young that motor boats were bad and could really hurt them. But, instead of avoiding them, the manatee lobbyists had them go *towards* the boats and get hurt – just a little, tiny bit. Then, they surfaced up where people could see the terrible scars, take pictures of them, put them in the papers and news, and send letters to the state legislature.

"How terrible it is that these innocent creatures are so badly injured by careless boaters! We must make more laws!" So the legislature, being politicians, cater to the loudest voice and punish boaters.

The older and wiser manatees teach the young ones that the water is their birthright and they can go anywhere they want and do whatever they want. Everyone else has to get out of *their* way. After a couple of generations of this, new manatees have this concept ingrained in their genetic structure. "The water is ours. It belongs to us. Boaters are bad. We can do whatever we want and they have to accommodate us."

It seems to have worked. The manatees have lobbyists in the legislature. Boaters are banned or slowed down. Still, no one can find a good use for the manatees.

Here are a few ideas we should try. First, tell the manatees that they are not all that great and when they hear boat motors approaching, take a deep breath and go 3 feet under water. Next, let them know that, while we have sympathy for their internal body thermostat, just as we do for menopausal women, they are just going to have to deal with it.

Lastly, introduce the Eskimos to the manatee. I'll bet THEY could find some use for them. Are they edible? We'll find out real quick. "Would you like carrots with that manatee steak?"

Send a few up North and let them see what *real* cold water feels like. Let them see what their blubber cousins have lived with for thousands of years. That should stop their whining and complaining when things are a little uncomfortable.

Free the boaters, who are not too lazy to go out in their motor boats on their days off. They worked hard for the privilege of using the waterways.

Yes, the gene pool wants life forms to be active and not lazy.

We are expected to fend for ourselves and not expect others to do our hard work for us. Societies cannot long survive having the lazy amongst them. The rest of us do not have enough extra energy to support those who won't support themselves. Let them die off. A lazy gene pool is a dying gene pool and that cannot be allowed to happen.

5 – The healthy ones win over the sickly ones.

It would seem obvious to scientists and engineers, and other similarly right-minded people, that the weak and unhealthy do not promote a viable and healthy future for any species. We just don't like those who can't keep up. They slow everyone else down.

If everything went at the speed of the slowest and sickest individual in the group, the covered wagons would never have made it across the Midwest plains, let alone over the two mountain ranges that followed. They would still be stuck in eastern Pennsylvania thinking about moving out west, but never quite getting up the nerve or energy to do anything about it.

Now, if you think a little bit out of the box (by the way – did you ever really SEE the box you are supposed to think out of? Me either.), you might be able to visualize our Universe U student, God, figuring out what his next steps are for creating intelligent life. Can you see him in your mind, pondering how to proceed?

Can you see him struggling with the intelligent life bit? Trying to figure out the best, selective bleaching to help the gene pool? God realizes that he is going to have to step things up a bit this semester and show some real progress. He has to produce or be left behind, just like in the gene pool he created.

God tried to clear out some of these folks with the Black

Plague, a couple of major flu's, and the little ice age. The strong survive! Wipe out the weak and sickly – we have progress to make! Reduce the burden of those who can't carry their own weight. We have progress to make.

In some species, limited care is given to the sick, but at some point, they are abandoned to their genetic fate and the rest of the group moves on. In other species, the sick or weak are simply left to their own fate. No "Good luck.", "Hope things work out for you.", "Get well soon.", "Send a note if you live." Nothing. Somehow, these species recognize that you can't fight genetics.

Yes, the gene pool can be very cruel indeed. But that is what it's for. To sort out those who are, and will remain, healthy and can survive injury. Remember: survival of life is the goal. After all, who would want a species of sickos lounging around the gene pool? Certainly not God. They tax the living, eat food that healthy individuals need, and they take up air and space unnecessarily.

That's why there is a built-in part of the genetic code that tries to eliminate them as individuals. It's kind of like a genetic trap door. If you aren't healthy, WHAM, the door opens and you disappear. Your species is safe from you and your bad genes. Your species is fit to continue to evolve and contribute to the gene pool – you aren't.

On a far grander scale, the gene pool provides examples where life evidently got way out of hand and large scale bleaching was needed. One example is the Black Plague, where millions of people died and the strongest survived.

God's thinking was that those who were susceptible to the plague were medically weak. His experiments yet to come couldn't tolerate that and his grades would suffer, so the weak had to go. The Black Plague had to happen. The sickly had to die.

The flu epidemics, like those of the early 1900s, also killed millions. In fact, the flu was the number one cause of death in America around 1900. It's a good thing we got smarter so that doesn't happen again (Yeah, right. Don't hold your breath. Don't forget your flu shot. And don't forget that the gene pool always wins in the end).

Chicken pox is another one that killed millions. It was also passed on to millions of American Indians, killing them, and nearly wiping them out of the gene pool altogether. Over and over, diseases have developed, as a sort of bleach, to help cleanse the gene pool. And over and over, the healthiest survived.

There were several other "bleaching" of the gene pool over the ages it took God to work through his curriculum. We still have a long ways to go to achieve the "intelligent life" status, so I expect more bleaching at any moment.

Bleaching can take many different forms. The odd volcano that disrupts the global environment and weather for years, killing thousands. And Tsunamis … are they to weed out the unlucky and those who can't swim?

The repeated cycles of ice ages and global warming? Maybe their purpose is to weed out those who catch cold easily or cannot deal with the travel to new places and climates without getting sick.

Or maybe, they are to find out who believes that the next cycle is here, NOW, and see who runs off the environmental cliff in a panic. Kind of like Shep's friends.

Then, there is the occasional big asteroid – now *that* is a whopper of a bleaching job, but effective. If you really want to know who can survive the tough times and weed out the weak, a good asteroid will do it every time.

Weed them out! Get rid of the weak! The strong are the future of all species! The weak ones hold the rest of us back. They prevent progress. They hurt survival of the species. Let them swim, or die, or heal themselves, or get a coat, or freeze. My, but the gene pool can be a harsh mistress.

We've seen evidence of the gene pool's tenacity for taking care of the strong and eliminating the weak, to the extent of creating "bleaching" to sort out potential survivors. Let's take a closer look at some of the gene pool "bleach" survivors and see if we can explain their survival. A sample list might include:

- Manatee
- Caterpillar
- Jelly fish
- Firefly
- Butterfly
- Poison ivy

- Mosquitoes
- Liberals
- Moles
- Babies
- Shrimp
- Locust

- Flies
- Moths
- Ants
- Armadillo
- Religious Zealots
- Lady bugs

These are all weak life forms that have survived, for one reason or another, sometimes against all logic. This gives added credence to the reality that no single gene pool characteristic is grounds for dismissal from the living and the future. Survival must be special combinations of characteristics that allow one to survive and another to die off. We'll explore this notion later.

First, let's look at some examples of where the weak and sickly are not automatically eliminated from the gene pool, in spite of obvious indications that they should be.

<u>Shrimp</u> – What have they done to hurt anybody? Nothing. Shrimp are food for everybody. No one doesn't like shrimp. Fish like them. Dogs, people, cats, and cows – we all like to eat shrimp. They are not particularly sickly, per se, but they are

kind of fragile. Take them out of water and they don't do so well. Rip off their heads and they don't last long, even on ice. Speaking of ice, if they get too cold, they die. If they get too hot, they turn a bright orange.

They don't have any natural defenses against getting eaten, or caught or getting their heads ripped from their bodies. Their thin shells are but a momentary speed bump to those who would apply the laws of the food chain to eat them. In fact, some people think that taking the shell off is part of the charm of eating them.

Why do they continue to live on? Is it just to feed the rest of us and provide specials at restaurants? There has to be something else they offer. They've survived the gene pool for millennia. They must be doing something right, especially with cocktail sauce. But, what is it?

Firefly – An honorable mention to the weakest of the weak list. No firefly ever hurt anybody or anything. Unless you got hit in the eye by one while riding a motorcycle with your goggles off (see the gene pool characteristic on good judgment).

They never started any fires. They are easily caught. A good late spring freeze does them in. A gentle breeze carries them off in an uncontrolled topsy-turvy flight to wonder land. A mild bug spray kills them off. They offer so little to the general harmony and continuity of life that one has to wonder why they are still around. But they are. What is it that they have? What is the secret of the firefly?

Manatees – Of course, we have to include these blubber wimps, again. They are so fragile that they panic and scamper, if manatees can actually scamper, to warmer waters if the water temperature drops below 75 degrees. They just can't handle it and have anxiety attacks and will actually die. All this trauma, in spite of the fact that they have more blubber, by percentage of body weight, than any other creature, except some humans.

What IS their problem? Why are they still here? They catch cold easily (and literally). They have no defenses, except eating them would take so long that predators just pass them by. They slow down boats. They aren't good to eat. They don't contribute anything obvious to the scheme of life. What is their secret?

Liberals – This one should not be a surprise or a stretch to anyone. They are weak to the point of picking on others as a way of getting what they want. Perpetual do-gooders, they only see the good that can come from using someone else's resources to help themselves, commonly while pretending to protest the plight of others. They feed on the emotions of others to survive. They are adaptable to the whims of those in power.

Their strength is the ability, through complex camouflage, to sacrifice the well-being of others for their own good; all while appearing to be just the opposite. Clever creatures.

But, they are weak when confronted with facts, logic and loss of resources. It's then that they exhibit their most clever survival trick. Liberals use this trick when faced with dire decisions and potential annihilation. They pretend to be anything, anything at all, to get something for themselves, and it's always at the expense of others.

They can be caring or harsh, racist or inclusive, rich or poor, conservative or moderate, socialist or democratic, oil lover or sun worshipper. It doesn't matter. They can convert themselves, seemingly at will and without conscience, into anything to survive.

They are amazing creatures that, for some unknown reason, the gene pool allows to continue. Perhaps leaches and chameleons are needed in the gene pool for balance. Liberals

THE LEVI GENES

certainly provide that. There is much more detail on liberal later in the book. Read on and stand by.

Religious zealots – A natural to follow the liberals in our little discussion here. Organized or not, these creatures are excellent examples of the weak and sickly who prey (pray?) on others using the bully pulpit of God. God created these creatures and allowed them to fester in his lab, maybe for the vanity of having someone enforce his name and rule when he wasn't around. What? You think God doesn't like attention and adulation?

What is so sickly and weak about religious zealots? Let's think on this a moment. Time's up. For one thing, like drunks and paranoids, they claim that they are NOT zealots. They are just doing God's work.

For another, like scavengers and liberals, they live off the spoils of others. They are especially adept at convincing lesser humans that it is their Godly DUTY to give to "God" some of their hard earned money, or crops, or goats, or daughters/sons or what have you. They've been doing this for a very, very long time.

Another trait of zealots is that they can't live as they preach others to live. What's good for the goose is NOT good for the religious zealot gander. They sit in judgment of others and crack the whip (literally in some religions) and offer nothing to society to improve it. Maybe if they grew crops or shared their money and assets with others, it would be different. Their benefit to the gene pool is not evident.

Related story. There is a very old, historical theory I made up that goes like this. God (the student, remember) had a couple of classes in cloning and social development of backwards life forms. This fit into his lab very well because he had a bunch of backwards life forms already made and ready to go.

As part of his cloning class, God took some of his sperm (don't ask how he got it, I can't stand the visual) and decided to clone himself in his lab. It had to be in his lab because having another one of him running around the universe just would not be right.

God put out the word and found a "volunteer" in his lab. This volunteer had to be virginal for the experiment to work and to get credit for it from the teachers.

With the social norms established at that time, virgins were easy to find because the religious zealots made a big deal of being virginal at marriage. She also had to be unmarried, because there were no such things as married virgins. (Duh!) The religious zealots made sure *that* matter was resolved on the wedding night.

When God met his "volunteer", he slipped her some roofies and artificially inseminated her. A while later – behold, a virginal birth that came from God. Just like in the biblical stories, but not quite like the humans tell it.

In this way, God introduced to us a peacenik carpenter-want-to-be, through surrogate parents, code named Mary and Joe. (Great Judaic-Christian names, I know, but he had to protect their real identities to protect them from rumor and gossip). Joe was there to protect the cover story and Mary's reputation.

Yes, he was the Son of God and created in His image. Yes, he was also a smart brat who went around spouting off God stuff and getting himself in trouble. Telling everyone he was the Son of God, of all the dumb things to do. What an ego … where could that have come from? But he did give us some neat guidance that the zealots have since repeatedly screwed up royally.

He didn't require money from anyone. He didn't wear a

Rolex (and he could have, if he wanted to). He could have created air conditioning and frozen foods. That wasn't his style. Of course, we didn't get the hint and put a human twist on it.

We created more religious zealots that sucked the life from others who worked hard just to survive. (Only humans have this type of character in their genetic lineage!) They gave nothing in return but platitudes and made guilt almost a genetic trait.

This experiment was a great innovation for God's socialization class that other students hadn't thought of. It certainly got the attention of the instructors. But, it caused all sorts of trouble for generations to come in the lab. It caused social stagnation and wars that almost ruined the entire experiment.

Imagine what would happen if God came back for a visit with us next Wednesday. Suppose he called the top leaders of all the world's religions together to meet him in quiet restaurant in some small town in Iowa?

He could set them straight, answer any burning questions, settle any arguments and give them some inspiration. I'm sure he would then tell the world's religious leaders to go forth, to be good to each other, and to play nice with each other and the rest of the animals on earth.

Every one of those "leaders" would go forth, all right. They would each claim that THEY had a personal discussion with God and got the real straight skinny directly from Him. Here is what He said "… blah, blah, blah".

Of course, each of them would have a different version of what was actually said, and all of them would be wrong. Each story would have a smidgen of truth, but not enough to ruin their particular "story".

Religious zealots are a lost cause and will manipulate anything and everything to a predefined point while continuing to make their own survival dependant on what they can get from others.

Babies – This one should be easy for everyone to understand. They are weak and susceptible to disease and danger. They can't fend for themselves or even feed themselves. They should be dying by the droves. This is one of those cases where another gene pool characteristic intervenes and influences survival. Even those that are supposed to die – don't.

We intervene with baby dolphins – yes, they are real cute and all, but if they can't pull their weight, let them go. Premature humans also continue to survive, in spite of the odds and the rules. We can almost generate babies from scratch without using humans at all (other than to burp the Petri dish and the test tube). Yet, we have this drive to save the ones who shouldn't be saved, cute or not.

Babies of all species are at risk of dying, yet they survive. They are weak, susceptible, helpless, need everyone else to help them, and they put the herd at risk. Yet, the gene pool keeps them around. Maybe the cute factor is under-rated.

Or maybe God has a soft spot for babies. He's figured out ways to save them through genetic teachings, as in the possum, where the little ones automatically migrate to the external pouch upon birth and stay there for safe keeping. Or like salmon, where millions of eggs are laid, with the probability (hope) that enough will be born and survive to keep the species going.

Chickens approached the egg issue differently. They only produce one egg at a time. They got smart and made themselves cute to humans and their eggs good eating. They sacrifice a few of their eggs to feed us and get us addicted to them. This way, we keep enough chickens around to ensure their continued survival. Pretty smart. All they have to do is cluck a little and lay an egg ... we take care of the rest.

Different approaches by different species, but all to protect the weak and sickly babies. As chickens and kittens have shown, cute counts.

Ladybugs – Now talk about cute ... have you ever seen an ugly ladybug? No, of course not! There's no such thing. There's also no such thing as a strong, decisive, lucky ladybug. There are plenty of animals who like to eat them. Children like to collect them. Adults squash them when they get inside a house or underfoot. They can't handle extremes of environments. They can't fly in strong winds or rain – in fact, many raindrops are bigger than they are!

Why are they still here? Do they have some special hidden strength or resistance to disease we have yet to discover? Why has the gene pool smiled upon them? It surely hasn't been the liberals, because they could care a rat's behind about ladybugs, unless there was money to be made from them.

Weak. Susceptible to disease. Of absolutely no threat to anyone, unless you happen to swallow one. Of no particular benefit to the ecosystem. Yet they're still around. Another mystery of the gene pool.

We could go on and on. In fact, I have gone on in my head and all it does is cause pain. The sickly and weak somehow survive. They survive in spite of the fact that the gene pool is clearly biased towards the strong and healthy. *They* are the ones we want to perpetuate the species and life here on earth. *They* are the ones that will win God an "A" and get him out of the lab. Why are the weak still among us?

6 – The adaptable ones survive changing times

If you are a species that's stuck in the mud, guess where you are going to end up. Exactly where you are, the beginnings of a fossil. If you're too stupid to know it, or too lazy to work to change, or too indecisive to make a decision of what to do, you'll die and all your kind will die, also.

But, if you are smart enough, and not lazy or indecisive, that may still not be enough, as we will see. If you just don't have the genetic makeup to adapt to changing situations, you cannot survive.

The caveman who didn't move out of the way of the glaciers or figure out how to stay warm, died off. The Jews who left Egypt for 40 years in the desert certainly had to adapt to survive. The Roman Empire knew how to adapt – mostly by assimilating others. They were the original Borg. How do you say, "We will assimilate you!" in ancient Roman Latin?

There were other assimilators, of course. But assimilation is not true adaption. Walruses and seals adapted to cold waters where manatees could not. (Manatees used the "cute factor" trick invented by the chickens.)

Some plants can deal with frost and others can't. Some people in Wisconsin and Minnesota have to go to Florida for the winter while others deal with the cold.

Adaptation and survival is all around us. But, so is extinction from the failure to adapt. Each year scientists find species that have become extinct or are on the verge of becoming extinct. Of course, every year they also discover thousands of new species. You choose your favorite part of that story. It works both ways.

Let me give you a real, honest to God story of an American Indian tribe that failed to adapt and died off. No kidding, this actually happened.

In the 1830, 40s and 50s, preachers and other religious zealots of all kinds were roaming around the American West. Their purpose was to make contacts and proselytize their particular religion and version of God.

They hoped to convert the many Indians and pioneers to their religion. Whoever got to them first got dibs on them, baptized them, and counted them in their membership rolls. The race was on full blast for market share of Indian souls.

One of these pioneering preachers was a catholic priest named Reverend P. J. DeSmet. Rev. DeSmet travelled around the west for many years, befriended many Indians, converted and baptizing hundreds, and ministering to the pioneers.

It seems that, in the land of the godless, there was a great need for a god. Many Indians converted to Christianity, accepting the mantra that the White Man's God was more powerful than the Indian Gods. It might have been more convincing if they'd kept small pox away and brought along air conditioning.

During his travels, Rev. DeSmet kept a journal and wrote letters back to Europe about his experiences. These letters tell many fascinating tales of life in the western wilderness and interactions with many different Indian tribes. One particular story demonstrates how the gene pool was at work before the White Man's organized society could screw things up worse.

In a letter dated August 3, 1854, Rev. DeSmet tells of the Soshoco Indian tribe. He had stopped to visit and befriend them, convert them, and learn from them (while slipping in a good word for the Catholic God, of course). Rev. DeSmet wrote of his experiences.

PETA would be proud of the Soshoco. They subsisted mainly on grasshoppers and ants. They also gathered the odd nuts, fruits, roots, leaves and berries that happened to be available where they wandered.

Other Indians, who lived off the flesh of animals, tended to be taller, more robust, more active, and better-clad, according to Rev. DeSmet. By contrast, the Soshoco were "... miserable, lean, weak, and badly clothed." He describes them as the "most degraded of the races on this vast continent."

You see, no one in this tribe knew how to hunt, trap or kill animals. They were true, pure gatherers. They didn't have animal skin huts, or homes, or clothes or shelters, as did other Indian tribes. The Soshoco didn't have the skills to make such things or know how to hunt and kill the animals.

They also had no killing weapons or tribal knowledge of fighting skills. Not a good situation for survival in the Indian Territories of the mid–1800s!

Their clothing was limited, since they didn't do the fur thing. They moved with the seasons, because their clothes were really only meant for one season – warm – if you know what I mean.

They didn't farm, because they didn't stick around long enough for things to grow. They also didn't have the farming skills since the tribe lived off what the land provided. They hadn't developed general life and survival skills, either. Which is why they've been lost from the gene pool.

In this particular letter, Rev. DeSmet tells of a special event the tribe held for him, because they were in a good mood and wanted to celebrate with a buffet for their new friend. Special food was ordered to be gathered and prepared. As he tells it, food specialists went out early in the day to search for special foods to go along with the main entre. Others went to find and gather the perfect main dish.

They found it in a large clearing in the woods. Many of the tribe members; young, old, men and women, were called to surround the far end of the clearing. While this was going on, a few people dug a large rectangular pit at the near end of the clearing.

At a signal, the people at the far end of the clearing started shouting and stamping their feet and making a large ruckus.

Then they started to slowly work their way towards the near end of the clearing and towards the pit, stomping their feet and beating at the scrubs along the way.

Watching this, the priest was perplexed, and also impressed at the coordination and cooperation all tribal members put into the effort. Everyone was working together, obviously knowing what was to come.

The priest asked one of the tribe members to explain what they were doing. It was explained that this particular clearing was chock full of grasshoppers and the tribe was driving them towards the pit. As they got close to the pit, the grasshoppers would be herded into the pit, at which point, the real meal preparation would begin.

In today's world, one can only imagine this taking place. But it really did happen this way.

As the pit started to get full, cooking fires were built and things really got under way. Some grasshoppers were taken away by the armload and cooked in large pans to make some crispy critters.

At one end of the pit, people were jumping in to squash the grasshoppers, creating a paste of them. This grasshopper paste was then cooked into a kind of grasshopper pancake. Grasshopper soup was made. Boiled grasshoppers were enjoyed. Roasted grasshoppers tied to sticks were also popular.

Now, what does this have to do with adaptability? Well, a lot, but I also think it's a terrific story directly from the person who was there.

The Soshoco moved around with the food supply, but could not fight to protect themselves from other Indian tribes. They never learned how to defend themselves, let alone carry on any kind of warfare. They didn't have good clothing to protect them from the elements. Fruits, nuts, leaves and grasshopper buffets didn't provide sufficient nutritional balance.

So this tribe, the Soshoco, was a victim of the gene pool. They all died off. They couldn't defend themselves when territory conflict came up. They couldn't ride off on their horses because they had none. They couldn't protect themselves against climate changes.

They couldn't adapt to a changing world that demanded they adapt or die. They choose "die". Not intentionally, of course. But the result is the same.

Adapt and you have a chance for survival. Fail to adapt and you have none.

7 – Good looks win over bad looks

Those who study these things, because they have nothing else to offer to the human race, say that there is a genetic tendency in animals driving them to mate with the best looking of their species. Is this a no-brainer or what? Was this study funded by the government?

If you've ever watched animals breeding on a farm or in the wild, there isn't a whole lot to choose from. When animals have the urge to mate, they have to choose the best looking from those available at the time.

Now, I'm sure that all cows do not look the same or have the same "attractiveness" to the bulls, but – damn – those cows are all UGLY! Maybe that's why they approach them from the back when mating – they are just too ugly to try to get belly-to-belly.

Is there a visual forming in your mind? Two cows belly-to-belly? Ugh! Is it even physically possible? Did God find out that some of his animals were way too ugly to face each other while mating? Even with their eyes closed, they just couldn't do it.

I suspect that he found that some animals were way too ugly, even for mating. So ugly, in fact, that the ugly overpowered the mating instinct. No mating, no babies, no survival. I'm sure he had to redesign some of the animals so they weren't so damned ugly. Others were redesigned so they didn't have to look at the face when mating.

Evidently, changing the mating positions was easier than changing the design of the "she's a babe" gene. Maybe genetic manipulation really is harder than we thought. So why haven't humans had "the change" put on them? We are designed to be belly-to-belly. (Yes, I know we can really go both ways.)

Maybe we're in the middle of a genetic change-over from belly-to-belly from belly-to-butt. Or vice versa. Maybe we have way too many ugly people and the gene pool is at work to give us an option, front or back, cute or ugly, lights on or off.

For evidence of what I say, take a look at the local Sunday newspaper and check out the section with pictures of engaged couples and newly married couples. Really look at the people. How many of them are ugly? I mean so ugly, that you need a couple of stiff drinks to look at the pictures again?

Now look at the baby pictures – even *they* are getting uglier.

Are we evolving into an ugly species? Is the percentage of ugly to cute increasing or decreasing over the years? Are we loosing the cute battle?

Is it possible that humans will evolve physically so that belly-to-belly is no longer desirable or even possible (maybe some people are already there)? Will our cuteness genes stay intact? Were the Greeks right or were they ugly?

Enough – back to important things.

Animal mating mostly works like with the cows. Whether they are buffalos, horses, dogs, cats, zebras, Greeks, ancient

Romans, sheep, pigeons, whales, etc., ugly doesn't matter. Remember that old saying about having a face that only a mother could love? Or the saying about being butt ugly? Well, there you have it. They're too ugly to mate with their eyes open. Just work from the back and look at the rest of the herd. And for heaven's sake – do not look down! Butt ugly!

The mating force is one of the most powerful internal, instinctual forces in any species. It is what drives all species to procreate and survive. Even with the "she's-a-babe" gene fully engaged, the surviving uglies of most animals overwhelm even that powerful survival instinct. They were too ugly to mate. So God changed their designs so they didn't have to see the ugly part when mating. He changed them from belly-to-belly maters to belly-to-butt maters.

Is it really true? Well, of course it is. I wouldn't lie to you. Now imagine how ugly the ones were that never got mated and died off without producing off-spring. The gene pool did really good work with that. If the survivors are still this ugly, one can only imagine what the others looked like. How ugly would an ordinary cow be if the gene pool hadn't intervened? Yuck – another bad visual.

What if they *could* do it belly-to-belly? My guess is that all the cows, and horses, and sheep, and Greeks and ancient Romans would be gay and entire species would have dropped off the face of the earth. (Wait, the ancient Romans did drop off the face of the earth! That just proves my point.) They would have been too ugly to mate with.

Masturbation and homosexuality would have been preferred. Neither of these options is very effective for creating progeny for the gene pool.

This trait is evidenced in fish, as well. Some of them are so ugly that they can't even stand to be close to each other during the mating process. Salmon, for instance, take turns (not a bad idea in the right circumstances). First, the female lays down millions of eggs then gets out of the way. Once she is safely out of eyesight, the male comes in and fertilizes the eggs.

He never has to even see her and, if you've ever taken a good close-up look at a female salmon, you would understand why. They are so ugly that when a bear catches them, the first thing it does is chew off the head so they don't have to see it anymore. Fishermen catch them and immediately stuff them into a box so they don't have to look at them, either. Obviously, ugly can be so ugly that it crosses species.

And what about all those millions of eggs and potential fish? Well, it seems that the gene pool has that figured out, too. If you look around at the different animals and plants, the uglier they are, the more eggs they have to produce to get a few to survive. Ugly fish have to lay millions to get a few to survive. The gene pool doesn't really want too many of these ugly fish swimming around, so the odds of giving birth to any goes way down.

The evolutionary design process is actually rebelling against the gene pool by creating more and more eggs so some can survive. In response to that, the gene pool made the fish really tasty to bears and humans.

"So there!" cries the gene pool. "You are so ugly! We can't stand to have many of you around."

Fish can make more eggs, but the gene pool will have the last laugh ... and a fish sandwich.

Now, at the other end of the spectrum, is the ultimate in cuteness – the panda bear. It is so cute that it generally has only one baby at a time, and then not very often at that. The world can handle only so much cuteness.

Once in a while, when a momma panda bear is exceptionally cute, she is given two eggs and has twins. The gene pool loves cute! It needs more pandas.

The percentage of eggs to good births is very high for the cute little bears. It is not high for the ugly salmon. And the rest of the animals and plants fall somewhere in between them, in terms of survival of cute offspring and the number of eggs needed for a few to survive.

No matter what, the gene pool does not want the ugly to thrive. There is a message here and we should be paying attention. Cute animals are special. And it works for more than cute bears. Consider other really cute animals like seals, prairie dogs, chinchillas, kittens, baby horses, and orchids. Cuteness pays off in the gene pool. If you can't be cute, you can't swim in the gene pool with the rest of us.

Do humans do this, too? Are we genetically programmed to search out for good-looking mates? You might not think so, if you look in the Sunday paper. How do some people get together and do the belly-to-belly with the lights on? They must have their "she's a babe" gene on all the way.

You aren't convinced? Go ahead and check out the Sunday paper, again. Or go to the local shopping center or airport and look at the people. How many belly-to-belly couples do you see?

The prevalence of divorce in the US gives us the chance to trade up from time to time. What do we do? We trade even. Or worse yet, we trade *down*. I'm telling you, the good looks gene is suppressed and it will have repercussions on all of us in the future.

We can't continue to ugly down the human species. We can't keep saving all the ugly people. If we do, they are going to mate and make ugly children who will grow up to be ugly people. If the gene pool wants them to die off, let them.

Still not convinced? Take a look at the process we go through to select a mate. We are always on the search for cute. Looks really do matter! It is genetic. There are even whole industries living off of cute. Examples? Sure. Hollywood, fashions, makeup, hair styling, magazines, Broadway, matchmaking, photo studios, and more.

Do you want to see it in action? Go to a bar or club where people gather to see and be seen. You know the ones. Every town has them. Stay sober, or a close approximation, and watch the action. People there are convinced they are cute and are looking for cute to hook up with. The uglies know they aren't welcome and don't even attend.

Early in the evening, everyone has high hopes and even higher opinions of themselves. The women pose themselves, and primp, and posture and check out the possibilities. They are the hunted, but they are also the hunters.

They are very good at quickly evaluating large numbers of men and sorting out the good-looking men from the not-so-good-looking men. They also look for other factors, such as, how they are dressed, if they are willing to spend their money, and if they act "smooth".

They gravitate to those who buy drinks and have dance moves. It's the genes at work. If he can't take care of her in the pursuit, how can he take care of her after the capture? A woman has to look out for herself in these matters.

They create a space around themselves into which the lucky few are allowed to enter and others are excluded. They didn't pass the cute test. The ones allowed in can stay and keep trying to impress her and better the competition. Eventually the woman either makes a choice to evaluate further one-on-one or gives up and wanders off to better pastures.

Could the rise in lesbianism be related to the increased

ugliness in the available men? Could the gene pool be reacting to the lack of cuteness? Or is it a genetic aberration all on its own in an expanded search for more cuteness?

The men, puffed up with their own sense of false cuteness and egos, bolstered by clothes, money and the right cologne, watch carefully. They're like the coyote looking for just the right prey and the right time to pounce.

Being visual beasts, men sort out the prey based on looks. Not too big, not too short, good figure, good boobs, nice hair, shapely butt, cute face. Does she dress to show and share? Would she look good in the morning before coffee?

They watch other men try and get rejected. They evaluate their chances and consider the tactics to use to get close to their prey.

They watch to see who is drinking and who is not. Which lady is accepting drinks from other men? What does the competition look like? Which women are giving off the "come hither" signals and which are playing hard to get? Which ones are worthy of their attentions and efforts? High hopes abound.

The selection and sorting process continues while they make their choices. Then they move in for the kill. Maybe some smarmy intro line to start conversation. A witty or snotty comeback. "Can I buy you a drink?" maybe, to which the response "No thanks, but I'll take the five dollars." is not a good sign.

The verbal dance is accompanied by hand and eye movements: a flick of the hair, the showing of the expensive watch, mention of an expensive car, looking for the hint of a smile, her looking at other prospects or checking him out more carefully, a brush against a hand. It's all choreographed.

It's also common among other animals. They all do it. The

mating dance of the herd. The natural selection of the cute. Saving the ugly for times of desperation. Will the coyote get his? Will his prey let him? Will male masturbation continue on the increase, like lesbianism?

Interestingly, these activities usually do not occur in a natural environment for humans. Other animals know when it is time for mating. The female is ready and sends off pheromones and signals. Winter is coming and the deer rutting season starts. Animals know when it's mating time and they go along with it.

Humans don't seem to have such instincts. Of course, we can tell when we get horny, but that happens all the time. No, we need some artificial help. If you'd notice, these places for mate selection are also excellent places to see how chemicals affect our genetic disposition; our judgment of cuteness, our ability to attract and respond, our mating chances, and our ability to survive in the gene pool.

Alcohol is the most prevalent drug used to turn off the ugly avoidance system. As we consume more and more alcohol, our ugly minimums decrease. Our ability to choose well goes down the tubes. We accept anybody left at last call. Everyone looks better then.

If we were to plot the use of alcoholic drinks in society over the millions of years, we would find that the human cuteness factor has gone up and down in direct correlation with the cycles of alcohol use in societies. The more we drink, the uglier we get.

Humans were the best looking during times when we had no alcohol and the ugly ones didn't get chosen for mating. Alcohol has hurt the work of the gene pool and continues to do so. Just sit outside your favorite bar at closing time and evaluate the cuteness factors of those coming out. Bad news to be sure … especially in the morning.

The same effects have been seen with mind-altering drugs. One good thing to say about them is they at least make the experience of belly-to-belly mating with someone ugly more enjoyable. They alter the brain and its workings so at least you think you are having a good time.

Just remember, when we need stronger drugs so we can mate with even uglier "options", the uglier the entire human species will become. The stronger the drugs in society, the uglier society becomes. Just connect the dots.

The effects of these chemical crutches are probably the primary reason so many people stay in bad marriages or relationships and keep ugly babies. The drugs make the situation, the other person, the "ugly" factor, at least bearable. Heck, with enough of the right drugs, you can be happy with the ugliest of the herd and still think you are cool, cute and desirable to all. Oh, what fools we are.

If you aren't convinced and want to see a purer study of this ugly avoidance trait at work, go to a junior or senior high school dance.

Most of the uglies don't even make it to the dance! They know they don't have a chance and don't want to be embarrassed. They know where they stand in the good-looking pecking order of the gene pool, without even taking biology. It's instinctual. The herd mentality and genetic awareness lets them know their position.

For those who actually make it to the dance, where there is no alcohol to influence the process, it is a brutal, open, unvarnished and impolite weeding out process. They quickly sort out the visually acceptable from those who do not have any belly-to-belly potential. No alcohol, no inhibitions, no sense of manners or attempts to be polite; just brutal sorting out of the herd.

They group together with others of similar cuteness and hang close for mutual protection. They haven't honed their stalking and hunting skills yet at this age, so it can be frightfully cruel for the uninitiated to watch. But they have to get through it for the human species to survive.

The cuteness of the human race is at stake. If this doesn't work well, they will follow their predecessors into the ugliness of the past and require large and regular amounts of various drugs. The human race needs more cuteness. The gene pool demands it!

Of course, looks count in all animals. No mother wants to have ugly kids. In some animals, mothers or fathers actually eat the ugly ones. Talk about tough love! But maybe this is something to seriously consider. The species has to come first and the gene pool has its rules. God does not want a bunch of ugly beings to show the professors and he can't just zap them into being pretty (that would be cheating). So he gave us some guidance in our genes that leads us to look for good-looking mates.

As we've seen, this trait is suppressed in many of us. But inside, deep inside, in private little places we don't admit to, when we think and dream of the possibilities and we dream of those we'd love to have, no one thinks ugly! No one hopes for an ugly baby. No one wants to say "Oh, what an ugly bride you are."

The good looks gene lives on in us all. There is hope … at least for the cute ones.

Conclusion

To wrap up this chapter, there are many motivations within all animals and plants that twist us, and steer us, and shape us, and guide us to support improving the species and keeping life going. These are powerful factors in determining who we are and who we will be. They are so powerful and important, that they are programmed into the very fabric of every life form on earth – and beyond.

They drive our most basic programming and motivations. They are so much a part of us, that we aren't even aware of them. Yet, we all have them and respond to them.

The gene pool has its rules. It must develop intelligent life and perpetuate life. Neither has been achieved yet, but we'll keep working at it.

One point to remember: no single genetic trait, all on its own, is a case for being included, or excluded, from the gene pool. The smartest animal, plant or person does not get an automatic pass into the deep waters of the gene pool. Neither does the most adaptable or industrious or lucky or best looking.

There is more to the gene pool than individual genetic traits. The rules are not so simplistic. The differences between survival and death are complex.

Chapter 4 – The Gene Pool Grading System

We've seen that the gene pool can be very cruel and … well … inhuman. It operates according to some very simple and straight forward rules. Remember them? Here they are again, just so you don't have to go flipping back through the book and getting yourself lost. I wouldn't want you to lose your place and have to start reading all over from page one. Don't laugh, it's happened.

The seven characteristics of the Gene Pool

1. The smart ones get extra points and do well.
2. The lucky ones live.
3. Good looks win over bad looks.
4. Lazy loses.
5. The healthy ones win over the sickly ones.
6. Those who make good decisions get extra points.
7. The adaptable ones survive changing times.

As we look at this list, we have to wonder – which one is most important? Which is least important? Are they all equal? For example, is lucky more important than, say, ugly? Is smart equal to lazy and ugly combined? You can see how this can get complicated.

This is why we can't get into God's school. It is just too damned difficult to make intelligent life and we're too dumb to qualify. Maybe we can blame all the social experiments the liberals foisted on our school systems through the last five decades. Are we any more intelligent because of them? (If you aren't sure, you probable attended those schools. The correct answer is no.)

We need to get to the bottom of the ranking system. To help ferret this out, I conducted a thorough, wide-ranging, purely scientific and unbiased study with several people who think like me to see if I could solve this conundrum.

They were asked to rank the gene pool characteristics. Which are most important? Which are least important? The results of their completely scientific answers were interesting and are shown below.

Rank   Gene Pool Characteristic

1. Those who make good decisions get extra points.
2. The healthy ones win over the sickly ones.
3. The adaptable ones survive changing times.
4. The smart ones get extra points and do well.
5. Good looks win over bad looks.
6. The lucky ones live.
7. Lazy loses.

Amazingly, the world's scientific community has never before measured these matters. They just haven't caught up with genetic analysis at this level. So, I did it for them and include it here for the first time ever, just for you.

Ranking the characteristics is one thing, an important thing, but it isn't enough. We need to determine how each of these relates to the others. This isn't an easy matter, as it turns out. But, it had to be done.

So, I also tackled the question of genetic relativity. Simply put, how important are these characteristics when compared to each other? For example, how important is number 1 – Good Decision-making, compared to number 3 – Being Adaptable?

From extensive analysis of the highly scientific, unbiased, broad-based survey, we now have the answers. To summarize, here they are: it's a tie for first place between Good Decisions and Being Healthy. Adaptability and Intelligence are close behind and are of almost equal value. Good Looks pulls off a surprisingly close tie with Lucky.

In a distant last place is Lazy. Evidently, Lazy is in a class all its own, but don't discount it, because it definitely plays a role in species survival. At least to the gene pool.

Now, we know. The gene pool doesn't like Lazy people and Smart beats Good Looks hands down. Are we vain? Are we selfish? Genetically speaking, it appears that we are. Does that surprise you? Of course not! You knew you were smart all along.

What does that have to do with survival of the gene pool? It has everything to do with it. Haven't you been paying attention? As humans, we are supposed to be the smartest of the livestock on the planet, made in His image in His lab. We are the salvation for God's grade this term.

Besides, we have a perspective on the topic that's better than any of the other species. Just to make sure, I tried to get input from other species on the topic. Invitations for interviews were sent to all the other species, Unfortunately, they were all turned down or were non-responsive. So, we work with what we have ... humans.

We should all be on the same page by now – that the gene pool is not simple. It depends on combinations of characteristics for the advancement of a species and its survival. But that, in itself, does not answer the bigger questions.

Why does a lazy, dumb slob like Uncle Nesbit continue to live on, when hard working Cousin Dorothy dies young? What is the genetic purpose of the firefly, the ladybug, the liberals or the manatee? What the heck is going on? Where is the fairness in it all?

To address these questions, I had to turn to some mathematical valuations of the gene pool characteristics. Using hundreds of seconds and tens of minutes of computer analysis time, the results of the scientific survey were re-analyzed to unravel the rest of the secrets of the gene pool.

So what are the answers? There is only one. Are you ready? The answer is, not all gene pool characteristics are equal!

There! Aren't you glad you asked? I am.

What good is this? Where's the math? Where is the data analysis? How can it be so simple? Well, it doesn't mean a lot to you as I stated it, but it is true! They aren't all equal. Also, it really IS more complex than, "they are all equal". Had you going there, didn't I?

Once again, I did the hard work and analysis for you. When we're done here, you'll be able to score someone in each of these gene pool characteristics and tell whether or not they belong in the gene pool. Now, don't you think THAT would come in handy? It's worth the price of the book all by itself, especially if it was a gift.

Consider all the scientific research, analysis and billions of dollars spent on genetic understanding over the centuries. I'm going to boil it all down for you. Right now. Ready? The secret to the gene pool is ... 35!

That's it! This is the first time that this particular piece of scientific data has been divulged anywhere! Be careful how you use it. But, above all things – remember that THE MAGIC NUMBER IS 35!

In the logic of the gene pool, animals and plants – in fact, all living things – are graded against a perfect score of 35 in each of the seven categories. Of course, only God can get a full 35 points.

Yes, Gretchen, we're created in his image, but not all that closely created. Remember, we also have something called original sin, free-will, and an imperfect lab environment. Besides, there are way too many fun things for us to do to get anywhere close to a perfect score.

It isn't as simple as 35 points for each category, either, I'm afraid. If you'll remember, we found that some characteristics are not as valuable as others. It wouldn't be fair to give Lazy the same weight as Good Decision-making, would it? So we have to factor in the importance of each category.

Don't worry, I did the hard work on that for you, too – again. When all this is put together, the theoretical maximum human score turns out to be 180 points!

This is important. The gene pool grades us against the maximum 180 total points.

The logical next question is: if 180 points is the maximum, what is the cut-off point between being a gene pool Innie and Outie? Good question ... glad I thought of it.

Again, more exhaustive research was required on evolutionary development and documenting how species and individuals live, die, prosper and survive. The years of data collection and analysis have revealed that the gene pool has its own scoring basis. Naturally, it is not as simple as you're a gene pool Innie and Outie. God just couldn't let it be that simple, could he?

The gene pool has four distinct groupings and *everyone* falls into one, and *only one*, of them. The groups are:

- Those individuals we must have to perpetuate the best characteristics of life, survival and the interests of the gene pool.
- Those individuals who have characteristics that are, in the whole, favorable for improving the goals of the gene pool.
- Those individuals who are irrelevant to the gene pool – their existence and perpetuation are of little or no consequence to the goals of the gene pool.
- Those individuals whose existence is a direct, immediate or likely threat to the goals of the gene pool.

Now, that wasn't too bad, was it? Pretty straightforward, huh? Clear and easy to understand? Hard to argue with it, too. You're either IN, or OUT, or IRRELEVANT or a THREAT. How could one ask for simpler?

But wait, there's more. All individuals have to be in ONLY ONE of these four groups, right? Yup. Hmmm. Just how are the groups calculated? By that, I mean, what's the breakdown? How can you tell which group you, I mean your friends, are in? If not in the Innie group, which one? Good questions.

After more careful study and analysis for tens of days, including research across four continents and almost exhausting the powers of my computer, I have the answer for you. The following is the definitive, unqualified, scientifically proven and accepted grading criteria for the gene pool's four groups.

- Those who MUST be kept in the gene pool – 8.17%.
- Those who are DESIRABLE to have in the gene pool – 13.32%.

- Those who are IRRELEVANT to the gene pool – 54.84%.
- Those who THREATEN the gene pool – 23.67%.

In other words, only 8.17% of human life is necessary to keep the gene pool going!

What about the other 91.83%? Who needs them? Not the gene pool. If push comes to shove, the gene pool doesn't need any of the rest of you.

Interestingly, 13.32% of life is desirable, but not necessary. Pretty sobering, right?

Well, the gene pool is a strict grader (and there is no curve). These statistics have been in place for eons. The effects of these criteria can be seen in fossils, bones and archeological digs as far back as we have been able to uncover. They are absolute and immutable. One could say that they are set in stone.

You should also note that almost one in four of you (23.6%) score in the bottom group. That means genetic doom on you! The gene pool will be actively out for your ass. You are a direct threat to the gene pool and *must* be eliminated. You do not deserve to live. You do not belong in God's gene pool!

What about the other group? The 54.84% majority group? They are irrelevant, remember? Nuff said.

Let's simplify all these numbers for you bottom feeders. I put them into grade school terms you can understand. If you need help, ask a 3rd grader. With a maximum possible score of 180 points, a grade of:

- 91.83% and above is an "A" and is NEEDED by the gene pool – congratulations!
- 78.51% to 91.82% is a "B" and is IMPORTANT to the gene pool – good luck!

- 23.68% to 78.51% is a "D" and is IRRELEVANT to the gene pool – sorry.
- 23.67% or less is an "F" and is a THREAT to the gene pool and the rest of us – go away!

Sober up – here's the real kicker. Based on the above, it is clear that *most life on earth is completely irrelevant to the gene pool.* Totally irrelevant! Ain't that a kick in the head?

You always wanted to be popular? You wanted to belong? Congratulations! If you are in the majority now, you are IRRELEVANT!

Irrelevant is not a good place to be when the gene pool needs cleansing. Even being in the top two groups provides no guarantees. History is full of examples of how necessary and important gene poolers have died off. In fact – now that I think about it – all of them have died off!

Where do you fit in the gene pool? That is a great question. The answer is – you DO NOT want to know. Trust me, you don't.

But, I'll give you a way to rate your friends and relatives and get *their* gene pool score. Here's how you do it. Use the form that follows.

For each of the seven gene pool characteristics, rate your friend/relative on a scale of 0 to 1. Assume that 1 is the best and 0 is the worst. You should be able to do this on your own by now. If you can't, seek adult help or ask a fifth grader.

For each characteristic, rate your friend in the column marked "Rating".

When you've finished with all seven characteristic, multiply each rating by the "Maximum Gene Pool Points" for that characteristic. Put that answer in the "Total Points" column. This gives you their characteristic rating points.

Add up all the "Total Points" and you have their "Gene Pool Score".

Divide this number by 180 to get their "Gene Pool Grade" and you'll see where they fall relative to the gene pool's survival groups: Needed, Important, Irrelevant or a Threat.

GENE POOL SCORING WORKSHEET

	Characteristic	Maximum Gene Pool Points	Rating (0 to 1)	Total Points
1	Make good decisions	35		
2	The healthy one	35		
3	The adaptable one	28		
4	The smart one	28		
5	Good looks	20		
6	The lucky one	20		
7	Not lazy	14		
Maximum Total Gene Pool Points = 180		Gene Pool Score		
		Gene Pool Grade (%)		

I know this sounds really complicated, especially if you have trouble reading, didn't get through high school or need a calculator to work on your check book. So let's walk through an example before we move on. Let's say you have a friend (Congratulations!) named Cedric. Cedric is nerdy, but only in the kindest, true sense of nerdness. Let's find Cedric's gene pool rating.

- Good decision-making: Cedric is not really good at making decisions, especially the ones about normal, everyday life matters, so we give him a 0.4.

- **Good health**: He stays healthy in spite of all the chips, and beer and brats he eats. He does not have any major issues, like asthma, diabetes or congenital stupidity, so he gets a 0.8. We downgraded him for his eating habits that will have to catch up to him at some point.
- **Adaptable**: Cedric is not very adaptable, unless it's about technical issues, toys, video games and things like that. Space ships could land all over the world and he wouldn't notice. But, change the IP address on his favorite techno-wiz bang internet site and all hell breaks loose … give him a 0.2.
- **Smarts**: For smarts, Cedric has to have a 0.9. He is not the smartest guy in the world, but he is certainly smart and has the potential to be a lot smarter. So, 0.9 it is.
- **Good looks**: What would you think with a name like Cedric? Any geeky gal who found him attractive wouldn't mind belly-to-belly with him. But, let him loose on the sidewalks of town and he may have issues. I make it a compromise at 0.5.
- **Lucky**: Cedric gets points for being lucky enough to not have been stillborn or sold by his mother. He didn't electrocute himself as a kid when playing with the electricity in the living room electric outlet. And he was not sold into slavery by his 7th grade classmates. We can give him a 0.7.
- **Lazy**: Cedric is kind of lazy in a physical sense, but his brain is always working on something. Let's give him a rating of 0.5.

So, what do we have for Cedric? As you can see in the rating table below, our friend Cedric got 103.8 points out of a possible 180 for 57.6%. Not good. This score makes Cedric completely irrelevant to the gene pool. He gets no breaks or help. The gene pool doesn't even care if he exists.

CEDRIC'S GENE POOL SCORING WORKSHEET

	Characteristic	Maximum Gene Pool Points	Rating (0 to 1)	Total Points
1	Make good decisions	35	0.4	14
2	The healthy one	35	0.8	28
3	The adaptable one	28	0.2	5.6
4	The smart one	28	0.9	25.2
5	Good looks	20	0.5	10
6	The lucky one	20	0.7	14
7	Not lazy	14	0.5	7
Maximum Total Gene Pool Points = 180		**Gene Pool Score**		103.8
		Gene Pool Grade (%)		57.6%

Try this with your friends to see who you should and should not be hanging out with. See if your spouse is gene pool material, for the future of your family and the sake of the humanity. Get a glimpse of what the future holds for your children. Do it for your neighbors to verify what you already think about them.

CAUTION: DO NOT do this on yourself. You WILL be very disappointed and we cannot be responsible for anything you find out or do as a result of what you learn!

Chapter 5 – Combining
Rules of the Gene Pool

We've established that the gene pool is not one-dimensional, it is complex ... multivariate, to use a fancy word. We also discovered how the gene pool's characteristics relate to one another. As an added bonus, we also know how to score ourselves, I mean others, to see whether they are a gene pool Innie or Outie.

The gene pool rules seemed simple and straight forward enough, at first glance. Some of the examples we explored were interesting, some funny and others were downright scary, and there's more to come. Without a doubt, stupidity, ugly and lazy live on, even though they shouldn't.

There is no rational explanation why some of the examples are still in the gene pool. They are definitely, without a doubt ... Outies. Why is this?

Well, it is like this. In the early days of God's schooling, and the beginning of the gene pool, he was still learning the basics of creating life. He used simple rules like: you live or you die.

That seems to have worked well for snails, snakes, amoebas, bacteria, fishes, leather covered birds, dinosaurs and cave men.

The lazy did not eat. The stupid died because they could not find food or the rabbit was smarter than them. (Don't laugh, I know some candidates for that category and they are not cave men.) The ugly never mated and died off (I know some of them, too).

But the gene pool did not stay simple for long. God found that life and genetic guidance are more complex. The good old days of one rule, you are in or out, are gone forever.

Is there something else missing? If so, what was it?

Are there more gene pool characteristics? I don't think so.

Is there something else that would cause disqualification from the gene pool, other than in vitro deformities and illnesses? I haven't found of any that occur naturally.

The bottom line is, the gene pool, as we have seen, will allow any idiot, fool, dummy, smart ass, lazy, sickly, ugly or weak individual to survive. We've also seen that the application of these rules is not as straightforward as it would appear.

Obviously, there is more at work here than is immediately obvious to a blind man. So, let's explore the gene pool a little more and search a little deeper into its mysteries.

To do this, we need to examine the effects of various combinations of characteristics, from the gene pool's point of view. If we only look at it from the PETA viewpoint, cute wins every time and cancels out all the other characteristics. Everyone would be cute, but dumb as a stone. On the other hand, if we looked at it from the MENSA point of view, everyone would be very smart, but they'd be ugly and have no common sense.

The answer must be in combinations of characteristics, not in the individual ones. So let's explore. Let's look at some of the combinations that we run into daily and throughout history.

Our daily lives are full of examples that confirm the survey data. From the dog that chases a car, with no clue what he would do with it if he caught it, to the person who can't find their car in an empty parking lot.

I think you'll see why 78.51% of you are irrelevant to the gene pool. Let's look at this a bit further.

Good Looks and Smarts

First, let's explore good looks and smarts. To see examples of this combination, just turn your TV to any channel, at any time of the day. The "entertainment" industry is renowned for pumping out, and using up, good-looking people. In fact, they are the ones we look to for advice on what we should look like, what to wear and how to act. They *define* good-looking. But, are there any brains behind those looks? Of course not!

Example – any girl who dresses in a tight, short skirt and *forgets* her underwear, knowing she is going to get her picture taken, cannot be considered smart, by any measure. How many times did mother tell you to make sure you had clean underwear on, just in case something like this happened (or you had to go to the hospital)? This is a no brainer. And that's exactly what it takes to pull off a stupid stunt like that … no brains.

These same people have a small army of minions running around after them to make sure they look good; to tell them what to do, where to go, how to act, what to eat or not eat, and when to throw up.

Even with all these people looking out for them, they're still too stupid to put on their underwear. This is something every 3 year old knows. What good is someone like that to the gene pool? After all, good looks are way down in 5th place on the priority list, way down in the bottom half. These people do not even make good breeding stock!

Hollywood is also known as the center of the insecure and paranoid. They are needy. They crave attention and positive reinforcement. Spoiled brats is just what they are! What they need is a good spanking and some discipline.

But, what do they get instead? Sycophants and drugs. Oh wonderful! Drugs will solve all your problems. If you aren't good enough for the gene pool, take some drugs and you'll believe you are. More stupid piled on top of stupid. Given more attention and money than all the 1st graders in any medium sized city, they are still spoiled, narcissist brats who contribute nothing.

Sometimes, we find a Hollywood type trying to sound serious, smart and educated. Interestingly, the more they talk, the dumber they show themselves to be. They, and those who pay attention to them, are certainly at the bottom of the gene pool grading scale and contribute nothing to its ultimate objective.

On the other hand, a relatively few really smart people, who may not be the best looking, are doing great things for health, society, economy, nutrition and education. They aren't necessarily beauty contest winners. But, they are doing something useful, for the most part.

They're helping in such activities as constructing better buildings and improving living conditions, curing diseases, improving the crop yields for farmers and finding new sources of energy. In short, these relatively few, not great looking people, are improving the well-being of all the rest of us.

You can see why the gene pool only really needs a little over 8% of the population to keep going. The other 92% are just a drain on the rest of the gene pool. Imagine what the really smart people could accomplish if we didn't have to solve the problems caused by the other 92%! Maybe we could get back to the moon.

Bottom line – if you are good-looking and you depend on that to get in the good graces of the gene pool, forget it. You need to have a lot more than that going for you to have a chance. Yes, good looks are nice to look at and help in the belly-to-belly arena, but for survival – give me a smart decent looker.

Lazy, Healthy and Lucky

Being healthy is an obvious benefit to the gene pool, as is being industrious. What do these characteristics have to do with each other? It's so obvious, if you think for a minute. Time's up. Industrious people and animals tend to be in better shape and are less susceptible to illness.

On the other hand, they also expose themselves to more risks. Like getting hurt. If you work hard at building houses, you are likely, at some point, to get a significant injury. Much more likely than someone who spends their life at a desk whose worst risk is getting the flu from a co-worker or getting crunched in the elevator doors.

Being lazy is not cherished by the gene pool, but it has its place, especially when combined with other factors. For example, a lazy bee would be a queen bee. She sits around all day being taken care of and sending hoards of other bees out in the heat, the cold, the wind, and the rain to collect pollen for honey. She also has thousands more bees that protect her, groom her and feed her. She has it made! What a life! And, she has a place in the grand scheme of the gene pool.

There have to be some leadership skills in there somewhere, too. She has to be smart enough to get all those male bees to do her bidding and like it. We want some of that in the gene pool.

If we translate that into the human world, maybe we really

don't want it so much. Human males are already serving at the whim of women, especially those women who know how to use their "bee-power".

Throw in some guilt with the possibility of sex and men don't stand a chance. They are genetically programmed to do dumb things for sex and guilt. Just ask their mothers, girlfriends and wives.

Back to the topic. Those who are industrious and lucky will work hard and avoid injuries. We want them. The smart and lazy? We have to take that on a case-by-case basis, but a definite maybe.

The lazy and healthy? What about those two? As your family doctor will tell you, if you sit on your fat ass all the time, it will get fatter, your arteries will block up with plaque and your heart will give out. Then you die or become a living burden to the rest of us. That's why the lazy are not very welcome in the gene pool. Someone else always needs to carry their weight. Unless they have that "bee-power" thing going for them, that is.

If they are just dumb and lazy, and otherwise healthy, maybe they have something going for them that we need to look at. Why would someone whose biggest exercise is walking to and from their car at work, or bending over to pick up their shoes, be wanted in the gene pool?

Only if they have something else to offer that outweighs the negatives of being lazy. Something like, never being sick or discovering the cure for cancer. Or they have a rare blood type and are only wanted in the gene pool as a blood farm. Or maybe they are just very, very lucky.

The bottom line here is, if you are lazy, there isn't much support or help you can expect, except from the liberals. They won't take you in, but they will harass the rest of us to take you in. Good luck, but not too much.

Good Looks and Good Decisions

At the top of the gene pool characteristics heap is good decision-making. This characteristic trumps all the rest. It doesn't matter if you are lazy, smart, dumb, sickly or stuck in the mud. Making consistently good decisions is a most valued characteristic.

However, in the animal, human and plant worlds, good looks are often more important. The good-looking fruit trees attract more bees to spread their pollen and continue their lineage, whereas ugly fruit doesn't. You don't want to be an ugly fruit, do you?

The best looking ones in the herd always get more belly-to-belly, or belly-to-butt, time than the uglies. Just check out the bars.

We humans have gone to extra lengths to screw up this simple system and put the gene pool into a tidal flail. We look for leadership based on looks more than on good decision-making, counter to our genetic heritage.

Look to politics for more examples of this than you can shake a stick at. Through all the bluster and rhetoric of campaigns, it turns out that looks and image are the most closely cultivated and controlled features of a campaign. Clothes have to be just right. No sweat stains showing. Get that $400 haircut to look $300 better than the opposition. We are drawn to the good-looking candidates.

If we look at the ugly politicians, we'll see, almost exclusively, that they were elected when they were still good-looking. They got ugly while in office and their constituents were too afraid of change to boot them out. To be sure, we have some very ugly politicians. Check it out for yourself. None of them was ugly when they first ran for office. We are real suckers for good looks.

Is it any wonder, then, that some of the things coming out of congress and local legislatures are dumb as dirt? It's because we elected a bunch of people based on their looks, or our fear of change, or both. We never considered that they have terrible decision-making skills.

You doubt this? Ok, look at the laws that have been passed. I mean, actually read some. You have to wonder what in the world they were smoking. This is what happens when we put 535 of our most egocentric narcissists, chosen for their looks and fear factor, in one place. You get the collective decision-making dumbness of the group, which is what we have today in the US (or in any other law or rule making organization.).

Nothing good comes from the politicians, except one thing. They can hardly ever agree on anything with each other, so they usually do dumb things slower than most other people.

Let's look even closer. What kind of decisions do these good-looking people make in their personal lives? That should give us a clue about the kind of decision-making skills they bring to the job.

Example: They somehow meet with a shady person and end up with tens of thousands of dollars, wrapped in aluminum foil, mysteriously sitting in their freezer. And they don't know how it got there. Duh!

Example: They diddle around with young boys and pretty girls and figure they won't get caught or that no one would ever find out. Duh!

Example: They fool around and actually have (or almost have) sex with that woman (or that man) and think that no one will ever find out. Double Duh!

Example: They accidentally "forget" to pay their taxes for years at a time. What!?

This is a funny one. Who, in all of the United States, doesn't know that taxes are due on April 15th of each year? Is there anyone who does NOT know this? Of course not! We learn about this as children. Illegal aliens even know this.

Yet, somehow, politicians manage to forget about April 15th! Or they forget to pay taxes altogether! Do we really want such people making decisions on our behalf when they can't even get their taxes in? Not late mind you, but "forgotten" for years on end.

What else might they have forgotten? Their wife? Their morals? Their promises? Who they work for?

At least they make good-looking crooks.

Why do voters consistently vote for good-looking people who are obviously not the brightest bulbs in the string? People who prove that they can't make good decisions, even when it means keeping themselves out of jail?

These observations verify our earlier findings that 78.51% of the people on earth have no place in the gene pool. They put an unnecessary burden on the 21.49% of us that the gene pool wants to keep and the 8.17% that it *needs* to keep. Why do we have to keep fixing the repeated stupidity of the other 78.51%?

Bleach for the Gene Pool

As we've seen, it doesn't take much of a bad thing to ruin it for the rest of us. Fortunately, the gene pool has factored that in. Yes, we want the lucky to survive. Luck is a good thing to have. As long as it is *good* luck, that is.

It takes a lot of luck to compete with health and good decision-making. Likewise, the lazy make it harder on the rest of us, and they aren't all that useful. Unless, of course, they just happen to have some other, very exceptional redeeming characteristic to counter their laziness, like great health or decision-making.

Life imitates the gene pool, of course. Because, that's the way God designed it. He actually got a B+ for that work.

It's apparent, however, that for all his good work, the gene pool became far too complex. From time to time, things went wrong. Somehow, occasionally the ne'er-do-wells and unwanted minorities kept becoming the majority. They grew to dominate and screw up the gene pool.

This has caused heavy pollution of the gene pool several times throughout history. To protect itself, the gene pool had to react; to eliminate the pollution, to stomp out the bad. It had to bleach out the gene pool to restore balance. Examples, you ask? Ok ... read on.

For one example, we can look at the meteor that was sent to wipe out the dinosaurs and rearrange the earth lab for new experiments. Some of the animals did not work right in the lab and others evolved too quickly. Fish learned to walk on land way earlier than planned. Leather-covered birds flew. From the gene pool's point of view, things were pretty intact and interesting, but life in general was pretty stupid.

Their brains were not much to write home to mom about. In fact, they could not write at all, and if they could, they probably already ate their mom. So much for the good decisions gene, right mom?

Some were lucky that the kids ate dad instead of mom. Some were not so lucky and were eaten by their next-door neighbor's kid. It was not a friendly time or place. It was time for things to change. The gene pool needed a good bleach job and the big meteor 65 million years ago was just the thing.

Need more examples? Ok, the Black Plague. The gene pool was overrun by people and animals in bad health. The general populous was also infested with a top echelon of the governing hierarchy who were lazy and preyed on those who could not defend themselves.

While this is in keeping with the general philosophy of the gene pool, it was skewed way out of proportion. This imbalance was causing consequences that were hurting the goals of the gene pool. Bad decisions were being made by a few at the expense of the masses – and of the gene pool. The few smart people were not allowing the smarts to roll out to others and a few dumb people would not listen to the smart ones.

In the days of old, only a few people could actually read, and they kept the magic of it all to themselves. This domination kept the masses under their control. The populous remained stupid and dominated. The brain functions of the masses were repressed because they didn't think much or get challenged mentally. Remember the saying "Use it or lose it."?

They were certainly not lazy. They were just too busy trying to survive day to day.

This domination of the many by the few stifled the natural evolution of the gene pool. The ones who made good decisions and were lucky had good crops and survived the winters. Others did not. But it was not enough. Things had to change, and in a big way. So the Black Plague was created to return the gene pool to a better balance. In the rebalancing process, millions of people were wiped out. Some good ones and many bad ones. Some were collateral damage. The others were people who just had to go.

Before that, there was the biblical bedtime story about God flooding the earth. Remember how he wanted to start all over again because he was unhappy with the way things were going? Actually, it was the fire suppression system in the lab that went off one weekend and caused it to spray down on the earth lab.

We know it had to originate from somewhere outside of

the earth. How do we know? Because there isn't enough water on the planet to flood it! Simple math tells us that.

Who knows why these things happen? Maybe it was one of those times when God was depressed at the way his experiment was going and he set the system off himself. Remember, God was under a lot of pressure in those times to get good grades. It would be no wonder if he got a little tense and depressed from time to time. We weren't helping much, either. Remember Sodom and Gomorra? Moral of that story? It's not nice to piss off God.

At some time in the past, the Middle Eastern and northern African areas were lush gardens and forests. This was supposed to be the center of where God's lab began, remember? It was full of life with lots of vegetation and trees. Animals and people flourished there.

What happened? Was it punishment for things people did? Things like not letting his people go? Or worshiping the wrong Gods? Or otherwise pissing off God? Did he get mad and turn it all into desert out of spite?

Interestingly, the climate change has been verified to have started around the same time that the Himalaya mountain range was growing. As the Himalaya's grew, they changed the wind patterns around Europe, northern Africa and the Middle East areas. The new winds brought drought to the cradle of civilization, cold to Europe and rains to the southern Asian continent. It changed the weather and climate around the entire globe. Just another example of the gene pool balancing things out.

And how about the flu epidemics of the early 1900s, among many other times? Many millions of people died in those years from the flu. It was just the flu for crying out loud. In 1901, the flu was the number one cause of death in the US. Still today, thousands die each year from the flu.

Mark my words, the gene pool is not yet done with its bleachings.

Some people believe that the AIDS virus is another bleach job from the gene pool. Have we gotten to the point where wars and polio did not do enough to balance out the gene pool? Is AIDS another "Black Plague" intended to kill off the enemies of the gene pool? To bleach it and restore a healthy balance?

There can be no doubt in any reasonable person's mind or heart that the gene pool is still active and that re-balancing is still taking place. If you doubt this, the gene pool will know and will find you. Non-believers are considered enemies of the gene pool. It uses bleach to cleanse itself in big ways, and it can do it in small ways, too.

Beware of becoming an enemy of the gene pool or you may just get yourself bleached. Remember the dinosaurs. You've been warned!

Chapter 6 – The Human Gene Pool

Human studies of the gene pool, and its effects on evolutionary development, are still in their infant stages. It is surprising how many people still do not believe that the gene pool is real or that evolutionary changes happen. Yet, the evidence of it is all around us and we rely on it every day. The ability to suspend belief in the obvious tends to be a very well ingrained defense mechanism for us humans. It helps us remain quietly stupid.

Humans continue to live in a state of denial, as we have done so for many thousands of years. This does not make God or the gene pool happy. The rules of the gene pool were carefully thought out. They were analyzed and simulated on the best computers God could get at Universe U. The seven characteristics, their values and meanings were carefully, and painstakingly, researched and chosen early in God's lab work. This early research work established the basis by which life will reach and maintain a balance and survival.

It was originally planned that the genetic balance for humans would be achieved within 14 to 25 generations. This determination came after long experimentation and engineering work with early life forms and the dinosaurs. Things were working pretty well with them. The sick died or were eaten, or both. Good decision makers lived, others died. The gene pool was working, at least for them.

But, the 14 to 25 generation plan didn't work out so well. Something was wrong. Things were no longer working as they should. More and more people and animals began living when they should be dying. Stupid ones thrived! Sickly ones lived to make more sickos. Gene pool bleachings were required more and more frequently when, in theory, none at all should have been required. What was wrong?

Careful forensic analysis of the lab notes and experiment data revealed to God just what had happened and where things went wrong. It all started going badly at the same time that God decided to give Alpha and Beta free-will. That was the beginning of the end. Everything went downhill from there.

It has been a constant struggle since that moment for the gene pool to maintain balance. It's been a hard struggle to counter the harm humans keep inflicting by their independent thinking and ignorance of the consequences of their actions. It's the free-will given to humans that has, ever since, royally screwed up the gene pool and God's efforts to obtain survival of intelligent life on earth.

How could God have been so stupid as to screw up a good system by giving the subjects influence, or even control, of the experiment? In his defense, he was a beginner at this intelligent life stuff and beginners, especially inquisitive ones, sometimes do stupid things just to see what happens. Hopefully, it doesn't ruin the original experiment. Maybe God, and we, can learn and salvage something from the experience.

The first mistake was giving Alpha and Beta a choice about

the fruit tree thing. If it was God's lunch, then he (being God and all) should just have put it out of reach, or put thorns around it or put it in the fridge. You'd think God could have come up with a better solution to protecting his lunch than by telling Alpha and Beta what NOT to do. It's like telling a child NOT to touch something.

Alpha and Beta were new to this human life thing, too. You can't blame them. Telling them NOT to eat something just peaked their (Beta's) curiosity. They had to eat it then just for the new experience of it and to find out why they shouldn't. (Duh!) Every parent knows that would happen.

Regardless of how or why it happened (please note that it was the female who could not follow directions, of course) it was a done deal. We have all been stuck with the consequences of it ever since. Some refer to it as "original sin", but I think it is more a matter of poor applied psychology in dumb animals.

The second mistake was letting Alpha and Beta have children. No matter how it worked out, someone was going to go belly-to-belly with someone related to them. I don't remember anything written or said about marriage back then, so all Alpha and Beta's children had to be illegitimate, as well as genetically corrupt.

A great start for humanity, huh? No clothes, rules about what you can and can't eat and no way to make the union legal. What if Alpha was ugly? Or maybe Beta was ugly and fat? I'm fairly certain she did not shave her pits or legs. Yuck!

But what choice did they have? "Not if you were the only man (woman) on earth!" had a different meaning in those days.

Another mistake was that God only made two of them. I guess this is ok, if you're working with hippos or rhinoceroses where the gene pool's search for intelligent life is not going to be very threatened by inbreeding. But humans are different. Alpha and Beta only had each other. Like it or not, ugly or not, dumb as a rock or lazy as the day is long. All they had was each other and nothing to do.

In time, probably within 3 minutes if Alpha was on the ball and Beta wasn't ugly as a stick, they did the belly-to-belly. Not knowing how long it took for things to develop, they probably did it a lot.

That is, unless Beta had her "moments" and refused. You know she had to have those "moments" – she was a woman after all. It's in their breeding. They could do belly-to-belly here on the rock, there in the tree, over there by the lake, but only if SHE wanted to do it.

That's one reason God invented masturbation. Note that even the word masturbation is male in its nature. It starts with the word "mastur", which we all know is old-world Latin for the word master – meaning man or male. God invented masturbation to give Alpha something to do during those times when Beta was "not in the mood".

Remember, this was the Garden of Eden (the E-den). They didn't have much else to do. Oh yes, they had to name the animals. Not exactly a time consuming task to fill in between belly-to-belly sessions. What a wonderful life they had before they screwed it up.

Eventually, a little Alpha was born, then a little Beta. God, being logical and all that, named them Gamma and Delta, respectively. As Alpha and Beta continued to stir the womb with belly-to-belly activity, little Gamma and Delta grew up to breeding age, as did their brothers and sisters. They watched Alpha and Beta, learning from their elders, and soon started fooling around and doing the horizontal crawl with each other.

With more little ones around from all Alpha and Beta's belly-to-belly sessions, the group faced a terrible conundrum. Alpha was getting tired of the same old thing with the same old Beta. His loins stirred for some variety. The female children started looking pretty enticing to him.

Beta, too, was a bit bored about the whole sex thing, as women are known to get. Maybe some young stud would be nice. The kids were at "that age". There was no rule against it (after all there was no marriage, either), so what the heck.

The first hippy colony was formed. No jobs, no worries. Free sex for all. Jump on in and enjoy. The term masturbation was lost from the vocabulary. There was sexual variety and complete flexibility about when, how, who, how much, how often and where. What a life that had to be! Woodstock and the hippy colonies of the 1960's had nothing on this group. In no time, there were more little Greek named humans crawling around than there were Greek letters and numbers.

But, a couple of the kids had cleft palates and some others were extraordinarily stupid. A few others also didn't turn out "right". They turned to God for some answers, as humans do when they want to know what went wrong and for someone else to fix it for them.

"Hey, God, what's going on here? Some of the kids aren't turning out so good. What gives?" Alpha asked.

"Yeah," said Beta "I carry these kids for nine months and some of them are broken. What's up with that?"

God thought about it some, did some research in his old class books, and came back with an answer. "You cannot do the belly-to-belly with your children, or their children, or their children or their children. You must have at least four generations between you and the ones you belly-to-belly with."

"You got to be kidding me!" exclaimed Alpha. "First, you

create us in this place with nothing to do except name some stupid animals and do the belly-to-belly mambo. And NOW you tell me that I can only do it with Beta? For four generations? What happened to paradise?"

Unfortunately for Alpha, Beta heard all this. As women have the knack to do, she keyed in on the really important words of "*only do it with Beta?*"

"And what is so bad about me? I was good enough for you all these years and now I'm no good for you? You want the children? Someone younger? With no stretch marks? Perky boobs? Is that what you want? I'm not good enough for you anymore? Is that it?" Beta screeched at Alpha.

Alpha now had a fight on his hands on two fronts. He wasn't the brightest of the first humans, but he did know which battle to fight first. "That isn't exactly what I meant and you know it. You've enjoyed your share of variety too, haven't you? What I meant was, back then you and I were the only ones around, there was no choice."

"Oh, shit!" Alpha said to himself under his breath, realizing his mistake way too late.

"No choice?" shrieked Beta, as only a wounded female can shriek. "You had no choice? What were you doing all that time by yourself behind the bushes? You think I didn't know? I saw you and what you were doing. You always had choices! Until now that is! Now you really have no choice. You can't have me and you can't have the girls, either! You can only have yourself behind the bushes! See how you like that for a few years."

Now at this point, if there had been any semblance of civilization, they would have invented incest, pedophilia, homosexual love, restraining orders, lawyers and divorce. Luckily, those things had to wait a while until we had a really good group of illegitimate and deformed people running around inbreeding, and arguing and going behind the bushes.

Instead, they had God. And God had taken Sociology 101 and Group Dynamics in Undeveloped Organisms. He was prepared for this situation. At least he thought he was. We know how it all turned out in the end, so it can't truly be called a success. Here is how it happened back then.

"Hold on there, Alpha. Calm down. I didn't say you could never do it with the others. You just have to wait a few generations. That's not so bad for a guy like you."

"And what's with dis'ing Beta? She didn't do anything to deserve that remark? She's still vital and good-looking, especially after having 26 kids. You think you look the same as you did way back then when SHE had no choice either? Come on now, look at her. Isn't she the true apple of your eyes (bad metaphor)? Doesn't she still stir up the feelings inside you? Come on now, admit it."

"Well, yea, she does a bit. It's just that the others …"

"STOP right there! Do NOT say another word. Just look at Beta. Tell her you are truly sorry and that she is plenty woman for you. I'll tell you some secrets about how to deal with your other feelings later."

"You will??? Well then, I guess maybe I did say a couple of things that didn't really sound like I meant them to." Turning to Beta, he continued "I'm sorry, Beta. I didn't mean to put you down. You know you are my favorite and always will be."

God rolled his eyes. Beta glared. Her hairy pits dripped from the emotional strain.

"That isn't a very good apology, but because you are too stupid to know any better, I accept. But, you still sleep in the bushes for a while till I get over it. Got it? No touching, no smooching, no nice baby-talk trying to get into my fur. Well, maybe a little. You just have to wait!"

"Yes, dear one." Alpha muttered in defeat. He knew when he was beaten, having been beaten so many times before.

Walking a few steps towards the bushes, Alpha asked God about those tips he promised for getting through such tough patches with women.

"Well," answered God "you've learned the first lesson, always let her win. Next thing to remember is that you can still do it with the girls, just don't get caught. For other variety, you can check out one of the guys. There are no genetic issues there and, technically, you are not cheating on Beta with one of the girls. Last, and most important, alone in the bushes is not that bad of an alternative, as long as your hand isn't broken."

So, here we have, in short order, the reestablishment of masturbation as a reasonable alternative to facing a woman. Best of all, it was sanctioned by God!

Also, homosexuality is suggested, by God, as another alternative to women, especially those in the next four generations.

Most important of all, the wisdom of the universe – always let the female win the argument! Perhaps, if Moses had been around during this time, the commandments might have ended up a little differently.

Happiness was once again established in Hippyville. Deformed babies stopped popping out, the bushes shook regularly, Alpha and Beta were happy again and the men started getting along together … surprisingly well, in fact.

So how did it go south from there? Remember that part about free-will? That was it. That's what did it. Hippyville was a happy place, but as the number of people grew, they developed different ideas and wants. These soon grew into rules. With rules, as we all know from momma's house, someone has to enforce them. Without enforcement, the rules have no meaning.

With enforcement, they had to develop keepers of the rules and enforcers. In the beginning, these were moms and dads. As we started to become an actual society, mom and dad weren't enough, something more was needed. The result was the first form of police and law-makers and people to judge the law breakers.

The keepers of the rules and laws tried to keep everyone in line and following a single interpretation of what was good and bad; acceptable and not acceptable. Inevitably, it came to pass that some folks in society had different ideas of what was right and wrong and who had the right to decide and to punish. Unable to change things, these good minded people tended to move away and form their own societies.

If you look closely at history, going way back to the very beginning, well, almost to the beginning, you will find something very interesting about all these breakaway societies. They all, each and every one of them, claimed that they were unwanted in their old society. They were driven out from society and were persecuted for their new ideas and ways.

It's always the "others" who were cruel, and mean and unfair. "They" made dumb laws. "They" wouldn't listen to reason or to dissenting opinions. "They" wouldn't let people do what they wanted. It all sounds like a bunch of 6 year olds or preteens. "They keep picking on us and won't let us do what we want." Waaa, waaa, waaa. Want some cheese with that whine?

In time, the people who left the original groups had groups leave them with the same complaints. Imagine that! Over and over this same scenario was repeated. Look at the Pilgrims. They left England for "religious freedom" because others told them what to do and wouldn't let them do what they wanted.

They took their religion and ran away across the Atlantic to New England. Not great navigating, if you ask me. I would've headed for Bermuda or the Bahamas myself. But, what do I know?

Anyway, at last, they could do whatever they wanted. Soon, they were freely roasting witches, hanging people for having sex and punishing people who said anything against them. If this is their form of freedom, I'm glad they didn't stay in England and pass it on to the English. This was radical stuff.

As soon as rebellious Pilgrims had a chance to meet others or get away, they did. And they carried with them the same complaints as the original Pilgrims ... no freedom, people were mean, no one listened, no one understood them. Waaa, waaa, waaa.

What does this have to do with the topic? Well, a lot. If you are smart, you have already figured it out. If not, please read on.

As societies grew and their populations expanded, especially with the population explosion after the fourth generation, there have been some people telling other people how to live. As things went on, some of these people had the power to impose their own opinions and wishes on others, at least for a time.

From the time we are little until we die, there is always someone telling us what to do or not do. Sometimes, these people have controlled the lives of others to great extents. The Catholic Church, in the early days and middle ages, was one of the greatest of these types of offenders.

Ganges Khan killed and destroyed all across the Asian and Eastern European continents. But, he was never so hypocritical as to do it in the name of love and the one true God. He was straight-forward. "You have it, I want it. I'm meaner than you ... therefore, I win." Even the simplest of peasants could understand that!

The Church controlled far more people than Khan and probably killed more, too – all in the name of freedom, and love, and forgiveness and peace. They controlled people through the imposed fear of eternal damnation, no food, taxes, pain, torture, no education, no freedom to think on their own, and more.

Perhaps worst of all, they suppressed free thinking and free-will and denied education to the masses. In the global ways of the gene pool, this skewed things dramatically and unnaturally away from a properly operating gene pool.

The gene pool can handle normal evolutionary developments, as we've seen. It was designed to promote it, in fact. It has rules and processes to keep things under control and in balance. Before humans showed up, things were going quite well. Dinosaurs came and went. Bugs and fauna came and went. The best survived and the others died. Simple and easy. Even ice ages and asteroids had their places and purposes.

Things changed when people were created. The gene pool had a very difficult time keeping things in line once humans, with their "free-will", showed up. There are three major applications of "free-will" humans exhibit that ruined it all for God's gene pool plans:

- The ability to ignore the rules, like free-will.
- The desire to do things different than the gene pool would have them do – the application of free-will.
- The ability to do as they wish and mess up the purpose of the gene pool – the power to impose free-will on others.

How has this messed up the gene pool? Come on – you can't seriously be asking that question!

Let's look back at the poor Pilgrims again, that group of

malcontents from England. They replaced some of the gene pool's rules with their own. If you were smart and could see through the crap they were spouting, you were called a heretic. If you were declared guilty of heresy, you were burned at the stake.

As an alternative, developed to show just how fair the Pilgrims really were, you could prove your innocence by being drowned in the dunking pond.

So much for natural evolution.

If you were sickly, they found a way to kill you rather than save you. Maybe the gene pool could have used the healing genes of those killed. Too late, though, the Pilgrims intervened.

If you were too lucky and always got game when hunting, or always got the first seat in the bathroom, or didn't get hit by Indian arrows, you were tortured and killed as being possessed by the devil.

According to historical writings, the men who governed the Pilgrims also gave special preference to good-looking women and killed off the good-looking men. They were no dummies. Good looks wins, again – at least for the ladies.

They trashed the gene pool in the name of freedom, love, tolerance and knowing right from wrong better than anyone else. Sound familiar? Kind of like parents and certain religious groups.

We have other religious groups around today who believe they are close to righteousness and deny the gene pool's rules. For one of these groups, "wait and see" seems to be their version of the gene pool. If the person, or child, is supposed to live, they will. Either way, it is God's will … so they claim.

Well, I don't buy all that God's will stuff. Good genes, bad genes, luck. Yes, I can work with that. Sure, God set the rules, but he also gave us free-will and the ability to intervene for the good of the gene pool and to preserve life.

The rape of Islam has brought to the current world similar concepts of strict and baseless religious demagoguery and cruel control, all in contravention to the gene pool.

Ok – the gene pool doesn't care so much if you want your women covered from head to toe. Truth be told, it would be doing men a favor if more religions would follow suit. But denying education? Withholding medical help? Controlling people's freedoms in the name of God? Killing others who may be different, in the name of love and God! How grossly stupid!

They have gone back into the Middle Ages and recreated the Catholic Church by another name! It also prevents the gene pool from doing its job of maintaining survival and balance, with some intelligence intact.

How can the gene pool compete with such human created problems? Humans are taking things into their own hands and we aren't doing such a good job of it. Religious fanatics, who don't have half a brain, are making bad decisions for selfish reasons that make the bleaching of the gene pool look like a daily shampoo.

The search for whale parts almost wiped out the whales. The buffalo in America were almost lost over the same selfish, unthinking greed. The Dodo bird *is* extinct, but we cannot blame that on man. The Dodo was just too stupid to survive (see gene pool characteristic number 4).

Whole civilizations have been wiped out by man's quest for power and control, despite the efforts of the gene pool to counter these actions through plagues, ice ages, etc. Mankind continued to get the upper hand and screw things up.

The results on the gene pool are seen in our everyday lives and in the results of the scientific poll, discussed before.

Remember that? Remember, it showed that 78.51% of life on earth is irrelevant to, or an active enemy of, the gene pool. Think about this a moment.

The gene pool, which was created by God to maintain a balance of life on earth and to perpetuate intelligent life, was once in control of life on earth. This was before "free-will". Now, after eons of that "free-will" crap, more than three quarters of life is *irrelevant!* The gene pool has lost control! How can 21.49% of us counter 78.51% of them?

Is a big "correction" looming before us? Maybe a huge bleach job will restore the balance by wiping out the other 78% and give us back the natural order of things? As bad as things have gotten, it can't be very far off. Remember the dinosaurs.

The Rise of the Liberals and the Fall of Society.

How did this genetic juxtaposition happen? The cause is evident in our history books and our daily newspapers. Those in power worked to keep power. They killed others to get and maintain their power. This had nothing to do with the gene pool, except for those few occasions where some lucky individual was hiding from the bad guys and wasn't found. Or when the guys on horses captured a beautiful woman or pretty young boy and kept them for their leader. A little luck and good looks were able to slowly creep back into the gene pool that way.

In the last few hundred years, we've seen something more sinister than all those who have come before. Something more powerful, more controlling, so sneaky that people don't yet realize what's happening to them. We have seen the rise and conquest of the liberal, again.

Yes, the left-leaning, stick their nose into your business, goody-two shoes, champion of those who don't have a clue, or a life, or both … liberal. The liberals have been the largest contributor to the decline of the gene pool since the Pharos of ancient Egypt and the Roman Empires.

How did they do it? How did they ruin the gene pool, cause chaos on earth, and destroy the balance of nature itself? They combined free-will with bad decisions, heaped with excessive sentimentality, excuses for everything, and guilt for everyone, except themselves. How, you ask, could this be a bad thing? You *are* kidding, right? Follow me.

The building of all civilizations in history, the real building, was done by people with vision. These were the people who were not lazy. They made good decisions about where things were to go and how to make them happen. They understood the social needs and how people got along. They understood that individuals had to be responsible for themselves and their actions. They knew that people had to be able to band together for mutual protection, survival and growth.

They also knew that people had to pull their own weight. If they weren't willing, or able, to support themselves, they would be a drag on the rest. For much of human history, the world just could not support those who would not, or could not, contribute to their own survival.

The sick died. The strong survived and shared with the others. Unlucky, but hard working, people who had crops ruined by hail-storms got help from others. People too lazy to care for their crops had nothing to eat in the winter and got no help.

These were the golden times of human history. The times when the gene pool thrived. You worked for your survival and improvement or you were left behind. You made good decisions or you died from the bad ones. This is the way the gene pool was designed to work. Yes, life was a bitch, but people, as individuals and as societies, were able to adapt, and grow and stay strong and resilient. They evolved as the world changed.

As civilizations improved and made life better for all, the free-will of the less fortunate and those with too much "stuff" clashed to bring the civilizations down. We started to take care of those who could not, or would not, take care of themselves.

Old people who spent their lives working and giving to others got help. But, so did those who did nothing to help themselves. We have to give thanks to those who had things and felt guilty and went out of their way to look after those who had too little.

Often, those with "stuff" (money, land, food, slaves, weapons, women, boys, gold, water, etc.) wanted to do something about those who had nothing. But – they did not want to give up anything *they* had to do it. So they badgered the working folks to donate *their* "stuff", instead. Feed the hungry. Shelter the homeless. Teach the dumb. Cure the sick. Just don't use *my* "stuff" to do it.

Over and over, throughout history, the same cries have gone out. Over and over, those who have the good life, and no clue about reality, have been the mouthpieces for giving every-one else's "stuff" away. In this way, those who have "stuff" get to keep it and still feel good about themselves for helping the down-trodden.

Their efforts are completely hollow, of course. They've contributed nothing of consequence of themselves. In the process, they've made the rest of us, who work hard for our own "stuff", give it to those who have done nothing to earn any "stuff". Nothing, except to look and act pathetic.

Over the thousands of years that this has been going on, the result of this meddling is to skew the natural genetic populations. This is mostly seen in the dramatic increases in people who really do not deserve to still be here.

Thanks to the recurring surges of liberalness, we heal those who should die. We spend resources teaching those who will never be smart enough to use it. We use food that others worked hard to grow to feed those who are too lazy to get a job or do the work to earn that food. We make working people spend their resources to house those who are too lazy or stupid to make a home for themselves.

Sometimes the excuse given is that they are just "down on their luck". Well, if things are that bad for them, the gene pool has a solution – die and quit sucking the life out of the rest of society. If you are a consistent drain on society or continuously take more than you give, die and let the best live. Let the gene pool work!

We have numerous examples throughout history of how this has brought down societies. Consider the extreme examples that brought down the Egyptian Empire, the Roman Empire and the Inca Empire. As free-will proliferated, people gave more of their personal responsibilities to others, the leaders.

An insidious career path developed that is considered the height of liberalness. A career path that has done more throughout history to bring down civilizations than any other form of employment.

No … not hookers. This is worse. Politicians!

Repeatedly, politicians put themselves above all the others. They dictate how everyone else should live, where they should live, the work they do. Then, they take your "stuff" (money, or crops, or cattle, or children) to give to others.

Their goal? Stay in control and in power.

Their process? Take from those who have some "stuff"

(you) and redistribute it to those who don't have any "stuff" – all the while without pissing off those who have a lot of "stuff".

Because politicians have the power to make thing happen, they need to protect that power in order to keep it. They also like to live large. Pyramid large. Coliseum large. White House large. Palace large.

They have access to the fruits and toils of others and don't have any "stuff" to show for their own work. The currency for politicians is other people's money and hard work. They trade it, barter it, control it, collect it and distribute it to maintain power and control.

To live large, they need others to pay large. Politicians always work with people who have a lot of "stuff", such as people who have a lot of money and want to keep it, the rich.

The rich keep the politicians in power so they (through politicians) can continue to manipulate the populous unhindered. This way, the rich stay rich and make sure no one makes rules to get at their money, their "stuff".

They help the politicians and the politicians help the rich. One hand strokes the other guy's stroker.

This system is as old as civilization itself. In the old days, someone just went in and said "Beware the Ides of March" and stabbed the politician to death.

Things aren't so easy these days. There are procedures for getting rid of corruption in politics. Even if caught diddling a young boy or girl, the politician is not automatically guilty or kicked out. They have different rules to protect the guilty than those to protect the innocent.

When the great civilizations have failed, and they all have, it's because they forgot what it was like to struggle and work to survive. They got soft and uncaring.

The politicians got carried away in their excesses and forgot what real life was like. They took more and more from those who actually worked for it and gave more to the rich; to those who don't have anything; and, of course, to themselves. All this time, they refused to take any responsibility.

Of course, the populous was not all that dumb. They kept turning to the politicians for handouts and help. They came to rely on the politicians for life itself. This, of course, fed right into the ego of the politicians. As has been said, "We have them right where we want them." The politicians sucked on the teat of their world till it was dried up and then demanded more.

When 22% of life on earth is carrying the other 78%, things are bound to collapse. And they did – over and over again.

We are at the same point today. Those who do not have to worry about their own welfare have taken over the reins of power based on a simple promise: to get everything for everybody from someone else.

Didn't "Animal Farm" teach us anything? If not, why did we all have to read it in school?

We have come to the proverbial slippery slope of all great civilizations and we are on a sled ride to oblivion. Just look at the gene pool for the evidence of it and a glimpse of our future.

It should give everyone major worries that only 1/5th of human life matters to the gene pool? The rest are in the way or working against it. These are the ones who take power and continue to wreck life as it was intended. Indeed, as it was designed to be, by God himself when he created the earth and the algorithms that guide the gene pool.

It is the liberals who bear the greatest responsibility for putting us in this situation. It is they who want to ruin a good plan, God's plan, by saving those who should die. By taking from the productive few to give to the useless many.

It's not the gene pool of the liberals to control and manipulate. It's God's gene pool. God certainly has to be preparing something big to restore the balance of HIS gene pool.

By the way, has anyone heard of someone building a big boat or a space ship? Or maybe a deep, meteor resistant underground shelter? Is there a large migration to the Antarctic area to survive the coming bleach by fire? Buy land in Greenland while it's still cheap.

Something has to happen. We cannot screw around with God's gene pool like this without consequence. I think I smell genetic bleach being poured.

Remember the dinosaurs, the ice ages, the floods, Krakatau, the continental shifts that separated continents, the Black Plague, and the year with no summer? Have we forgotten so soon? Put the gene pool back in alignment or face the consequences!

Am I just crying wolf? The sky is falling? Yelling fire when there is none? Of course not! Have you not been paying attention up till now? Come on, stay on task.

Let me give you a few examples of how the liberals have put muck two feet thick on the waters of the gene pool. Muck that suffocates it and destroys all hope of achieving intelligent life and long term survival. This muck perpetuates the worst of the gene pool and protects the stupid and unlucky teat suckers. They then grow up to make more little stupid and unlucky teat suckers. These are direct threats to the gene pool and to humanity itself!

- If you are bad at making decisions while driving, the kindly liberals add more signs and lights so you cannot make a mistake and hurt someone. So much for letting those same folks kill themselves off and save the gene pool. If they aren't good drivers, let them die – the surviving drivers will all be better drivers by default.

- Regardless of whether or not you are a safe driver, or just a passenger, the government is going to save you by making you wear a seat belt and not allowing you to use a phone while driving. Next thing you know, they will mandate a sensor on the steering wheel to make sure you have two-hands on it. If a driver can multi-task and do it well, and not kill themselves in the process, good for them. We need those skills in the gene pool. If they can't do it – they die off and solve the problem for us.

- About the passengers. If they don't have the good sense (they make bad decisions) to stay away from bad drivers, let them die off, too. If they don't know the driver is a bad driver, then they are unlucky and we don't want them in the gene pool anyway.

- The current tax structure is similar to those in other failed great societies – if you have a lot, you can afford to find ways to pay little. If you have little, you pay nothing. If you are somewhere in-between, the government takes as much of it as it can get away with.
The original plan was for those who "have" to share their extras. Those who don't "have" would get some from those who do. And those who don't try to help themselves would get bleached by the gene pool and no longer be a drain to the rest.
But, the do-gooders have changed all of that. Instead,

if you don't work, you pay no taxes. In fact, the government will GIVE you money for food and living, and will even give you a place to live, for NOT working.

If you work and don't make enough to take from you, the government will give you more money for food and living.

If you make enough to take care of a house, a car and college for the kids, the government will take more than 50% of it from you to support the of the rest of the ne'r-do-wells, including those who do nothing but drain the gene pool dry.

What is the incentive to work at all? Play the game and take from those who work. This is not acceptable to the gene pool … work, share or die.

- In order to protect all the real dummies out there, we've been forced to write 8 pages of warnings on appliances that need only 3 pages of instructions, including 4 different languages. Does something sound wrong here?

  If people were smart enough to actually READ and UNDERSTAND all those warnings, they would be able to understand the instructions. They would use the product correctly and take personal responsibility for their misuse or mistakes with it.

  This all started because some guy lifted up his RUNNING lawn mower by hand to trim some hedges. In the process, he trimmed himself (big surprise!). He sued and WON because there was no warning against lifting the mower while it was running or that it was not intended to be used to trim hedges. This is wrong on so many levels. Unburden the gene pool. Let the dummies die off.

- The liberals want to save everybody, regardless of the cost. (Remember, it doesn't cost *them* anything.) We now have extraordinary medical procedures done on infants and fetuses to save them when there is no reasonable expectation for them to live, let alone to contribute to the gene pool.

  They were not intended to survive. The genetic system was established to be probabilistic … some make it, some don't. Deformed babies are supposed to die.

  Instead, they pollute the gene pool and suck more from society's teat while giving nothing back. The same thing goes for those who are badly hurt or diseased. Let things happen the way they were designed to and stop screwing around with the gene pool.

- Motorcyclists are forced by laws to wear helmets. Some decide not to. If they don't want to wear helmets, let them be. If they're good and/or lucky riders, we won't have to worry about it. If not, let them die the honorable death of a motorcyclist with a smashed-in skull and half their skin gone.

  Let them feel the pain of having all the skin scrapped from their bodies by the asphalt as they go to the big motorcycle rally in the sky. Give them some Jack Daniels and let them be. Float them out with the tide into the gene pool, like the Vikings of old.

- Contrary to the basic rules established way back in Alpha and Beta's day, the governments have made it illegal to have anal sex. This is a left-over remnant from the Pilgrim days. How unenlightened we've been led to be. Sodomy fits with the original warnings to Alpha about the first four generations of his daughters. It cuts down on the consequences of inbreeding. It's approved by God! It also helps people make more friends. No worry about the belly-to-belly ugly issue either.

- Criminals are another group that takes from others without giving back. Unfortunately, we've become a society of apologists. We believe there are no bad criminals, just those unlucky ones who, due to "life's circumstances", actually get caught. If they're that stupid and make those types of bad decisions, we do not want or need them. Follow the guidance of the gene pool and cancel their membership in society, permanently. Kick them out of the gene pool.

- General lack of adaptation of the individuals. The liberals have convinced governments that it is their primary role to adapt to, and provide for, the needs of the individuals. This counters the proper leadership role of holding a steady course and having individuals adapt and grow with society. Remember, if you cannot adapt, you cannot stay in the gene pool.

You should get the point by now, unless you're as dumb as a rock.

It's not that liberals are the roots of all evil. It's just that they foster it and add to it, unnecessarily. The philosophy of the liberals can best be summed up as "Give unto others as you would have someone else give unto them."

To be sure, the liberals are not the only wrong-doers on the earth. The more conservative groups and individuals contribute their share of trouble for the gene pool, but they tend to be more in line with the original intent of the gene pool. This is why more of them are going to be saved for the future, if the gene pool has its way.

The conservative groups have two major flaws. First of all,

they tend to attract and perpetuate fanaticism. Extremists can often be found in this group and extremism is not in line with the balance the gene pool tries to maintain.

Of course, we all know that the liberals have their share of fanatics, too. Just ask the spotted owl and the soft-beaked woodpecker. But, in sheer volume of extremists, the conservatives win.

The second flaw of the conservative extremists is that they are very black and white about things and tend to be very vocal. Their beliefs are that you should believe as they do or you are wrong. Simple and straight forward. Black and white.

They also tend to believe that it's their divine purpose and destiny on earth to convert everyone else over their way of thinking, regardless of how extreme it is.

Examples? Ok, back to the Pilgrims. They couldn't have it their way, so they came over here and made everyone they ran into conform to their way, or else.

Back a little further and we have the Muslim and Catholic wars and crusades. Fanaticism ran wild.

And before that? Let's see, there were the Egyptians, the Incas, and many more tribal issues on smaller scales.

More recently, the hijacking of Islam by extremist conservatives is a prime example of this. If you don't believe as they do, they believe they are justified, indeed duty bound, to kill you. They are very black and white about that. And they would be just fine taking the world back to the 1400s, or earlier.

Where the liberals cannot justify their positions on logical grounds; the conservative extremists try to justify themselves with the pronouncements of God, or just kill, to make their point.

An interesting note about the conservative fanatics. Almost all of them believe they are in direct contact with God, and that they alone have the only correct answer and interpretation of God's intent and guidance. This is an interesting position. God created the gene pool and the extremist positions work counter to that purpose and, by extension, counter to God. You try to explain it to them.

I cannot figure out either position and believe that somewhere in the middle is the safest place to swim in the gene pool. Do unto others, but please do unto thy self first!

Chapter 7 – Humans vs the Gene Pool

C ats and rabbits and birds – Oh My! A little humorous side trip is needed after all the serious stuff we've waded through. So, for your amazement and entertainment, I present a true story of man's stupidity while playing God. There are so many to choose from, but this one kind of struck a nerve. Read and enjoy.

This is a classic case of man not being up to the standards required for even minimally competent operation of a gene pool. The story comes to us from Macquarie Island. Macquarie Island is a wonderful, rugged little island south of Australia. Macquarie Island has an abundance of wonderful birds and water animals, including penguins, seabirds, fishes, and more. They love it there and they thrive.

These animals have been decreed to be there "naturally" by the divine guidance of the gene pool and the local government. "They BELONG there! It's THEIR island." say the human inhabitants, who have taken over the rest of the island. (Unnaturally, it is presumed.) It's interesting that no one seems to ask how the "original" animals got there in the first place.

Anyway, on with the story.

A problem has developed recently. It seems that, over the years, non-native animals have been showing up on the island. Most have arrived by boat as stowaways.

As a result, the island became overrun with cats, rabbits, rats and mice. One or two is ok. But, you know how prolific these animals can be. It is impossible to have just a few. Soon, they overwhelmed the island.

It should be noted that these "pests" got to Macquarie Island the same way that other Pacific islands, such as Hawaii, developed new life forms, including human ones. Existing indigenous animals and fauna were supplanted by seeds from migrating birds and animals from human travel. People brought animals with them on ships. Birds deposited new seeds from other places in their droppings. It's been happening like this throughout history all around the world.

This process allows a species to expand and find new places to live. Of course, man added new scope and speed to the distribution process, but it is the same process that's been at work all along.

In the case of Macquarie Island, mankind decided to interfere with the gene pool and to "correct" the situation. Of course, they didn't start getting upset about things until the situation got out of control. But, once things were out of control, people had to set it "right" again. I guess we still haven't learned that it isn't nice to fool with things we don't understand and cannot control. And nature and the gene pool fit nicely into these categories.

Back on Macquarie Island, the feral cats, rabbits, rats and mice dominated the "natural" food chain and caused all sorts of problems, including impacting the tourist trade. (Do we think we may be getting to the heart of the problem?)

As we know, there is a delicate balance to nature. These interloping stowaways were ruining it. The people evidently couldn't wait to see what the gene pool would do about it. That would take too long. The tourists were coming.

Besides, they might not like the gene pool's answer. Anyway, the birds were here first and were the natural inhabitants! Things had to be set right!

"By God, them cats and rabbits just ain't natural and they gots to go! The birds need our help!"

Man to the rescue! We're here to save you! Look out gene pool!

How I cringe when I hear those words. Go birds, go! Fly away and hide. Go far away and don't look back. Get away while you can. Man is here to help you!

The islanders charged ahead with their plan to make things right and restore the balance of nature. Unfortunately, they did so without the knowledge of a God or the planning one would put into a 5 year olds birthday party. But, charge ahead they did. Full steam ahead to save the birds and the tourist trade.

What was the plan? How did it work out? What do *you* think?

There wasn't much to the plan. A reasonably intelligent reader can guess how it turned out, partially because it's in this book. Big hint: man screws with nature and the answer is? Of course, we screwed it up, killed lots of animals and made things worse.

The original plan was to "eradicate" (their word, not mine) all the cats because they were hunting down and killing the birds. Simplicity itself, right? Cats are killing birds – kill the cats and the birds are free again. How hard can this be?

I guess it took people by surprise that cats would kill the birds. Or they didn't care if it was just a few birds. It took a while for it to become a real problem. I surmise that the tourist impact was the deciding factor, not the actual number of birds killed by the cats.

Eventually, the people got riled enough to take action. When they finally decided to act, they really went gung-ho.

With some well placed poisons, they killed many feral cats. Bummer and so sad. But at least the birds were safe once again. They probably got a stray domestic cat or two, but some collateral damage is to be expected. I'm sure someone got promoted or reelected for "correcting" this terrible horror of nature. Maybe there was a lottery to guess how many feral cats would be killed.

Finally, all was once again well in Macquarie Island and the tourists could come back.

Not so quick. Something unexpected happened. Sure the cats died. Well, not all of them, but a lot of them died. However, the *rabbit* population on the island exploded. With no cats to chase them around, to eat their food, and to keep them at bay; and with the extra vegetation now available, the rabbits flourished, as rabbits will do. Nice rabbits. Pretty rabbits. Right? Well, there can be such a thing as too many rabbits, as Macquarie Island found out.

The rabbits were everywhere. They ate the vegetation (because that's what rabbits eat) without hindrance. However, the vegetation is what the birds also relied on for food, for protection from predators, and for cover. On top of that, not all the cats were killed. They didn't get them all, not by long shot. Oh-oh! I smell a plan going bad.

Biology question: which animal reproduces faster, rabbits or birds? Oh yeah! You know the answer to this one – the rabbits! Well, in accordance with the rules of the gene pool, the rabbit population grew. And grew. And grew!

So did the rat and mice populations, because there were no cats to chase after them and kill them. The birds were in distress! More distress than before man "helped".

"Oh me, oh my. Where shall we eat and sleep and hide? The rabbits are everywhere." Cried the birds.

This, of course, upset the liberal nature worshipers. The birds were distressed. That will not do. Never mind the thousands of cats they already killed – that was ok because the birds were here first.

Besides, tourists won't come to watch a bunch of cats. Duh! The birds had to be saved at all costs.

After scratching their heads for a while, a new plan developed. Something had gone wrong with connecting the two simple dots of the first plan.

Dot 1 – cats eat birds.

Dot 2 – kill the cats to save the birds.

Even the Borg could deal with that. But, it was more complicated than the two dots. In all the head scratching, someone realized the reason the first plan failed was because they didn't "eradicate" all the cats AND the rabbits at the same time.

Boy-o-boy, when man gets focused on a goal, he just does not want to let go? Finish off the cats and eradicate the rabbits at the same time! Finally, the birds (and the tourist industry) will be safe again. This plan is sure to work.

Question? How does one kill all the cats and rabbits on the island? And how do you do it without changing anything in the gene pool's balance of nature? Let's find out, shall we?

In another brainstorm, that had to be studied all of 37 seconds or so, it was decided that poison would do the trick, again. They could use guns, or traps or people with sticks. But, someone might get hurt or the cats and rabbits might suffer.

"What harm could come from poison, if we are very

careful? And no one suffers – much. The cats and rabbits just go to sleep and never wake up, right?"

A little research revealed that the plan had to be carried out with very special and selective poison planted everywhere the cats and rabbits lived or hung out. They would have to spread the poison liberally to be sure they got them all the first time (well, the second time). No brainer, right? After all, they knew where the cats and rabbits were.

A great plan, except for a tiny little unforeseen (but not unforeseeable) problem. The cats and rabbits were also living and hanging out where the birds were. Can you see where this is going?

I'd like to see the backup plan for rescuing the birds that ate the poison. Maybe there was a poisoned bird patrol with little stomach pumpers, and charcoal, and ipecac, and tiny little vomit bags to save the birds. Maybe even tiny little defibrillators for the very sick birds.

Of course, they couldn't be used on the cats and rabbits. This is a bird saving operation. Get the picture?

Of course, the poison has to be a *very* special poison to kill cats and rabbits and not harm the birds. And what about any dogs, children, bats or tourists? Will it kill them or just make them a little sick? Will it only taste like carrots and catnip, so other animals don't eat it? How, exactly, is this going to be done? Does the poison become harmless after 3 days? How do you clean it up from the area afterwards?

I haven't heard how this second part of the plan worked out. But, I have my doubts that the folks on Macquarie Island knew the answers to these and other questions. Such careful considerations take time and the tourist season was coming up quickly. They had to act, now. There was no time for details or to research to hold up the plan.

Let's fast forward a little and assume that the cat and rabbit eradication plan was successful. They still have the rat and mice problem. In fact, it has to get worse with no cats to eat or kill them. And with all the extra food now available? The rat and mice population has to explode.

Now, what do they do? Poison them, too? Do they go around poisoning everything they don't like? The mean dog next door? Mothers in law? Eventually, this has got to backfire on them.

While we're thinking ahead a little, what happened to the bodies of all those dead cats and rabbits? Were they buried? If so, did the rats and mice dig into them and eat them? If they did, which is highly likely, they probably developed a natural immunity to the poisons used?

Remember, "What doesn't kill you just makes you stronger."? A favorite saying of mothers to their young rats. This means the same poison won't work again. The rats and mice will just laugh it off. The now-immune rats and mice will take over while young children and their favorite pets die from the poison. Nothing like a well thought out plan.

Perhaps, instead of burying the poisoned bodies, the cats and rabbits were dumped into the ocean. Could the fish and other critters that eat such things have become poisoned themselves? Do we now have poison-resistant sharks and food-fish swimming around down there? Are they being caught and eaten by humans? Are they back-door poisoning the local humans who eat these fish?

Or are the fish dying from eating the poisoned cats and rabbits? Are their carcasses poisoning the sea bottom? Will giant clams develop that have fur on the outside and a tail? Will starfish develop long ears and eyes to see in the dark?

Who knows what the evolutionary impacts could be of

dumping thousands upon thousands of poisoned cat and rabbit carcasses in the ocean? Certainly we don't. At least not yet.

Sometimes, there are unintended consequences to a plan. We've certainly seen that on Macquarie Island. I hope the kids are safe and the tourists are happy. Just remember, the gene pool always wins in the end.

Chapter 8 – Evolution and the Copy Machine

What does the copy machine have to do with evolution? For one thing, the gene pool is the *original* copy machine. I'll bet you didn't think of the gene pool that way, did you? For another, as you'll see shortly, man imitates the gene pool by striving to constantly improve things. We just cannot leave things as they are. We are driven and inspired by our built-in genetic nucleus; the same nucleus that keeps the gene pool driving to evolve and improve.

The genes make us do it! A great excuse, but it is true. As happens in the gene pool, some man-made results are better than others.

This chapter provides insight into how human evolution works its magic, without our even trying to make it happen. It demonstrates how adaptation and evolution are genetically motivated within us. We don't have to think about it.

Often, we aren't even aware this is going on or that we're playing a role in it. It is an instinctual force within us – change, adapt, improve, evolve … or else.

The evolutionary history of the copy machine is a story of gene pool ebbs, flows, whirlpools and sandbars. It's a fascinating study in human interactions and genetic maneuvering.

The development of the copy machine is an excellent example of what I call: "subliminal evolution".

Today's copy machines are ubiquitous. Even the corner coffee mart has one you can use. We count on them for everything from copying a love note to mortgage settlements. Despite the development of the electronic "paperless society", we are anything but paperless. Making copies wasn't always so easy, you'll discover, as you read about the evolutionary path we took to get where we are today.

The story begins.

Long, long ago, in the cave dwelling days, to copy something from one wall (like the tale of Sherman killing the giant jack rabbit) to another wall was extremely difficult. Especially for a caveman. It isn't like you could put some rock over it and trace it. You couldn't take it over to your cave and copy it. After all, rocks are pretty heavy and, once taken out of the wall, they are *really* hard to put back in place without lines showing that they were moved. Life was tough back then.

At some point, Ferd's lady, Rockface, wanted a copy of Sherman's jack rabbit painting on *her* cave wall. She pestered Ferd until he finally gave in, as all men eventually do.

Rockface had to rely on Ferd's memory as he went to Sherman's cave, tried to memorize part of the story, then went back to his own cave and tried to recreate what he was supposed to remember. I say supposed to remember, because they didn't have the memory thing worked out all that well back in those days.

Then, back to Sherman's cave Ferd went to memorize another part of the picture and back home to paint his version of his memory. Back and forth, back and forth. Ferd even got lost twice as it was getting dark.

We've all seen pictures of the final results of the paintings. Yuk – they were terrible painters or terrible story tellers, or both. I guess they didn't have that art stuff figured out back then, either. If you look at their pictures, can you really tell anything from them? Is that really a jack rabbit Sherman is killing or is it an azalea bush?

If the paintings ARE accurate, Sherman was one UGLY dude! You'd think that, when telling a big story about killing the great giant jack rabbit, Sherman would want to have his best presentation in the paintings! Then again, maybe, that really IS Sherman at his best. If so, I can see why they all died off. Way too ugly for belly-to-belly. Procreation had to be really tough back then.

Of course, they didn't have all that much to choose from. One can only imagine what the women looked like, if Sherman was *that* ugly.

Anyway, trying to repeat what someone else drew left a lot to be desired. Thankfully, there isn't much that survived from that time period. If Darwin was right and only the fittest survived, it is probably for the best.

They weren't good at drawing or remembering. They also had terrible caveman names, they weren't anything to write home about in the looks department and they got excited over little things – like a jack rabbit.

What a boring life it was just sitting around in a cave all day. With all that time on their hands, why couldn't they think of anything better to do, or come up with better names or figure out how to make better drawings?

The take-away from this vignette of history is: the caveman died off and the jack rabbit survived. There is a lesson in there somewhere.

Let's fast forward a few millennium and a few cycles of the gene pool tidal process to the days of tents made from animal hides. Now *these* people were a lot smarter. They somehow figured out that painting on caves made it hard to move from place to place to follow the animals.

They also figured out that starving isn't fun, even to a caveman. While sitting in the cave, rock or skin, all day doing nothing (except painting ugly pictures of ugly people) was cool, it didn't feed the family.

The animals didn't just walk into the cave and say "Hey, caveman! Here I am, come and eat me!" If the caveman wanted to eat and survive, he had to go to where the animals were. Then, *he* could jump out of a hiding place and say "Hey, animal! Here I am and I'm going to eat you!"

Back in these old days, it was cold and polyester hadn't been invented. Our forefathers had to find ways to keep warm. Along the way, they figured out ways to make and control fire. They learned how to bring it inside, under cover from the elements, to ward off the chill.

But, they couldn't carry the fire with them for warmth while hunting. After all, it was pretty hard to sneak up on the jack rabbit when carrying a big fire stick. If they weren't very careful, they'd end up setting fire to the bush they were hiding behind. Tended to ruin the day and made the jack rabbit laugh. (Now, THAT would be a story worth drawing on the walls!)

Anyway, old Rolaf got to thinking one day. (Note: thinking was a new skill that developed as people sat around talking about the dumb paintings in the old caves and how to catch a jack rabbit.) Rolaf was sitting by a fire he'd accidently started while hiding behind a bush, hunting what was supposed to be dinner.

Rolaf was thinking about some dots, the dots of fire stick,

bush, no dinner and cold. Those were a lot of dots for poor Rolaf. He kept losing one or two, since the memory ability still hadn't progressed all that far. It took a while for all four dots to line up for him.

How do those rabbits stay warm? They don't have fire. They run around in the snow and cold and don't have a care in the world. What's up with that?

That's when Rolaf made a giant mental leap that changed mankind forever. Rolaf thought about what was different between him and the jack rabbit. I know this seems like a no brainer to us today, but back then, with few mental skills, bad memory and cold feet ... this was HUGE!

Rolaf continued his thinking: Rabbit – man. Man – rabbit. Two ears, two eyes, mouth, nose, bushy tail (oh, yes, we were REAL hairy back then), four feet versus 2 big feet, lots of hair versus fur all over, small and fast versus big and not so fast, fire versus no fire.

Wait, go back ... fur. What's up with that? Furry tail – hairy butt. Rolaf remembered that his butt didn't get very cold and it was hairy. "Hmmm, maybe there is something to all this." he thought. "Next time I kill one, I won't eat the outside stuff. It tastes bad anyway. Maybe I'll put it on my butt and see what happens."

This was the beginning of the first scientific experiment ever conducted. That is, if you don't count people going around saying "I dare you to eat that berry or that root." just to see who lives and who dies from it. It just isn't the same, but think about it and I'll bet you smile, too.

The next time Rolaf killed a rabbit (without starting a bush fire), he remembered that he was not going to eat the fur this time. So he put it on his butt, and other places, experimenting.

Back in the mid–1700s, archeologists found some very,

very old writings in a dig that relates to this fur event. Because of these writings, we know Rolaf's name and what happened next. These writings tell the story of Rolaf and the rabbit fur. The writings are in a chanting style that was popular long ago while sitting around the old skin tents at night.

> Translated and partially repeated here it goes like this:
> Made them with the fur side inside,
> Made them with the skin side outside.
> He, to get the warm side inside,
> Put the inside skin side outside;
> He to get the cold side outside
> Put the warm side fur side inside.
> That's why he put the fur side inside,
> Why he put the skin side outside,
> Why he turned them inside outside.

Following Rolaf's breakthrough about fur and which side is in and which is out, evolution moved rather fast. Soon, it was discovered that other animals were just like jack rabbits and that their fur was also not edible. (Remember, the smart ones survived!)

They also discovered something that survives to this very day and is as true now as it was way back in those days of innocent discovery. Size DOES matter!

Little rabbit furs were good for a little mitten or an earmuff, but not much else. You had to string together a lot of rabbit furs to make a decent blanket, let alone a good pair of slacks.

That's a lot of rabbit hunting and, more importantly, a lot of rabbits to eat. If you haven't tried it yet, try eating rabbit day in and day out for a week or two – or longer, as if you are trying to make a blanket for the kids. That's a lot of rabbits.

With evolution's constant march to keep only the best and brightest, things continued to change. Someone figured out that killing only one animal, one that was bigger, meant hunting only once and yielded a big fur. Enough fur for a blanket for the kids without sewing!

Now they were really onto something. Kill the bigger animals, less sewing, share the meat. With some imagination, a little sewing and bigger furs, they could even create their own portable cave (tent) made from animal skins.

I say skins, because they found out that the fur-side-inside adage just doesn't work well when it comes to tents. Plus, it is hard to draw the stories of Rolaf and *his* jack rabbit on the tent walls when there is fur on them. Skins are so much easier for paintings.

And thus explains how mankind discovered:

- that fur is not good to eat,
- that fur can keep you warm,
- that the fur needs to be on the inside when dead and outside when alive, and
- most important of all, bigger is better.

Of course, today we know that men have a defective gene in their DNA that started developing during this evolutionary period. It's known in pseudoscientific circles as the "bigger is better" gene. This genetic factor motivated the hunters, who were male, for thousands of years.

The male gene is infected and permanently imbued with a natural drive to have bigger, to do bigger, to compete and to show off their bigger ...

To this very day, males repeat this innate natural urging, this compulsion, in almost every facet of their lives. No wonder women can't figure them out. They can't help it, ladies. It's in their genes. It started long, long ago with Rolaf and his rabbit fur.

So, ladies, when you see men exhibiting this natural drive of theirs, have pity and try to focus their attentions onto more productive matters, like diamonds and, of course, furs.

Let's fast-forward again, this time to the Egyptian days when writing was on papyrus and on large stones.

It seems like mankind took a step forwards and backwards in this era. We learned to make a form of paper from papyrus so we could pass on the stories of Egyptian jack rabbit killers, or their equivalent. The papyrus was very portable, so one could take it anywhere to copy a story, a few jokes or new laws.

We also practiced communicating in pictures, just like Ferd and Sherman.

While progress was made in portability of words and stories, we also took a giant step backwards with paintings on big stones and stone-walls. The stones weren't very user friendly, for writing or for distribution. Extra copies of something carved in stone weren't normally carried around.

I have to give them an "A" for longevity, but an "F" for portability. Does this sound like Sherman's cave days? Why do Déjà vu and Darwin both start with a D? Is there a connection? Like history whispering in our ears "Don't do that. We tried it and it doesn't work."

A whole new career was created around this time in history – the scribe. Always a man, the scribe would write down what he was told and make copies of documents.

There were two types of scribes: the papyrus scribe and the stone scribe. The stone scribe usually had big muscles and strong hands. He also had to be an excellent speller, because it was really hard to erase mistakes carved in stone. Historical factoid – there is no known ancient Egyptian word for collate.

In Egypt, there are lots of terrific carvings and paintings telling stories, testaments to those who were in power and had money. How do we know they had power and money? Well, for one thing, we know they had to have money, because that's what it took to have a story or a picture of themselves carved into mountains. Lots of money.

If they had even more money, they had the mountains brought to them. The pyramids are good examples of this. In case you haven't looked lately, Egypt is not exactly filled with mountains. At least not anymore. Where did they go? The rich folks took them all. They were the only ones who could afford what few hills there were.

The filthy rich would have people go out, find a good mountain, and have it brought to Egypt, as a canvas, or a pyramid or as a big pile of stones. When someone is THAT rich, what does it matter what they do with their new mountain? It took people with real power and money to get others to drag those large stones around and stack them up. Think about it. Ok, that should be enough. If it isn't, then to the shallow end of the gene pool you go.

Since large carvings and stone works were so much a part of the social structure in those days, we have to credit them with creating another career path for willing and industrious young Egyptians: stone carvers and painters. (Stone pullers and haulers come in a close second, with whip makers in third.)

Stone copies were hard to make and required a lot of back and forth effort. It was easier to make up a brand new story, which is what the stone masons did. This explains why Egypt is full of stories about battles, and kings, and Gods, etc., but no two are the same. The folks in power were cheap when it came to making copies. So rather than pay for all the back and forth, they just had the masons make up new stories. A little secret from the ancient stone masons union.

What do we learn from this short visit to the gene pool? The shallow end is teeming with life and bad ideas never die. Also – bigger is still better.

Another leap forward in history and we're at a time when things started evolving fast indeed. More and more people wanted copies of things. This is partially because there were more people and partially because more of them could read. Evolution of the gene pool continued. People needed to know more.

This led to the development of the first, true mass-producing copy machine, first made popular by the Catholic Church: the monks. They were the first true modern day copy process, albeit completely manual.

To be successful as a copy monk, one had to have some very special genetic skills that allowed him to successfully survive the inevitableness of the gene pool. Unfortunately, most of the monks weren't allowed to pass on their genetic talents, which is why the Church needed new monks all the time

What was so special about the copy monks?

- They were not bored with doing the same mundane thing over and over again. This genetic trait resurfaced itself in the US in the mid to late 1800s in mines and factories. An interesting genetic footnote: this trait was formally recognized in the 1900s and became the basis of organized unions and government employment.
- Copy monks were not very ambitious. This helped keep order in the order and control in the monk house. It also contributed to the future creation of unions and government employment.

- They were obedient to a higher authority. This trait was important to be a monk. After all, they worked for the highest of authorities. This also meant that they followed the chain of command without question. "Just following orders." could have been their motto. I wonder how that worked out during the Crusades, yelling "Just following orders." as they killed some other-God loving infidel.

- They were very detail oriented. In order to accurately re-create the documents required extraordinary attention to detail. This genetic trait has, sadly, lost favor in the genetic evolution of the last hundred years, or so. "Just the bottom line and don't bog things down with details." is the motto of the day.

- Copy monks didn't talk much – communicating more through their artistic expressions. No talking, no arguing. A few prayers and a "Yes, Brother." here and there and they were set for the day. This worked out very well for monk-dom, but not for the success of individual relationships and social development. This trait successfully made it to the shallow end of the gene pool.

- They were not very creative. They seem to have given rise to the adage "monk see, monk do." They did what they were told and copied what they were given. No embellishments, no editorial comments, no insertions of "You got to be kidding?" or "There once was a monk with a duck …" in the margins. Just copy what's in front of you with no questions asked. Does this sound familiar?

- They were not very fashion oriented. Really, they weren't. You've seen the pictures. Basic brown all the way. Some say that this genetic marker can still be found among engineers who, DNA studies indicate, also lack a developed sense of fashion and color matching.

The monk copy process worked well for a few hundred years. Then, it smacked directly into the path of a competing genetic evolution – the evolution of independent thinking and increased intelligence. It seems that no good deed goes unpunished.

In trying to help the copier business and promote more portable stories, they inadvertently fed the genetic evolution of brain usage. The more the brain was fed and used, the more it wanted and the better it worked. And we all know that, once a genetic evolutionary trend starts, it's hard to stop.

People wanted more and they began to think more. Then, they began to ask questions and to challenge authority. Well, there goes the hope for a compliant people who respect authority. It was the beginning of the end of that genetic marker.

The first tangible evidence of these changes was the development of a printing press. Like the monks, the printing press was detail oriented, didn't mind doing the same thing over and over again, did whatever it was directed to do, didn't talk, wasn't creative and came in basic woodland brown. Who could complain? Who could possibly have any issue with this? It's like having your own group of monks in the basement without having to feed them or take care of them.

A no brainer, right? Well, as it turned out, this is another of those historical turning events in genetic evolution, similar to when fish learned to walk and women learned to talk. Once this step was taken, there was no turning back. Evolution took a turn and it wasn't going back.

Oh yes, some people tried to put the toothpaste back in the

tube, but it didn't work. People wanted stories, and jokes, and gossip and much more.

One could think of the printing press as the first semi-automatic copy machine. It changed the world and led to wars. It is single-handedly responsible for the creation of what is known as the fourth estate (one wonders what the fifth estate will be) with all sorts of divine rights claimed by those who labor under its veil.

Despite all the benefits of the printing press, it had one major deficiency. It was not easy to create new text and pictures on it. One could not just sit down and start typing away at a keyboard using new, wonderfully imaginative words with which to boggle and amaze people. Oh no – after all, the keyboard hadn't yet been invented. Each letter had to be placed in the proper position by hand ... backwards!

Seeing the problem with the printing press and trying, for years, to actually create new words to describe the problem, some smart, genetically advanced person (an engineering type to be sure) actually solved the problem. He sat down (all the best thinking is done sitting down) and focused on the solution instead of the problem. He created the typewriter.

Problem solved. Now, new words and thoughts could be created with ease and, if you wanted a lot of copies, you could always go to a printer and have him make a thousand copies for you. Sounds great, right? Problem solved, right? The gene pool was safe for another thousand years, right? Of course not. People had to piss in the gene pool and ruin things, again.

There are a couple of important genetic points that we can get from the above:

- bigger is still better and more is better than few,
- if they have it, you want it, whatever it is,

- everyone wants the ability to write, even if they don't have anything to say,
- if you have a good thing going, don't tell anyone — they'll only screw it up for you and the rest of us.

About this time, thinking and originality really came into vogue. Typewriters were everywhere. Anyone with two fingers thought they had to write something that everyone else wanted to read.

You know the gene that some people have? The one where they just HAVE to tell you their life story or every nanosecond of their MRI experience? They can't help it and you just HAVE to listen, every damned time they re-tell it. Connect the dots between them and typewriters. Straight line, I promise you.

A side-thought. One language I don't understand is mimes. Mimes are in every country as a classic form of entertainment. But, how do you translate a French mime into German, for example? Or from Pashtu to English? Or from Swahili into Comanche? Why don't they have sub-titles? Or interpreters for the deaf? Of course, you'd need interpreters for the different languages, so the deaf French, German, Comanche, etc. listeners can understand what is going on.

Hmmm, does a mime have listeners? Would a mime make a good witness in a criminal investigation? What does a mime say when someone sneezes? How does the college mime debate team work? How do they communicate when they have sex and want to mime sweet nothings in their partner's ear? For that matter, how does a mime whisper? How does a mime call their dog? How does a mime call 911? Why would a mime have a phone? When it's dark, how do mimes communicate? Glow in the dark face paint and gloves? Just wondering.

Back to business.

Eventually, typewriters made it into the business world and some guy (it had to be a guy) figured out that women were better than men at typing (a new word created for what a person does with a typewriter). They assumed that women's small fingers and attention to detail (like the monks who copied and their moms who sewed) made them DESIGNED to be typists! In fact, it was claimed that women were genetically PREDISPOSED to be typists and that typing was a waste of brain-power and time for a man to do such work. True!

Men think. Women, like the monks before them, only had to copy (type) what men wrote for them. Now we know how the women got pulled into this mess. A man decided. Sound familiar? It should.

Shortly, there came the development of the typing pool, a place where lots of women typed in a big room. This is where women went each day to work at their divinely proclaimed typing, while men lorded over them and trolled for fresh fish in the typing pool.

Need copies made? There was a printer down the street for many copies and a typist in "the pool" for a few copies. Businesses rarely need hundreds of a document and typists were cheap. So, for only 2 or 3 copies, they'd just have the ladies type it again.

This led to the phrase: "Type another copy for me, will you, Sweetie?" came into being.

I wonder if they ever went home and said that to their wives, perhaps when asking for more corn. "How about some more corn, Sweetie?" He'd probably get the pan upside his head, if he did. Anyway, I digress.

Women got tired of listening to this sort of demeaning and demanding crapola and also got tired of listening to complaints that all copies weren't *exactly* alike. Women aren't perfect, ya know. Mistakes happen.

The women complained to each other, which didn't do any good, other than make them feel better for letting off some steam. They also complained to their bosses, the men, who got tired of listening to the bitching (man-speak for complaining) and the grief they were getting. But, the men also weren't getting the copies they wanted. Copies were important, after all.

All across the world, these complaints were heard and listened to. Research money was spent to find a solution.

One idea that didn't work too well was to put a woman in charge of the typists. We all know what happens when a hen is in charge of the hen house, instead of a rooster! Things didn't improve. The squabbling just got worse and louder.

More research money was spent and new ideas were tried. Nothing worked. Then, somewhere along the line, a miracle occurred. Straight out of the engineering research department. It demonstrated one of the many reasons God invented engineers. It was another of those turning points in evolution that changed things immediately and forever.

Behold – carbon paper. From now on, all copies could be *exactly* the same and the copies were made at the same time as the original typing! No re-typing. The typists were ecstatic! The bosses were ecstatic! Everyone had what they wanted. Evolution had once again proven itself as the guiding truth of progress and development of intelligent life. All was well, again.

Well, not exactly *completely* well. If you didn't handle carbon paper right, you got black carbon on your hands and it was tough to wash off. Even worse if it got on your dress, or blouse or sweater. Then you had the dickens of a time getting it off, if at all.

Clothes were ruined. The women were unhappy. Again! Bosses were unhappy. Again! Evolution hiccupped. Call in the engineers. After all, they were the ones who caused this mess. More head scratching and research.

And the engineers came thru again. Behold – NCR paper. No Carbon Required! Even the name of it made the women happy. Just having it around the office made everyone happier. No carbon required! How can anyone get carbon on their dress when there is no carbon required?

Problem solved. Pat the engineers on the head and send them back to the lab. Life is good again.

You see, the gene pool had to be stirred a little by the women, who were at the forefront of evolution's impact, in order to get change. The prior tidal cycle, remember, had the men doing the work. By shear genetic genius, the men passed the work to others (the women) and convinced them it was progress. It was the women's natural genetic destiny and talents at work. It was evolution at work.

What a load of crap! But it worked!

The gene pool was still not done being stirred. At least not yet.

To help make peace and settle down the continuing complaints, the engineers continued to contribute to the progress of making copies. The old mechanical typewriters were a marvel of mechanical genius. They had levers all over the place, four-bar-linkages galore, gave consistent results, and worked for years without electricity.

All cool and wonderful things – except they required strong fingers. And, if you had carbons or NCR paper in the typewriter, you had to press extra hard on the keys so the pressure of the letter would pass through all those pages.

Make no mistake about it. The typists of old had very strong fingers. They typed 60 to 100 words per minute all day long on those mechanical beasts. Heaven help the kid whose mom was a typist back in those days. She could grip the blood out of your arm without thinking about it. She could make orange juice in the morning just by squeezing the orange in her hand. Her handshake was like that of a longshoreman. Don't piss her off!

But the new gals coming into the "pool" were too dainty for this. They didn't want bulges between their knuckles when they flexed their fingers. It just wasn't feminine. They wanted to have finger nails. The new wave of typists just would not hear of it.

Again, the engineers to the rescue. Voila! The electric typewriter! Same silly QWERTY keyboard that all typists had in their muscle memory, BUT very little pressure was required for the keys to work! Making copies? Just move a switch to the number of copies you want and the machine does it all!

They solved carpal tunnel syndrome before anyone ever knew it existed! A boon to business productivity and to workers compensation costs, all in one master-stroke. The human copy machines could now continue to work without a hitch, with increased productivity and…the bosses had copies! The engineers did it again!

Thank God we had copies. I don't know how in the world those Egyptians and Rolaf ever got by without them. Who could live without copies? How could businesses survive without copies?

Did we learn anything from these gene pool developments? Probably not, if we are to be consistent with history. But, let's assume we *could* learn something from this:

- bigger is still better, but faster is even better than bigger – sometimes,
- just like forks, God invented engineers for a reason,

- don't piss mom off,
- women evolved from finger bulging muscular mommas to dainty divas,
- a vocal majority can create change among the controlling minority, especially if sex is involved.

For a while, the mechanical-electrical-human copy machine had few minor improvements made. Little tweaks to a good thing. Little fixes to the complaints of the women. That was all.

A bit of time went by before the next big copy making change came along. And it was indeed a huge evolutionary leap. It involved making copies with *no typing* and very few brains. Excellent! We had the environment and women for this invention already in place!

You could make as many copies as you want – all the same, all perfect (well mostly) and all easily done.

The first commercial copiers were very simple devices. They were big and had lots of technical breakthroughs built in. But, that was for the engineers to marvel about. The intended users were the women in the office. They certainly would not understand, let alone appreciate, the engineering features built into the machines.

Technology features, such as, how copies were made in spite of all the static electricity generated just by moving the paper through the machine. How paper had a right side up and long and short grain orientations that made a difference in copier performance.

How the heat bar fused the black toner material to the paper so it would not come off. (Remember all the grief about carbon paper? They weren't going to make that mistake again!). How the toner got hot and didn't catch the paper on fire – usually.

How a dot for dot picture of the paper was made and transferred to a blank sheet of paper in only ~30 seconds. How all this happened in a small cabinet-sized box.

No, the engineering feats achieved in the copier were never going to be appreciated by anyone, except other engineers.

With the targeted user being women, the interface with the copier was made simple. VERY simple. After all, women were known for their notorious fear of technical things (men did technical things). In addition, everyone *knew* their brains just wouldn't be able to operate a complex piece of machinery.

So, the first copiers had a big green START button, a bigger red OFF/STOP button, and a simple thumbwheel to tell the machine how many copies to make. Copies were made one piece of paper at a time.

The process was very simple. Lift the cover, place paper on the glass, make sure it is aligned properly, close cover, push the green START button, wait (~30 seconds), lift the cover, remove the paper, place another piece of paper, make sure it is aligned properly, close the cover, push the green START button. Over and over, page by page. Boring, repetitive, unskilled work. Just right for the women.

All machines also had a prominent sign telling who to call in case anything went wrong. Most operators were known to be too simple to understand the insides of the copier and were forbidden from opening it. Only specially trained women were allowed to add paper or toner.

Remember the carbon paper fiasco? What is toner, but millions and millions of very, very tiny pieces of carbon? In these first machines, toner was added only by a specially trained female employee (who called a man if she ran into trouble). She was called every time the toner ran out.

At first, it was an honor to be this go-to toner girl. They

were special and were trusted with knowledge about the copier no one else had. Everyone called on her for help. And she *had* to be smart because she could make the machine work again!

This lasted until the first time the toner was spilled while pulling out the toner holder or someone sneezed and blew it around. They learned quickly that you did NOT try to wipe it up. That just spread it around and it didn't come off.

Some copier toner ladies were known to wear lab smocks and lab gloves when handling the toner, so as not to ruin their clothes. It was terrible. It was carbon paper all over again! It was worse than carbon paper!

Did we not learn anything? Maybe the design lessons never got copied and distributed to the new engineers to prevent them from making the same design mistake again. Very bad juju.

The ladies roared. Again! The boss men were not happy. Again! Offices, in general, were not happy places. Again! The cry went out, again, "Get the engineers to fix this!"

Eventually, they did fix it. Again! Sometimes we just have to go back and swim in the gene pool over and over because evolution didn't work the first time, or the second time, or the...

Genetic lessons?

- Carbon is bad. Millions and millions of itty-bitty pieces of free carbon are badder. (New word. It means more worser than bad).
- We repeat history because the gene pool is shallow and we think we are smarter than history.
- Engineers aren't perfect (but don't tell them).

An interesting thing happened as the copier machines were introduced to businesses. The bosses (the men) thought they were doing the women a huge favor by getting copy machines. And the women grabbed onto the machines like they were new fangled frying pans.

"Mine!" they exclaimed in a shout of ownership heard across this great land. The copiers were the exclusive domain of the typist ladies. No ifs, ands or butts about it. And the boss men were fine with that. "Let them have it. It's just an administrative job that doesn't require any skill, just right for them."

Little did the bosses know that, within the rank and file of workers, the men workers that is, festered a revolution. You see, the bosses, as is typical in all organizations, did not actually *do* the work. Their job was to take credit for the work of others.

The real work back then, as it still is today, was being done by lower level men. Still chauvinistic, still filling offices with a blue haze from smoking, still trying to accomplish things within the system, still hitting on the women; but men just the same. They were the ones who got the real work done. Just ask one of them.

Anyway, they had a process for getting typed products created and produced that would make Darwin sit up and smile in his grave, saying, "I told you so." It went something like this.

The man wrote out what he wanted typed in long hand on paper. (Some of you may be old enough to remember actually writing on paper.) He then gave it to one of the typing girls to type. She typed it and gave it back to the man who made changes and returned it for retyping. It went back and forth through this process a couple (or more) times until he was happy.

He then asked her to type however many copies he needed to satisfy the bosses. The bosses added their changes on the document, like dogs pissing on a fire hydrant just to let others know they were there.

Then, the original man had to integrate all the inputs from the different bosses and go back to the typist to have her re-type the document all over again, with the changes included. Then, she had to make copies again, after the man approved the newly retyped document.

These worker level men were caught in the middle between the two struggling power brokers in industry: the bosses and the typing girls. There was no way to win. There was no way they would be allowed to do their own typing. They could not even make their own copies! The borders were set. The lines were drawn. They were men caught in no man's land. They had to be nice to both sides of the war. It was a no-win situation for them.

So they did the only thing left for them to do. They talked to the engineers and convinced them to make copiers more and more complex!

At first, it was little things, like do you want darker or lighter copies? Then different paper sizes came into play. Then the great international turmoil of A4 paper had to be ad-dressed. (What the heck is A4 anyway? I thought it was a road in England.)

Next, collation was introduced. Then, scaling was added for making the copy bigger or smaller than the original. Automatic stapling came along. Before long, the copier was a veritable printing press right there in front of you.

With every new feature, the copier became more complex and the ladies tried to keep pace. Sometimes, when the copier broke, they even reached out to a man, or an engineer if a man wasn't handy, for help.

New technologies brought even more new features. Copiers were connected to your computer. They were un-con-nected and went wireless. The "typist" became extinct. The men didn't even have to have a secretary or admin anymore. They could do it all by themselves.

Wait! What a great idea – that could save money. Get rid of the secretaries and admins and let the higher priced men do their own copying and business will boom. After all, copiers had obviously exceeded the natural, genetic capability of women. So claimed the bosses. The men could take it from here. They had won the war!

Oh my. Have we heard this before? Is this not a harbinger of things to come? Did we not learn anything? Evidently, not.

Today, you can have all the copies you want. Just select the number of copies you want to print (Notice it is called printing and no longer called copying?) and you have it. The printer is at your desk, or just down the hall or across the country.

No special skills needed. Any man can do it. Of course, faster is still good, but smaller is now better (no reflection of the male influence). I can do it myself and don't need any help (definite reflection of male influence).

Where does this lead? If history has taught us anything, the gene pool will swirl around over and over, repeating itself, until the pool finally dries up from exhaustion or shallowness, or both. Let's try to take a peek forward, based on what we've seen of the past.

- No – we won't write on walls made from animal skins (we have to make nice with the animals). Unless, we are hit with a large asteroid or start a nuclear war. Either one bleaches out the gene pool and we start over.
- We will tend towards simplicity. Computer software and office tools are so complex that the average person uses no more than 8 to 10% of the available functionality. It's cool to have all that available, and it's a testament

to the engineers to get it all to work, but it overpowers people.

- New generations will have complex brain function genes kicked into high gear, so they can multi-process, but they'll miss the details behind the processes. Stay tuned for the big picture generation. Ask one of these folks how big is a font point? (Answer: 1/72 inches) Or what is iron? (Answer: What you use to make steel. It's not a verb to describe what mom used to do to clothes).

- Information will be more important and data will be less important. "Just the facts." will be replaced with "Just the answers." Gigabytes will be replaced by megabytes and then by kilobytes as the gene pool evolves towards answers and away from data.

- Copying will merge with text messaging, IM'ing and email, eliminating the need for physical copies, especially after secure digital signatures are perfected. Think about going to a mortgage closing and using no paper!

- The need for paper will finally go down and the electronic, paperless office will actually develop. Trees will make a comeback and we won't know what to do with all of them.

- More copies of results will be sent to more people so that, eventually, everything will be available to everyone, whether they want it or not. Caring about results will be overrated and brains will atrophy from lack of use. The genetic pool will respond by dumbing down the brain capacity to the level where it only deals with the answers important to the moment. We won't be able to see past our noses. We will become the modern versions of Ferd and Sherman.

- The third world countries, who have been mostly sheltered from all these genetic influences, will rise up and take over the world. They will be the only ones who know how to grow cotton and make cloth, or make steel or grow food. They will have written the processes down on the walls of their animal-skin and stone houses.

Darwin and the gene pool win again!

So to summarize ... what did we learn? In the end, nothing. Again! The gene pool keeps evolving to perpetuate, to reward, to punish and, most of all, to survive. There are some tidbits worth taking away, though.

- Bigger is better, but faster is better still.
- Size matters, but only if it has lots of functions and special features.
- History repeats itself, because the genetic basics it works with haven't changed all that much.
- When one genetic trait suppresses another (bosses and typists, men and women, rabbits and fur, etc.) evolution is triggered and the suppressed genes evolve to deal with, counter, or even control the oppressor. The cycle repeats, as necessary.
- We always want more, even if we don't know what to do with it.
- The fur belongs on the outside if living and the inside if dead.

Remember the dinosaurs.

Chapter 9 – Mating and the Gene Pool

Sex. Mating. Copulating. Belly-to-belly. Screwing. Doing "it". F***ing. Hooking up. Shagging. Balling. Getting laid. Banging. Making love. Whatever you call it, procreation is a genetic instinctual drive in all of us. The gene pool relies on mating, more than anything else, to keep itself going, to pass on adaptations – to survive.

Without mating, the gene pool dries up and turns to dust, just like the first kangaroos.

In our little discussion here, I use the word 'mating' so we can be clear of the distinction between 'mating' and 'sex'. Note: humans are the only species that maintains a difference between the two.

The key to survival is to genetically replicate the good results and remove the bad ones. Of course, in order to even have results, there has to be mating. It is truly a fact of life. In fact, it is the cornerstone of life. We have to do it! For the sake of humanity! For there to be life on earth – we have to mate! It is not just natural, it is necessary.

I'll bet your mother or father never explained it to you that way when you were a teenager. You're natural instincts were right after all. Do it and do it often for the sake of humanity. Do it in the car, under the bleachers, at the beach, in the woods, in the janitor's closet. Do it for the gene pool! Imagine how different high school would have been if only we'd known this little gene pool secret!

Of course, God knew about mating. He'd gone thru galactic biology in his early classes and survived adolescence. Life forms must reproduce to have continuance. That is why he experimented with so many different forms of life and methods of reproduction as part of his Universe U studies.

You don't seriously think microbes happened all on their own, do you? Snakes and birds, too? Of course not. There was a plan to all of this, as laid out in the curriculum at Universe U. The students start with simple life forms of varying basic chemistries and expand from there to cover many other different life forms. They then learn to design variations to suit the environment and characteristics desired.

To be a successful graduate of Universe U, God has to be able figure out what the best life forms are for a situation or world. Then, he has to be able to create those characteristics in viable living entities. Tough job.

There are so many things to consider, a few of which include:

- Does the entity live in the water, on land, both or neither?
- How does it get air to breathe? Does it breathe air? Does it breathe at all? How does it get oxygen from the air and use it? Does it use oxygen?
- How does it store energy? It has to store some energy or it would have to feed all the time – like our friend

the humming bird. If it stops eating for more than a few hours of rest, it won't have the energy to fly to get more food.

- Does it move in the water? With fins and tail, or shoots of water, or bobs up and down with the water currents, or crawls on the bottom with legs or squirms around in the dirt? Does it ever go on land? If so, why? How does it move on land and what do you do with the legs?

- Does it move on land? Crawling? 1 leg? 2 legs? 3 legs? 4 legs? 8 legs? 100 legs? Zero legs? Maybe it digs its way around. Does it ever go in the water and, if so, how does it move? Does it like trees or cliffs? How do you keep it from falling out of the trees? Does it hop, or crawl, or walk or lumber?

- Does it move in the air? Soaring? Gliding? Floating? Beating wings hard and fast or slow and easy? Big wings or little wings or no wings? Does it ever go on land? If so, how does it move on land and what do you do with the legs? Does it have legs?

- How does it keep warm and cool? Does it pant? Does it sweat? Does it have fur? Fat? Can it only live in very temperature controlled places like the manatee in Florida and the polar bear of the arctic? Can it adjust to extremes like humans and black flies?

- What does it eat? Is it a vegetable eater? Or a meat eater? Or both? Does it get nutrition from the blood of others? From the ground? The air? Maybe the water? Does it chew or just swallow? Fresh meat or rotten meat? Raw meat or cooked?

- If it eats others, how does it hunt and kill? By smell or sight? By day, or night or both? Does it use teeth and claws to kill? Or poison? Does it just squeeze the living out of you? Does it swallow you whole and digest you later? Does it pick you up and drop you from a height to kill you? Does it drown you? Does it bash you with a rock or a stick? Or does it kill you with guilt, like a Jewish mother or a Catholic Priest?

- How does it see? With eyes, or infrared sensors or motion sensors? Day or night? Can it only see part of its body or the whole thing? Can it see all around or a narrow area? Can it see close up and far away? Does it key on things that move? Can it see colors? Which ones?

- How does it defend itself? Teeth and size are popular. What about the electric eel? Camouflage? Hard shells? A bad temper, where the best defense is a massive, fierce offense, like a pissed off mom? Does it spit poison? Does it roll over and play dead? Does it give off a terrible stink? Does it stay with a herd of others?

- And the biggie – how does it reproduce? As I said – without this, there is no future, so this is a big issue for the gene pool. Does it reproduce on its own? Does it need another of its kind? More than one? Does it have eggs? How many eggs? Hard eggs, soft eggs or poached eggs? How are they fertilized? Inside the body? Outside the body? By Petri dish and test tube? By a third party, like flowers use bees? By luck, like with weeds and flower seeds?

As you can tell, creating life is not all that easy. If you looked around at life on earth, as it is and as it used to be, you would see all these, and many more, design options that God has tried. Some failed, like the first, pouch-less kangaroo. Others succeeded, like the black fly and mosquitoes, unfortunately.

There's more variety than we can understand. There's a method and an alternative for just about every situation on earth.

Every living thing finds a way to reproduce or it dies off. And it adapts or it dies off. Reproduction is the method by which adaptations get into the future generations. The two are linked because life on earth cannot exist without either of them.

Unfortunately, it is too late for us to adapt, genetically, to our lives. Genetically speaking, we are who we were at birth. Well, at conception, actually. Evolution only happens when we pass on our genetic experiences and knowledge to our offspring. This is the only way to protect and improve our species (or any species). The only way, at least, until we learn how to introduce genetic changes into living animals and humans to create genetic changes without reproduction.

Do we need to be taller? Faster? Stronger? Less susceptible to disease? Hairier to protect against the cold? Immune to small pox? Good eyes? Good hunter? Patience? Meat eater or grass eater? Carry extra fat or remain lean?

We could look at birds for a quick look at how they've adapted different capabilities and needs to survive. Some birds are good at long distance soaring. Others, like Canadian Geese, are not only good at long distance flying, but are excellent navigators. They've also learned to share the lead position so they all make it to their winter or summer grounds together. Pretty smart of them to figure that out and communicate it to each other.

There are hunting birds that have great eyesight and have the ability to loiter and then strike their prey by zooming in on them for the kill. Their entire bodies are designed for hunting.

It's easy to see that a duck is very different from an eagle or a pelican. It's shaped differently, its beak is different, its wings are different, even the way it flaps its wings is different. This is because its mission in life is very different from the eagle or the pelican. It evolved in the best way to be a duck, not an eagle.

They each evolved by mating to make little changes over time and evolve into whatever it does best. A duck would make a terrible eagle, and vice versa. The rules of the gene pool dictate that this process must continue, passing genetic changes on thru mating.

Since ducks don't interbreed with hawks and sparrows don't interbreed with humming birds, and no self-respecting bird of any kind would interbreed with a mocking bird, each breed continued to develop within its own special bird species. Genetic adaptation, passed on through mating, ensured the survival of the best of the best.

In this way, humming birds keep making better humming birds, who don't know the words. And mocking birds continue to be mocking birds, without a bird song of their own.

A little aside about the mocking birds. Do you know why they don't have a song of their own? Because, when God was assigning songs and sounds to the different birds, the mocking birds kept jumping in and making a big racket, wanting everyone else's song. First this one, and then that one, then the next one. They just wouldn't wait in line until God got around to them.

Eventually, they pissed off God, who was more worried about getting his assignment finished on time than pleasing these noisy pests. So, in a moment of anger, God gave the mocking bird no song.

He took away their genetically embedded song memory and replaced it with a short-term memory repeater. Their short term memory was set so they could only remember 22 seconds worth of the last song they heard. This doomed the mocking bird to forever repeat the song it heard recently, but with no long-term song memory. This is why mocking birds have no song. Honest.

Since I mentioned interspecies mating, it might be a good idea to remind you that it doesn't work. You don't have to worry about that dog humping your leg getting you pregnant. Or those young ladies down in Tijuana, who reportedly cavort with ponies and large dogs.

In spite of what some people have reported, there are no people walking around who really have the face of a dog or the hung organs of a horse. They just look that way because the gene pool allows for variety. The closest thing we have to a true interspecies animal is the duck-bill platypus. It's the one surviving interspecies animal God created.

Second in line to the duck-bill platypus, in the interspecies arena, are liberals. Liberals are a genetic mixture of humans and the laughing hyena, believe it or not. Honest!

As we know, the hyena slinks around in the dark trying to take what others have, without doing any work for themselves. Then, he laughs about it to the other hyenas. No guilt, no conscience, no cares.

Somewhere in the distant past, genetic materials of humans and hyena combined to produce liberals. The current scientific thinking of how this occurred revolves around a massive volcano eruption in Africa that incinerated many, many hyenas. Their genetic material got caught up in the ash cloud that spread around the world.

Somewhere, somehow, this genetic material got onto some clothes drying outdoors and got mixed into a woman's private area during mating. It got mixed with human sperm during the "process" and produced a liberal. From there, it was just one genetic aberration after another as these genetic defects continued to evolve.

Today, liberals are a large part of the social population, proving that genetic interspecies anomalies can still occur.

Third in line in this category, is the mule – a man-made combination of the horse and a donkey. Fortunately, unlike the liberal, the mule is sterile, but it looks strikingly like the donkey, the liberals chosen symbol. Coincidence? I don't think so, but you connect the dots for yourself.

A major part of the mating activity is selecting the mate. Just what do the female and the male find attractive? In some animals, it is the ability to fight and beat up on the others. This is the "strongest buck wins" mating choice. After winning, the buck gets his choice of all the females of his herd.

Many animals choose mates in this manner. Among them are deer, buffalo, lions, puma, elk, young humans, knights of old, and gang members. Some of these actually *have* a herd to work with. For others, the herd is in their imagination and is fueled by ego. Not necessarily a bad thing for the gene pool.

Some species don't fight it out – they go for looks, pretty colors, the ability to dance and showing off. These characteristics are most often seen in many forms of birds and gays. It's not so much what you bring to the gene pool, but how good you look doing it.

Unfortunately, as we've seen, looking good isn't way up there in the gene pool selection criteria. Eventually, it gets muted out over time through natural evolutionary selection. Nothing personal. Just for the good of the gene pool, you understand.

If we look at ourselves, we may have a reason to be optimistic about the future of the gene pool. Or maybe not. Most humans tend to have the right idea in mate selection and, genetically speaking, pick fairly well. As long as they don't try it until they're over the age of 28, that is.

Can we find a way to help our future generations make better mate selections? Can we help the gene pool?

Along this line of thinking, suppose we try the following. When we find someone who has the genetic characteristics we really need in the gene pool, we should put them to work popping out babies. This way we can reduce the pollution of the gene pool and have a better chance of survival.

This would, of course, require a special government agency to assess the make-up of the gene pool and determine which characteristics are in demand and which aren't. Those in demand would fuel a search for the right genetic people for breeding. Those characteristics deemed "harmful" would get sterilized.

As generations go by, the make-up of the gene pool would change. From time to time, this special government agency would have to re-assess its "in-demand" characteristics list. Can you imagine it?

"Sorry, Sarah and George, your eligibility for the government's gene pool enhanced breeding program will come to an end at the end of this fiscal year. Your in-demand genetic characteristics have dropped from 8th place to 14th and we only have money for the top 9. If things change, we'll let you know. At least you still have desirable genes and we don't have to sterilize you. Thanks for caring and sharing. Have a nice life."

"Oh George, what do we do now? All we know how to do is breed and now we aren't even wanted for that. What will we do?"

"Say, Mr. Government Man, Sarah has a good point. What will we do? We don't have any other skills. All we've done is breed for the good of the gene pool. Do we get some money? A job? What do we do?"

"Well, gee, George, you too Sarah, I don't know. That isn't my job. It's possible your genetic characteristics will become needed again, but it isn't likely. It's also possible that they become prohibited and then you'll be sterilized. I've seen that happen twice in my career. Not pretty. You better figure out something 'cause we don't tolerate people not carrying their own weight, unless they work for the government. Hey, there's an idea – you need work and don't have any particular job skills. You'd fit right in with the government. Go down to personnel and see what they have and tell them I sent ya. Good luck."

It almost sounds like a repeat from history or from science fiction stories. But, can it really happen? Is it so farfetched? Once we learn to completely decode and understand human and other DNA, are we really very far away from this scenario? Remember, the engineers are always looking for something to do.

And don't forget the propensity of governments to step in and do what's "right" to you, whether you like it or not. Genetic tagging at birth? Certainly likely. Mating prohibitions based on genetic characteristics? Of course! Already been done. Forced sterilizations? Also already been done.

Making some people better than others, or more privileged than others, based on genetics? Been there and done that. Government lists of acceptable and unacceptable genetic characteristics? Already been done and right around the corner, again.

Increased attention and funding for euthanasia programs? Already happening. We do it for all sorts of animals around the world, especially those we love. Why not for humans?

Just as soon as people really understand the gene pool, someone is going to figure a way to really screw it up worse than it is now. Be careful world … we're here to help you.

Chapter 10 – The Ten Commandments and the Gene Pool

Mankind has tried to make sense of things beyond our comprehension from the very beginning. Alpha and Beta tried to make sense of where God kept his lunch. They progressed to wondering why they could not mate with their sons and daughters. We've always known there was a higher power at work in this world. Some people even thought *they* were the higher power. Silly, of course. After all, God told us all that *he* was the top dog.

With free-will, imaginations and hefty fears of that-which-we-cannot-understand, we've created some doozies for explanations of why things are the way they are. The Gods of the ancient Greeks and Vikings. The UFOs who visited the Eskimos, the Egyptians and the Incas. The Jewish heritage and the Christian outgrowth. The religions of the Far East and south Asia. And let's not forget the recent renewed interest of the Muslims.

They all try to make sense of why we're here on earth and

try to find ways to guide us to a better place.

One might wonder, are things really so bad here that the best these religions can do is preach about how to tolerate life and encourage people to look forward to death? All in the hopes that whatever happens after death is better than what we have in life?

If this IS the case (which it is), a reasonable natural extrapolation of that thinking would be – why are we waiting around for death and the afterlife? Why don't we take things into our own hands and go there now? The "Reverend" Jim Jones had this idea when he quenched the religious thirst of his followers by giving them poisoned kool-aid. Now, that's religious conviction!

Even better than that would be for the religious leaders to actually "lead" their followers into the next life instead of just talking the subject to death. They should show some real leadership and religious conviction by killing themselves first, supremely confident that the others will follow shortly. (Yeah, right, be right there after you, O great leader.)

Maybe the followers of the radical Islamists should demand that their leaders show this same conviction in their beliefs and demonstrate their leadership skills – by going first. "You know that suicide bomb you want me to blow myself up with? You're the leader – you go first – lead by example."

You can bet this form of stupid extremism would come to a halt real quick-like if some of the followers weren't as dumb as rocks and had an ounce of independent thinking.

Anyway, let's look at the role religion and the Ten Commandments have had in the evolution of the gene pool. Let's start with the first written guidance from God recorded in our records.

It's a little known archeological and theological fact that

there were originally 13 commandments, not 10. This historical fact has been covered up by religious leaders for thousands of years to avoid embarrassment and to simplify the teachings of religion.

Ten worked out just right, because the people tended to have 10 fingers. One for each commandment. Very convenient for the uneducated sheep of the flocks. Thirteen commandments would be three too many for them to follow. They didn't have enough fingers.

By the way: Does anyone besides me wonder how two stone tablets got "broken" by accident and lost? This was the only direct evidence from God of what he wrote and somehow it is – gone. Missing. Lost to the ages. Strong stone tablets of *immense* importance and they just *happen* to get broken and disappear. If you believe that story, I have some desert land to sell you, only used for 40 years.

Here is the true story of the Ten Commandments.

The basics of the story of Moses going up to the mountain and getting the commandments from God are true enough, as far as they go. The burning bush? Naw – that was a laser pointer God used to try to get Moses' attention and it stayed on the dried bush too long. Sorry to spoil it, but that is what really happened.

Once Moses got up to the meeting place, he took a rest because he was an old man and the climb wore him out. After eating a fish sandwich (a favorite of God's, as we all know from his son's work) and some wine (great trick, that water to wine thing – comes in handy at the frat parties at Universe U), they got down to things.

Moses started off by complaining about the climb, "Geeesowiso-witz, God, can't we meet somewhere besides the top of a mountain? I'm getting too old for this crap. Besides, I live in the desert, in case you forgot, and we don't have many mountains there. I'm out of shape."

"Man up!" Replied God, ever the concerned, benevolent, caring individual that he is.

"But I'm old and you do have the power to meet anywhere. Why always the mountains? Why can't you just stop by my tent? I'll send everyone out for a while and you can just pop in while they're not looking. It'd be a lot more convenient and comfortable. Which reminds me of something I wanted to ask you."

"We've been living in this here desert for some years now. It is so hot here and there is no good water. It doesn't rain. The land is barren, making it hard to grow crops. There is no scenery. The only colors we have are desert brown and sky blue. Everything is so flat. It is depressing. Did I mention about how hot it is?"

"But, Moses, the humidity is very low. It is a dry heat." God responded, not exactly feeling the love. "Flat is good so you can see enemies far in the distance. And it allows the nice breezes to flow through your villages and homes."

Moses tried again. "Dry heat is still heat. Dry, hot breezes do not cool. They just move the heat around. It would be nice if we could move to somewhere cooler and more temperate. However, if we really must stay here, could you at least invent air conditioning?"

"Why sure I can, but what will you use for electricity?" answered God.

Moses thought for a bit and answered, "What is this electricity you speak of?"

"You see?" said God. "What would a blind man do with bifocals?"

"Huh? What blind man? What does he have to do with it?

Should I go find a blind man? What are these 'by-fog-owls' you talk of? Will they help? Should I go look for some of them?"

"For crying out loud, Moses. Get a grip, will you? Now, let's talk about why I asked you up here. Oh, and sorry about the bush incident back there. I was trying to get your attention." God responded.

"Right, burning bush. It did get my attention, and also my beard. Good trick though. So, what is up? What is it that is so important?"

"Well," God started "it seems like your people are getting restless and fidgety. I think they need some structure and guidance in their lives. After all, they're going to be in the desert for a while longer and we can't have things getting off track. You know what I mean?"

"Yes, yes, I see your point. But, I didn't think we were going to be here all that long. I mean, we suffered enough in Egypt. I was thinking maybe we deserved a break. Perhaps something by a nice ocean with great beaches, good fishing, places for boats to travel and explore, not too hot, not too cold. Don't you have something along that line available?" Moses asked.

"This isn't a Med cruise or a Boy Scout Jamboree, Moses. At least you aren't building any pyramids. You and your people, MY people, are here for a reason. Besides, you need to stay under the radar screen for a while till those Egyptians calm down. They're mighty pissed at you and me right now. They put the word out to other tribes to report back if they see you. You don't really want to be found by them now, do you? If you do, I can arrange that. Just say the word."

"Oh shit, I hadn't thought about it that way." Moses replied. "By the way, what's a 'Med cruise' and a 'Jam-bo-ree'? And what the hell is a 'radar screen'? Sorry about the hell thing. But, why do you keep talking in these strange languages?"

"Moses, my dear, dear Moses. This is why I am God and you are Moses. Why I am here and you are there." God answered. "Now, let's get down to things. I want you to implement 13 rules for the people to follow. These rules, I call them commandments, will guide your people, MY people, to get along together and help keep them in my favor. These are important and must be taught to all and be instilled in the young."

God continued, "I wrote them down so you, and my people, won't forget them. You know what happens when you folks forget things, right? They're right here on these three stone tablets. They'll last a long time and no one can change them. This way, everyone will remember them with no excuses."

"I remember." Moses replied, adding, "You've always been big on the 'no excuse' thing. When are you going to give us a break? Let bygones be bygones. Forgive and forget?"

"Don't start with me, Moses! Just read and we'll discuss." God responded with a little anger in his voice, causing Moses to cower and read.

Here's what Moses read on the tablets.

TABLET 1

Commandment I

I am thy God. Do not forget that. Thou shalt have no other gods before me for I brought thee into this world and I can smite thee out of it.

Commandment II

Thou shalt not make unto thee any weird images or any strange likenesses or idols, except of me. Thou shalt not bow down to them nor serve them, except for me (refer to Commandment I).

Commandment III

Remember the Sabbath day and keep it holy. Sleep in late if

you want, just keep it holy and be nice to each other.

Commandment IV

Thou shalt not take the name of thy God in vain for it shall piss Him off. So you'd best mean it if you do.

TABLET 2

Commandment V

Thou shalt not kill my people, unless there is a damned good reason of which I would approve. Otherwise, thou shalt be punished for killing my people.

Commandment VI

Honor thy father and thy mother for they caused thee to be born into this world.

Commandment VII

Thou shalt not covet thy neighbor's wife or house or goods.

Commandment VIII

Thou shalt keep thy eyes within thine own house.

TABLET 3

Commandment IX

Thou shalt not commit adultery with a neighbor.

Commandment X

Thou shalt not commit sodomy.

Commandment XI

Thou shalt not bear false witness against thy neighbor.

Commandment XII

Thou shalt not gossip, unless it is confirmed to be the truth by at least three others.

Commandment XIII

Thou shalt not steal or break anything thou hast borrowed.

Moses read through the list of commandments, slowly. After several minutes, because he was old and slow, Moses turned back to God.

"Interesting idea, God. Good forward thinking. You've obviously given this some thought. Wish I'd thought of it. What have you got in mind to do with these?" Moses posed to God.

"Quit trying to kiss my ass, Moses. It won't work and I don't swing that way." God reproached. "Now, let's go over my commandments. They really aren't too onerous. There are a couple about remembering who is really in charge here – ME. Some are family friendly, like don't covet your neighbor's wife and don't cheat on yours."

Moses interrupted "What about coveting their daughters or sons? Or their nieces? Or sheep? Or someone from a different part of town who isn't a neighbor? And on the adultery one, is oral sex real sex? "

"We know where your mind strays, don't we Moses? You have some very strange people down there. Then again, I've seen your wives and can't blame you for the questions."

"Let's see. Sheep are ok and so are other animals. Relatives? Well, in those cases we have to go back to the four generation rule established for Alpha and Beta. If they aren't in that group, go for it. Neighbors? Hmmm. What exactly is a neighbor?"

God pondered for a moment and then declared his answer, "Ok, here it is: neighbors are people living within a 4–hour walk."

"Now, as for oral sex and real sex. Hmmm, a ruling needs to be made here as well. I have it. Oral sex is not real sex as long as there is no swallowing. Incompletion, spitting or leakage is not sex. That should take care of that. The rest of the commandments have to do with stealing, lying, cheating. Stuff like that. Read them again."

Moses re-read them while muttering under his breath about how heavy the big tablets looked. The commandments seemed pretty reasonable, but being Jewish, he had to make a complaint about something. So he started the negotiations, knowing not to pick on the commandments themselves and risk pissing God off.

"These are reasonable 'commandments', as you call them. But, I do have to protest about the three tablets. Oy vey, they are so thick and heavy and there is only one of me. Can we not have them on papyrus or Styrofoam? Something an old, not too healthy man could carry with ease? Or maybe I could go get a couple of young fellas to help me carry them."

"Christ almighty, Moses. You whine worse than a little old lady waiting for someone to get out of the bathroom. Don't you ever give it up? There are 13 of them. They're in stone so they will last. Duh! Did you think I wanted these to just fade away the first time they get wet? Come on, man up!" God retorted.

"Oh, but my back hurts just looking at them. They are so heavy. If I had a cart or an ass to help, maybe then ..." Moses complained, hesitatingly.

"Maybe, if there were only two of them and they were thinner." he continued. "Then, they would still last and I might be able to survive the trip back down this long, dangerous mountain trail. Do you think you could do that, and maybe make the print a little smaller so they would all fit better? Maybe shorten some up a bit? Like that first one. It seems a little wordy for the point you are trying to make. Maybe you could cut out the 'smite thee' part."

Chuckling, God said, "Moses, I want people to remember the dinosaurs."

"The dinosaurs? What are they?" Moses asked, fearing he already knew the answer."

"Exactly my point, Moses. They lived long ago. I smitomized them one day. Used a big rock and wiped them all out, along with most of the rest of life on the planet. I brought them into this world and I took them out. And they didn't piss me off. Imagine what I could do if I really got pissed off. As Commandment I says, don't piss me off! It stays like it is and you and your people need to heed that."

Being appropriately chastised and feeling like he couldn't push some things any further, Moses changed tactics.

"Ok, God. Message received, Sir. But, I still have the problem of trying to carry 3 such large and very heavy tablets. I am but an old man who has to use a staff to steady my walk."

God rolled his eyes in exasperation. "Will you never tire of feeble excuses and trying to negotiate with me?"

"It is but the nature of the Jews, as you well know, God." Moses explained. "For example, take Commandment 12. 'Thou shalt not gossip…' Gossip is a genetic part of who we are. It is part of our cultural identity. We have no newspapers or other way to spread the news. Without gossip, we have no identity, no cultural cornerstone."

"But you are the Chosen People, Moses. Did you forget that? Does it mean nothing to you and your people?" God challenged.

"We do not forget something as important as that, God! Never!" Moses quickly replied, sensing a trap coming. He had to salvage this discussion quickly.

"But, when we go to the market in town and try to trade for food, tools or clothes, we have so little to trade with. Believe me, God, it means so very much to us to be Your Chosen People. But the vendors at the market, they will not give us a discount of any kind when we invoke the 'Chosen People' moniker. It just doesn't carry any weight with those non-believers. So, we have to be a bit practical to survive. We trade information, or gossip, to be able to afford food and clothes."

"You have a good point about the tablets and their weight, Moses." God responded. "Perhaps I was a little heavy handed in the stones I chose to use. And I see your point on the gossip thing. It is a tough situation I gave you, having to deal with all the non-believers. Ok – Commandment 12 can go."

"Oh, thank you, God!" Moses gushed. "That is so very generous and magnanimous of you!"

"While we're talking about this, can we also talk about number 8? With no air conditioning or windows, we have to use sheer curtains, if any at all, to allow the breezes of the desert into our homes. It is impossible *not* to see into a house, unless one only looks at one's feet. This seems impractical at best and impossible to enforce? If I were to look into my neighbor's house to see if he were home, would I not be subject to this commandment and any punishment it brings?"

"This commandment is there to keep the perverts under control and keep the peace among neighbors. Perverts cannot be tolerated in a civil society. The people should not have to worry about such problems." God explained.

"A point well taken, God. But, let me counter with this point, if I may. We live in the desert. There is little that is civil around us, except, of course, ourselves. We are a very close society. If a pervert were to exist, all the mothers would know this when he was very young. His wrong ways would be corrected immediately and effectively. We cannot afford, as you say, to have such among us and we do not. I would offer to you that we have the processes to deal with such problems without having to create a commandment just for that."

Moses continued, feeling himself on a roll "Can I also bring to your attention Commandment 10. Not that I am a fan of sodomy, you understand, but it does help keep the rape crimes down. It has also been a big factor in our low instances of inbreeding problems. It gives a person options that, in the big scheme of things, you might not want to take away."

"Sodomy has also helped many men make new friends they would not have otherwise made. In at least three cases, it has also been a significant factor in resolving lingering anger over perceived wrongs, creating new friendships where only anger existed before. If you are looking for a balance in social matters where we get along together, I would suggest that you remove this one as well."

"Enough!" God cried, "I have a lot to do and I'm getting tired of your prattle. I admit you make some good arguments and I can live with some of your suggestions. You rest for a while and I'll redo the tablets."

"Excellent, Sir! They will be, perhaps, a bit thinner and only 2 tablets? That is all I am able to carry at my advanced age."

"Just go to sleep and leave it to me and do not come to me about these commandments ever again. You and your people must live with them. Got it? We are agreed?"

Looking for a place to rest, Moses replied with a smile "Huh? What? Oh, yes … yes, Sir! Whatever you say, Sir. After all – you are God and are all knowing."

And that, my dear readers, is the true story of how we got the Ten Commandments. In the final version, they were written (in a smaller font size) onto two, rather thin tablets that proved to be fairly fragile after all.

Some of the words have changed slightly over the many years from the many languages that have touched them and interpreted them. But, they remain basically good rules for the gene pool that help people get along.

They were fairly pragmatic, at least until the extremists got to them. Take coveting of your neighbor, for example. God set a quite realistic condition on this – if it takes more than four hours to walk there, they are not your neighbor. It is ok to covet all you want. This has since been modified to be ... no coveting at all. How is someone supposed to live, I mean *really live*, if they cannot covet a little now and then?

As originally intended, adultery with a neighbor was taboo because it messed things up among the locals. The word God actually gave was just don't do it in your own town. This way, the family image can remain intact, at least in theory, if not in fact. The extremists took out the operative words there, too, changing it to: don't do it at all!

Where's the fun in that? Where is the old fashioned friend-liness that we saw in California in the 1960s & 70s? How is a person going to share their happiness and neighborly affec-tions? We can't keep a village happy if all we do is keep to ourselves. It got all twisted around.

Extreme views put it in black and white – don't do it at all – keep it in the home. How boring! How unfriendly! No wonder the world is so unhappy these days. People are keeping their love and friendliness to themselves and not sharing. We need more sharing in the world. This needs to be changed.

While we're at it, maybe we should also take a good look at the definition of adultery. Does it only include someone of the opposite sex? Is same sex ok? Do they have to be of a certain age? Do they have to be consenting? Does it still count if they get talked into it or have one too many drinks? Do sheep or large dogs count? If you think of your spouse while you do it, does it still count?

Suppose, just for argument sake, that you haven't had

marital sex for more than, say – two months. Is it ok to stray then and not call it adultery? I mean, like if your spouse wasn't doing her marital duties, it's kind of *her* fault, right? So, that should make it ok? Almost like you have her permission. If God thought it ok to have some flexibility here, who are we to argue with that or to change his intentions and words?

At least sodomy is still ok, even though it is against the people law in many places. Hmmm, does sodomy with your neighbor's sheep count as sodomy? With their large dog? Consenting spouses or children over 14?

See how these things get all messed up when people get involved and start thinking about this stuff? They just have to pick it apart and try to figure out what God really meant. Like God isn't smart enough to say precisely what he meant. Oh no, that isn't good enough for humans.

Then, there are the people who have to try to make us live by their own personal interpretations of God's word, as part of their own power play. What do we end up with then? Thousands of different versions of what God meant. Kind of like when someone whispers something in your ear and you say it to someone else and they tell it to another person, and so on. In the end, the final version is nothing like the original.

Does no one else see the idiocy of this? God has to be falling off his lab stool in laughter at the stupid things we've done to his original words. And we do it with such sureness, confidence and ego. He's rolling on the floor I tell you.

I say – get past it all. God said what he meant and he created the gene pool. They both work hand in hand. Let things be as they were meant to be and above all – remember the dinosaurs.

Let's take another peek at those 13 commandments God started with. Let's consider the intelligence that went into their creation and how they fit so well into the purpose of the gene pool.

We can lump the **first 4 commandments** into one topic for this discussion. All four of them are intended to help us remember the dinosaurs and to remember that God put us here and he can take us out – or smitomize us, to use his term.

The bleachings of the gene pool are not some random happenings. God causes, or allows, them to happen and always for a reason. Things are going wrong, the experiment is over, someone pisses God off, curiosity, whatever the reason. It does not happen by accident.

It's interesting that God used up four complete commandments to make this point. Do you think that maybe, just maybe, he thought that this point was important? Something that he didn't want us to forget? He even set aside one day a week so we could remember. It had to be important to him.

Remember, the dinosaurs did not have cognizant thought capabilities like humans have. They could not have pissed God off on purpose, or by negligence, if they wanted to. It didn't matter! Look how they turned out – God turned them into oil, coal and diamonds. He made them. He liked them. They didn't piss him off. Still – oil, coal and diamonds.

Maybe we should change Sunday into Dinosaur Remembrance Day and make offerings of oil, coal and diamonds. If he used up four commandments just to get this point across to us – maybe we should pay attention. Ya think???

On to **Commandment 5** – you should not kill people. In the original text, there was a clear "out" if you have a really good reason. If you look at the acceptance God gave to some of those who made war and killed others, there can be no doubt that there are a lot of reasons where God considers killing justifiable.

He also left it a bit unclear for a reason. This command-ment comes right after the four admonishing us to honor God. Its placement is intentional – if we've paid attention to the first four commandments, we should have a pretty damn good idea of what is good and bad in God's eyes. God also left the punishment open-ended – obviously, some punishments are worse than others.

God expects us to have a clue. It's kind of like when your mother wonders about what kind of birthday present you are getting her *this* year. What? Are you supposed to read her mind? Duh – of course you are! After all this time, if you weren't such a selfish bastard, you would know what would make your dear mother happy. Not like last year when you bought her a two-year subscription to the "Tampon of the Month Club".

Get a clue, dude! Just like with God. Get a friggin clue!

Moses, with God's help, did his own share of killing when God parted the Red Sea for Moses and his peeps. Being desert dwellers, the Egyptian army dudes couldn't swim a lick and all drowned. Just another historical example of killing that's not only justified, but was done by God himself. The message? Don't pick on my peeps!

Remember King David and all the thousands he killed on the battlefield, just so he could keep the holy land in his grip. From this, and many other such examples throughout history, we can ferret out some of what God's intentions were. "If you kill to protect me and honor me, I can live with that."

It's like when you got into a fight at school because some-one said your mother is ugly or a lesbian. How can mom be mad at you for defending her honor? Go ahead, smite away.

Suppose those kids talking trash about your mother are also picking on you and taking your lunch money. Your big brother steps in and starts smiting away. This is also obviously ok! Mom will understand and will thank your big brother for watching over you and protecting you. From God's example to mom's lips.

How much clearer do you need it? The gene pool is ok with certain killing, because it strengthens the overall human species and life on earth, in general. Just have a damn good reason. Or else.

Commandment 6 – Honor mom and dad. This is common sense extension of the first four commandments. It also comes from some advice God's uncle gave him when he was a youngster being punished for some infraction of his parents' rules. His guilt lived on through the eons and God passed it down to us in this commandment.

It's also an acknowledgement of our superiority over other life forms. Some, like sharks, are known to eat their young. No respect there, just pure gene pool. Those little ones who are not eaten grow up to have their own life. They don't hang around the home nest. They go out on their own, as it should be.

You don't see adult lions coming back to *their* parental pride, trying to join back up with mom and dad, because some lioness threw them out. Or because the other lions teased him. Or because he couldn't find anything to eat. Or couldn't find a mate. No indeed. They man-up (or lion-up) and make their own way in life, applying the lessons their parents gave them.

If they listened well when they were young and honored their parents' lessons, they became good lions with plenty to eat and lots of little lions to aggravate them. Without such honor, the young lion may one day come across his parents when they are old and eat them. There is no honor in eating your parents!

In the same way, God, and the gene pool, want us to grow

old with respect and honor and not have to worry about being eaten by our children. We should not fear the return of our young to the family home when they need help. If they honor us, that is.

If they don't honor you, don't let them in. It isn't as if the honor will magically appear where it was missing before. We have Commandment 6 to keep the gene pool intact and to honor God's guilt.

If this doesn't work, when the kids finally do leave home, wait three months and then send them a notice that you are moving to somewhere way off the beaten path. Somewhere like Billings, Montana or the Panama Canal. Invite them to visit if they get in the neighborhood. Don't actually move, of course. Just tell them that you moved. They won't show up and, if they do, you won't be there.

On to **Commandment 7**, coveting. As discussed earlier, the words and explanations exchanged between God and Moses provide significant clarification on this commandment. This is important to the gene pool, because it thrives on variety while weeding out the negative factors. Desire, such as hunger and having better things, are key motivators to life. Animals, plants and humans all strive for better shade, food, mates, water, etc. Humans are just more aware of it.

God had to provide us with some boundaries on this, for the sake of the gene pool. You can covet the wife of someone who is not your neighbor (a neighbor, remember, is someone living more than 4–hours' walk from you). Of course, you can always "admire" a lot without crossing the line into actual "coveting". Neat little out.

Also, if you are a female, there is no restriction on coveting your neighbor, other than their house and goods. Lucky women!

For the guys, though, there are still plenty of coveting opportunities. There is no prohibition about coveting your neighbor's daughters, sons, nieces, sister or mother. There are lots of opportunities in those.

Also, while the house and goods are off limits, anything borrowed or rented is ok. So, if your neighbor is having an affair, she is either borrowed or rented and you can covet her all you like. In this situation, he might even share, if he's a friendly sort of fella.

Coveting is a good thing to motivate us to do better for ourselves. If you think about it, isn't that all the gene pool is trying to do, to make us better? Sometimes we need some motivation. Your neighbor's daughter may be just the motivation you need.

Don't let all the extremists and liberals mess this up for you. God was very clear on what is and is not allowed in legal coveting. The extremists would have you slit your wrists for having a wet dream, for crying out loud. The liberals would have you believe that anything goes as long as it's consensual. Covet with care and remember the first four commandments – and the dinosaurs.

A word of caution. While God and Moses don't mind a bit of coveting or admiring from time to time, your spouse, your loved one(s), or even your neighbors, may have some objections of their own to your coveting. In fact, they may react rather "aggressively" if they found out. And if you do more than passive coveting, like maybe actually doing something about it, you risk all sorts of trouble.

Keep this in mind, coveting is a *passive* activity and a *solo* activity. It is NOT a couples or team activity. So, be careful in your coveting, enjoy the thoughts and smile when no one is looking. And sometimes even when they are.

Commandment 8, keep your eyes to yourself, does not need a lot of explanation. Moses talked God out of including it in his masterful example of negotiating with higher powers. This example of negations should be taught in every business college. It is virtually impossible to keep your eyes to yourself. Especially if you are in the process of coveting! After all, some of the best parts of coveting include looking.

The intent of the original commandment was to keep the energy of the gene pool going by limiting the energy spent on useless ogling of others. The thinking was that this activity is not time and effort well spent and takes away from real work. It also promotes laziness and doesn't make for nice neighbors.

In the end, though, if one wants to spend their time watching others, whether coveting or not, the other rules of the gene pool will eventually come into play and correct any extremes or excesses which lead to laziness. As we all know by now, the gene pool does not like laziness. So having this commandment dropped from the original thirteen commandments is not that big a deal. God and Moses were wise to let this one go.

Coveting and looking are great transitions for discussion of **Commandment 9** – do not commit adultery with a neighbor. Adultery could be looked at as *active* coveting – taking coveting to the next level of actually doing something with someone else. Kind of like mutual, active coveting with physical contact involved. This is definitely not an individual sport.

Once again, similar to the coveting commandment that was dropped, one has to look carefully at the words and guidance God gave Moses. First of all, there is the definition of neighbor, someone who lives less than four hours' walk from you. Now, if one's conscience were so inclined, one would realize that there is a lot of room for interpretation available in this restriction.

I believe God did that on purpose so that the smarter people would figure this out and pass on their smarts to their children. The dumb ones would get caught and castrated or stoned by their spouse.

If one were to walk VERY slowly for four hours, they could find opportunities just about around the corner. Also, if one was too dumb to figure that out, but was a real fast walker, chances are they would get away with it, once again reinforcing the goals of the gene pool. Smart and in good shape. We need them in the gene pool.

There is another aspect of this commandment we need to look at. What actually *is* adultery? Is it just consensual sex with someone who is a neighbor? Does it count if both people in a marriage participate, like in a three-some? Is it really cheating if everyone does it or does it with permission?

God was silent on these points, leaving us two possibilities to consider. First, that he was relatively innocent about real life when he wrote this commandment. He had never been married nor experienced the heartbreak of married life. How could he know that some added spice might be needed in a marriage from time to time?

The second possibility is that he really did know what he was doing and stayed silent on the subject to give us some room to flail as we grew as a life form and the various societies we became. At different times, cultures have taken a lot of license with this commandment, some making it an actual governmental law, others taking a hands-off approach. Perhaps this is one of God's great gifts to us – to allow us room to interpret as the world changes and as we change.

As we discuss the interpretability of this commandment, we should look at what was left out. Coveting included, specifically: wife, house or goods. The adultery commandment does not include house or goods and is gender neutral.

Again, why did God use these specific words? Let's look at it for a moment. We are allowed to commit adultery with a neighbor's house, if that were possible. Ok – easy one – no brainer, except to those of you trying to figure out how to have sex with a house. When you figure it out, let me know.

Sex with the neighbor's goods? Well, maybe it depends on what the goods are, doesn't it? I'm sure there are *some* goods that could be very interesting. And none of them are included in the adultery commandment. So, if you have a hankering for your neighbor's giant cucumber – go for it – it's ok in God's eyes.

Same thing for their candle sticks, bed posts, door knobs, rake handle, and so one. As a matter of fact, your neighbor's goats, sheep, dog, pony, etc. are all ok with God. Have fun and don't forget to protect yourself from disease and splinters.

Being gender neutral, this adultery prohibition is aimed at men and women alike. You can't do it with your neighbor. Period. However, it does seem to leave open to iterpretation whether, by the term "neighbor", God meant all neighbor people, or just the adults or just those who are married. Do their kids count as adultery? Do their nieces, or the cute nephew that stayed for the summer last year, count? If they are visiting, are they truly neighbors? After all, they don't actually *live* there, do they?

If you can't get permission – you might think about letting this one go and just stick to coveting. But, if you are determined to tackle this troublesome commandment, you better be very good with your interpretations of the written words, or learn to walk or like animals. This one could get you in serious trouble. Not so much with God, but within your house and with the neighbors.

Either way, God knew what he was doing and gave us a lot of room on this commandment. Use it carefully, because the consequences at home are a lot worse for adultery than for just coveting. People have been known to have lost body parts and their lives over this issue. Mostly because the aggrieved party tends not to be very understanding and accommodating. Not like God is.

And now for another point of view.

If a man and woman were truly sexually and emotionally satisfied and into each other, there would be no coveting or adultery. If people kept each other happy, why go anywhere else? While the gene pool rewards those adulterers who are good thinkers, or slow walkers, or really fast walkers; we should remember that it rewards good, strong, loving relation-ships even more. (*This editorial comment was brought to you from the Religious Council On Equal Time, because they did not like the perceived idea of God endorsing adultery. Well, gentlemen and little old ladies, read the original text from God and get a grip.*)

Okay – on to the next commandment. **Number 10** – don't do sodomy. Any asshole can figure this one out. Don't go in the back door! There are no loopholes in this commandment. For very good reasons. It is not good for your health. The gene pool and God want you to be healthy.

Some people will argue with God on this commandment, saying that the anus is not a dirty place. Well, let's look at it this way – would you eat from it? Not me! Wipe all you want, no way! The shit that comes out of it is dirty and full of things bad for your health!

Also, it's designed with special safeguards in the intestines so that the bad germs and other crap don't get into the body or the blood stream. If that happens, the body gets infected, becomes septic and you die. This is why doctors are so worried about problems like perforated bowels and similar issues. Those things can kill you. God knows this. He did the original design work, remember?

Part of the design of the anus is for the lower bowel and colon to take the material out and away from the body. This means that the anus is an *outie* – not an *innie*. It is, by its basic design, not intended to have things go in it. As many of you have found out, bad things happen when things do go IN, instead of OUT, things like disease, hemorrhoids, tearing of the intestine walls, pain, emergency room visits, uncomfortable explanations, and more.

If we read the commandment words and the definition of sodomy closely, we see that sodomy means putting your sexual organ into someone's anus. This part is pretty clear. But, into your own anus? Sounds like that's ok. Evidently, you cannot illegally sodomize yourself, so have at it, if you have the reach, that is.

Another gap in the definition is: what about sticking other things into it. Fingers, tongue, dildos, hamsters, flashlights and bottles are evidently all certified by God for anal use. Now, even though such things are physically possible, as evidenced by our growing population of happy gays and adolescent experimentalists, one still needs to be careful with this commandment. The consequences are potentially high.

Some people think AIDS is one of God's reactions to interspecies and anal sexual experimentation and lifestyles. That he created AIDS to bleach out and punish ass holes that are misused. Maybe yes. Maybe no. Either way, perhaps he should have thought it through more carefully back when he wrote this commandment.

This commandment could just be the results of a bad boyhood experience with some of God's classmates, or upper classmen or a religious leader in his early teen years. Maybe this commandment is nothing more than a visceral reaction to that experience. A bad anal experience has haunted more than a few young boys into manhood.

Perhaps, God is just anal-phobic. Well, I'm not going to ask him about that one. You can if you want. Let me know what he says. I'm good with what we have in writing and will let it go at that.

Commandment 11 – don't bear false witness against thy neighbor. This is just common sense in how to get along together. The gene pool doesn't work well with lies and falsehoods. Whether you are family, friends, lovers, spouses, workmates, whatever; we, and the gene pool, can't work properly without the truth.

Now, being Jewish himself, God left some room in this commandment, knowing how the Jews like to talk about others. Of course, he doesn't want people lying, but if you really believe something to be true – is it false witness if you tell others?

Is it false witness if you really did think the girl was 18 years old? Or if you really, truly believed that Saddam did have weapons of mass destruction? Or you really do believe that suspect #3 *was* the guy who raped you?

This wording leaves plenty of room for Jews and non-Jews alike. If you know it to be untrue – it is false witness. If you aren't sure or you don't know – it can't be false witness! Even a 3-year old can figure this one out, so it should not be all that difficult for adults.

In fact, there are three prominent professions that are centered on this very concept: politicians, lawyers and religious leaders. They all play loose with the truth, especially because they often don't have it, but proclaim they do.

We also can't ignore the neighbor definition again with this commandment. It appears, from the wording God gave us, that it's perfectly ok to give false witness against someone who is not your neighbor. This is an interesting item to consider.

As discussed earlier, if someone is just visiting, are they your neighbor? Or if they haven't lived here for very long – can you lie about them? How about those folks more than a four hour walk across town? Can you lie about them, too?

What if someone lives close by, but you hate them? Aren't neighbors supposed to look out for one another and help each other? Well, if you hate them, or they hate you, how can you call them a neighbor? Is it ok to lie about what their dog did in your yard? Or what their boy did to your daughter?

It's interesting how something as simple as those nine little words can be so confusing. Was it left open to interpretation on purpose? Was it a "give" to the Jewish leadership so their people would not complain so much and could still function in the ways of old? Was it an oversight that just has never been corrected? Regardless, it is what it is and I think it speaks for itself. And that is that.

Only two more commandments to go, so hang in there. If I can, you can, if you are true gene pool material, that is.

Commandment 12 – Gossiping. Gossip makes villages, towns, families, industries, societies and religious organizations work. Whether it's a couple of nosey old ladies telling stories about the cute, sexy thing with the perky boobs three doors down or two kids talking dirt about the smart kid with glasses in the class. It could be the gossip papers, the White House, military disinformation efforts, the 6 o'clock news or the morning paper. It's everywhere and all societies are addicted to it. It's not a genetic trait that God created for us. No, it is much more.

You see, ever since the cave man days of Ferd and Sherman, it was important for survival to share information. This included where the good berries were, where animals were for hunting, when the woman of the cave was in a bad mood and it would be a good thing to go on a hunting trip for a few days. Survival depended on such information.

As Ferd and Sherman met others like them, they shared such information to get smarter. This increased their food supply, they found places to get protection from the elements, they identified who the bad guys were (sometimes the wrong way) and they could sometimes trade-up their current women to the new and improved models, some with fewer "miles" on them.

This thirst for more and more knowledge helped fill in the quiet times when they were stuck in a cave with nowhere to go and nothing to do, except fool around, tell lies and draw graffiti on the cave walls. Survival depended on collecting information, making good decisions, being smart, lucky and not lazy.

The early Ferds and Shermans of the world didn't have a lot of mental capacity. Little things threw them off track. Things like, the moon changing, lightning, fire, oral sex, snow and which side of the rabbit went on the inside of the gloves. It didn't take much.

They were the original and classic "duh" guys. In fact, that was their favorite word. Duh! Duh this. Duh that. Duh could mean anything, including east, west, north or south – that is, if Ferd and Sherman had any concept of what a direction was. But, they did thirst for more information.

Early in the evolution process, as God found out when dealing with Alpha and Beta, once the human brain bucket got filled up, it just sort of tossed any new stuff on the ground and some old knowledge went along with it. It's kind of like that movie "Fifty First Dates" where things started over new again each day.

Over the many years and generations of human development, God was able to start increasing the capacity of our brains, while also improving its ability to hold onto what it had. This had a great impact on human survival. We could remember, from one hunting season to the next, where the big game was and how to kill it. We didn't do so well at how to get it home, but hell, at least we got a kill.

As we learned and remembered more, we grew smarter and were able to improve our existence. We moved with the ice ages and the warm weather. We built better homes. We made better graffiti. Men taught women how to plant crops so they could sit back and watch them do the hard work for a change. (See how well that one worked out?)

Throughout all this time, information continued to be shared. The best way to get crops to grow. How to make a boat (and what a boat was). The best women in the next village who will put out. How to keep warm in the winter when your woman finds out about the woman in the next village. How to build a bridge.

As we evolved and grew in numbers, there was more and more information to share with each other. We got better at learning and retaining knowledge. Life got better and better as the eons went by.

So what does all this crap have to do with gossip? Good question. Gossip is an insatiable need for information that has its roots with Ferd and Sherman. We've become programmed to want more and more information.

Even the kids in school want to learn. They just don't want to learn what *we* want them to learn, or *because* we want them to learn. Nothing new there. Watch them. They're already information junkies by the time they get into kindergarten. Look at this neat bug. What does dirt taste like? How far can you pee?

Why does mommy scream when she and daddy wrestle? Why is that lady fat? They are knowledge sponges.

Gossiping is just taking this evolutionary need for knowledge to a new level. A level where the information barter system is finely tuned. Information is power. It's been the medium of exchange for people all over the world for millennia.

So what does this have to do with God, Moses and the 13 Commandments? Well – God was no dummy! He watched us evolve – hell – he designed us to evolve. We *have* to evolve or he doesn't get a good grade.

For some reason, his favorite people, the Jews, had made gossiping into a religious experience like no other. They honed gossiping to a fine art form unequalled by anyone else in the history of mankind.

They're so good at it that it is synonymous with being Jewish. You think that circumcision is a Jewish thing? Oh no, no, no. It's the gossip.

Did God make a commandment about being circumcised? Of course not. He is a man and has some tender emotions about that particular item. But, he didn't make it a commandment. He did make one about gossip.

Why did he do this? Well, I'll tell you why. Because gossip can hurt. You see, when God was a little God guy, he was picked on by others who said bad things that were untrue about him and his mother and the family pet. In fact, he often came home crying from the pain of it.

He remembered that gossip hurts. He wanted to put a stop to it because it was getting out of hand and this was a great chance to do just that. So he created a commandment just about gossiping. The natural thirst for knowledge had to be controlled to stop people from hurting each other and to preserve the gentleness of the gene pool.

But Moses, who had spent a lot of time with his Jewish brothers and sisters, had a different perspective. Moses had a lot of experience with how words can hurt. He'd heard all the jokes and insults the Egyptians could throw at them all those years in Egypt. If you don't get a thick skin from that, you won't get one.

While in Egypt, the gossip system was the only way to pass information around the Jewish community. They had no newspapers to read, or pubs at which to gather and chat or public criers to exclaim information. All they had was the great Jewish gossip to quickly pass on snippets of information during short opportunities to talk. A few words here or there and another neighborhood got information passed around.

Moses well knew that he could no sooner stop the gossip system than he could carry three thick stone tablets down from that mountain. His people had to gossip and get it out of their system.

He also knew that God promised them 40 years in the desert so his people could chill out a bit and settle down after all the excitement in Egypt. They had plenty of time to slow the gossip down, but you couldn't just turn it off!

This was why Moses negotiated this one away from God and convinced him to give the Jews a break. After all, out in the middle of absolutely nowhere, who were they going to gossip about except each other? The Rabbis would handle that problem. Time for God to let it go, and also to let go of his own past "issues".

"So you were picked on as a kid." Moses told God one day. "You think we Jews know nothing of being picked on? Of course we do and you made it that way. We get it. But you have to let the past go. That was a long time ago. Get past it and move on. It's time to man-up!"

If you think that didn't take balls, think again. Moses really had a pair. What a guy. Because of him, the art of gossiping is alive and well around the world, especially within the Jewish faith. In fact, it's so entrenched, the other middle eastern religions, which are off shoots of Judaism, are now in competition for the best gossiping religion. Funny how things work out sometimes, isn't it?

Commandment 13, don't steal and don't break things you borrow, is a two-for-one kind of commandment. It's almost as if God was trying to slip something in on us when he was putting these together.

For getting along and being nice to each other, the first part makes lot of sense. Don't take what isn't yours. Well, that isn't what it says. It says steal. And that means taking something that isn't yours without the owner's permission.

Over the ages, however, there have been ongoing debates on what really constitutes stealing. If you take something "accidently", is that stealing? If you intend to bring it back, is that stealing? If you asked permission, but the owner didn't hear you and you "thought" he said it was ok, is that stealing? If you just came to their place and used it there, like, say, oh … their wife. Is that stealing?

Do you have to take it off their property for it to be stealing? What about if it isn't on their property to begin with? What if you had permission, but the owner changed his mind?

What about stealing one's virginity or innocence? Can you steal something that cannot be proven to exist or is gone afterward?

Many wise people have pondered these issues. Some governments have codified stealing and given it differing levels of severity, depending on the value of the item and if violence was used to take it. Most religions have also instituted prohibitions against stealing based on this commandment. It is, after all, good common sense and good manners for people who want to get along.

But, what's with this "breaking while borrowing" clause? Where did that come from and where did it go? Exhaustive, painstaking research in ancient writings of the period once again gives us a clue to the answers. Once again, God, in his young ways at Universe U, had a personal experience that colored his judgment and led to him including this clause in the commandment. Thankfully, Moses, the master barterer, talked God out of it.

His painful experience in the pitfalls of lending things came when God lent his lab, our world, to a fellow student who needed to get in some lab time. It seems that this other student, called D. Evil in the ancient writings, had burnt up his own lab in an experiment. He was left without a lab shortly before the end of the grading period. So, God lent D. Evil his lab for a weekend and D. Evil made a complete mess of things.

According to the ancient writings, D. Evil had a bit of a sadistic streak in him and liked to watch things go badly, rather than nicely. He would do things like, intentionally put two planets in almost the same orbit around a star, one just a little inside the other. He liked to watch the competition between them and watch them fight and argue – like who really owned the orbiting moons. Or watching as the planets got too close and infringed on their magnetic fields, ruining the environment on both of them. Or telling each planet that the other was stealing gravity from them.

Another favorite of his was to create great hardship in one part of a world and watch the life forms struggle and fight each other for survival. Silly, childish things like our kids do – ants under the magnifying glass, feeding Alka-Seltzer to a sea gull, toilet paper in the trees, hair remover in the shampoo, hair grower in the liquid body soap. Stuff like that – but on a much bigger scale with bigger consequences.

Well, when he borrowed God's lab, D. Evil focused on a little area in the plains of the River Jordan to do his work. This was in an area that we know as the southern limit of the old lands of the Canaanites. In this area were five towns that were close to each other and dependant on each other for trade, building and protection. These towns were known as Sodom, Gomorrah, Admah, Zeboim, and Bela.

Unknown to God, who hadn't asked and just trusted his fellow student, D. Evil's experiment was on applied psychology in making beings do bad things to others that were against their general character.

We've had our own modern day versions of D. Evil's little experiments. There were the Nazi experiments on civilian prisoners where a person was forced to hurt, and even kill, another prisoner or they were hurt themselves. There were people who were forced to watch their family members raped and killed. There have been many more recent examples of people acting completely inhumane to others for no good reason. This has happened many times throughout the history of mankind on small and large scales.

Well, this was exactly what D. Evil was up to. Historically, these five towns were peaceful and got along well. In his experiment, D. Evil applied some psychological techniques and some drugs to change the people.

He fed them rumors and lies. He caused problems and disease, that he blamed on the religious leaders, in order to turn the people against authority. He turned ordinary women into whores. He took away their inhibitions and fed into their animalistic instincts. In large part, he took away their humanity.

The results were not pleasant. In short order, the people of these towns became just plain wicked. No one worked. If they wanted something, they took it. If there was resistance – there was a fight and killing.

Animal urges created an orgy environment where no female (and many males) over the age of 11 was safe from rape or worse. The crops failed, food was gone, and no defenses were left to protect the towns. People were killing each other and no one cared, except to get what they wanted from someone else.

At the end of the weekend, God came to check on his lab and to see what D. Evil had done while using the lab. God was shocked at what he found! Where there used to be a pleasant area of people living in general harmony, he found complete wickedness. Where he had left things before the weekend in good order, he found this area completely ruined.

God spent a whole day mulling over what to do about the situation. First, he had to fix the lab situation up. He could, and would, settle up with D. Evil later. But, for now, what to do?

The more he looked at what D. Evil had done, the more appalled he got. Buildings can be rebuilt. But, the dead were gone. No sense bringing them back.

The rest of the people in the towns remained evil and mean. God conducted chemical tests to find out what D. Evil gave to the people. He found that the drugs D. Evil used to change the people had permanently changed them. They could not be changed back.

There was only one choice. He had to destroy the people and the towns. He had no option. And he was sooo pissed. Because of this idiot, D. Evil, God had to destroy five towns and start them over.

No, he thought, he would never rebuild them. They would

be destroyed and stay that way as a reminder about what had happened. So, God destroyed Sodom, Gomorrah, Admah, Zeboim, and Bela and all the people in them. It was one of his worst days at Universe U.

Later, God caught up with D. Evil and they had words. D. Evil was not sorry for God's problems, of course. In fact, his attitude was that if God didn't want anything to go wrong with his precious little lab, he shouldn't have let D. Evil borrow it in the first place. Simple as that. No remorse. Not even a "Sorry Chum." It was all turned around to be God's fault.

God and D. Evil never did see eye-to-eye on much and, after that incident, they didn't have much to do with each other, either. They ran into each other from time to time, but were always at odds with each other. This feud goes on to this very day and probably will for a very long time.

And that is the honest, true, real story of what we often refer to as Sodom and Gomorra.

Now, you might ask, why were we not told the real story long ago? Go ahead – ask. Why is the truth only now coming out about this incident? What took so long? Why didn't we know of this before now?

I'll tell you why – God was embarrassed about the whole affair. He misjudged his fellow student. He allowed his lab and his beings to be misused. He was forced to destroy five towns and their inhabitants.

God could not face his failings and certainly didn't want to have his lab beings know about this. Just imagine the impact on them.

"Oh great. God is going away for the weekend again. I wonder who he's going to let have at us while he is gone *this* time?"

"He said he would protect us and what does he do? He

turns us over to some schmuck to screw us over and then he destroys the evidence. Like we would never know or figure it out."

"What kind of God is he to let someone do that to us? Why should we listen to him after what he did? We should all go up to Sodom and Gomorra and demonstrate. Let him know he can't treat us like this."

They made up signs that said "REMEMBER THE SODOMITES" and "DON'T GET SODOMIZED BY GOD." And they protested the next weekend.

Yes, God was embarrassed and he could not allow this questioning to continue. So he did the only thing he could do – he made up a lie. Our politicians would be so proud of him they would make him an honorary senator. Except, God already had this religious thing going for him and we all know politicians believe that *they* should be the centers of all worship.

God concocted this story about Abraham and Lot and how only a few good people were in the towns and God saved them. Except for Lot's wife, who just wouldn't listen, being the curious little woman she was. God had to turn her, at least in his story, into a pillar of salt as a reminder to all that he still had the power to make you or break you. Then he got the story out through his network of religious leaders, and bartenders and gossip-mongers.

Soon, the real story was long forgotten and, to this very day, we continue to believe and teach the false story God planted. The story about how things went bad and God saved the few good ones who obeyed.

The angst of those experiences continues to haunt God. So, be careful about what you ask God for and give the guy a break. And above all – remember the dinosaurs.

And don't get sodomized by God.

Chapter 11 – Gene Pool Heroes or Zeroes?

E ngineers. They're geeky and squeaky. They're nerdy and weird. They're detailed and logical. They're dependable and predictable. They can manipulate electrons, but can't balance their checkbook. They're sitting next to you, yet somehow you get the feeling that part of them is ... somewhere else.

They have a sense of humor no one else can understand. They aren't very socially comfortable or adaptable. They harnessed fire, but not women. They appreciate a fast car, but are confused about a fast woman. They don't have a firm place in the world, except in their own world, which they are always trying to change and improve.

They're taught the secrets of the universe, yet can't explain them to a non-engineering minded person. They know about electrons, ozone, radio waves, quarks, material fatigue, computers, penicillin, and the laws of physics; yet they can't get the DVD player to show the correct time or pick up the right milk at the store.

They're the builders of things in societies, but not the builders of societies themselves. They're the inventors of things big and small. They have visions of things that can be and dreams of things no one else can conceive.

They figured out that the world was round and not the center of the universe long before anyone else. They designed pyramids and ways to build them. They found ways to mine underground, so we can have iron, gold, coal and more.

They brought us air conditioning and can pop-tabs. They brought us weapons to hunt more effectively. They got us gloves with the fur side, warm side, inside. They brought us efficiency in all aspects of our lives through the millions of years. Where would we be without them?

If there is such a thing as God's chosen profession, it has to be an engineer, because God is also an engineer. God is learning the secrets of the universe and he's building, creating and designing stuff all the time. He manipulates the world and materials around him to make things better, or as he wants them to be. He understands genetics, and chemistry, and biology and astro-stuff that we will never understand.

He learned to balance different life forms with tectonic plate dynamics, climate change, the earth's 3–D gyroscopic dynamics that control its wobble, errant genetic aberrations, and the free-wheeling things done by humans to each other and to his lab. This is serious Intelligent Life Engineering 101, to be sure. It's not easy. That's why he is there and we are here.

How can there be any doubt about God's true major at Universe U? It's certainly not religion. That's for humans and those of lesser minds. God is all about creating, building and designing things. Remember the first kangaroos that died off because they didn't have a pouch? God created kangaroo, Rev. 2.0, this time *with* a pouch, and it worked.

Having engineers run around our world these days is like living with a school principal – one isn't sure how to talk to them, or what to say or how to act. Thankfully, the engineers don't give much of a hoot about all that crap. If you don't like what they say or how they say it, that's your problem ... as long as they are right. If you don't like their analysis – show them where they are wrong. If you can't, then shut up.

Engineers don't fit neatly into normal society. And society isn't too sure what to do with engineers, either, except keep them together with other like-minded people. We certainly don't want to let them wander off too far alone in society.

To help with this, we created special schools just for engineers. All kinds of engineers. Engineering schools for computers, biology, medicine, teeth, feet, the brain, feelings, rockets, ships, planes, dams, roads, hair, ice, rocks, water, animals, food, tires, cars, engines, seats, bones, mines, air, space, society, thoughts, guns, butter, war, trains, and on and on.

We are smart enough to keep our politicians all holed up in a single place (like Washington, D.C., or London or the state capitals) and not let them mingle with the general public. We also try to keep our engineers grouped together, but for very different reasons. We have "engineering" companies and "engineering" schools and "engineering" societies and "engineering" industries. These are mostly run by people who are specially trained as "engineering" managers, who specialize in herding cats.

This treatment of engineers isn't as severe as we are with criminals or as obvious as we are with educators. We don't give engineers uniforms like we do the police and firefighters or military personnel. Engineering types aren't joiners and aren't much into uniforms, anyway. But, we want to be sure to keep them under some control and we don't want them running around mixing it up with everyone else. Why not? If you don't know – see below.

Question: What is an engineer's favorite word?

Engineer: Why?

Q: Because, I want to know.

E: Why do you want to know?

Q: Because, I do.

E: What are you going to do with the answer?

Q: I don't know till I get one.

E: Why?

Q: Because, I don't.

E: Why not?

Q: Well, because your answer will determine what I do with it.

E: That's just asking for the answer so you can make up the question.

Q: No, it's not.

E: Sure, it is.

Q: But, I don't do that.

E: You just did.

Q: Did what?

E: What I just said.

Q: What did you just say?

E: Why?

Q: Because, you said it.

E: I say a lot of things.

Q: Not those, what you said just now.

E: Why?

Q: Because.

E: What are you going to do with the answer?

Q: I don't know till I get one.

E: Why?

Q: Because, I don't?

E: Me, either.

Q: You either, what?
E: What, what?
Q: You what?
E: Why?
Q: Again, why?
E: You want to hear a joke?
Q: Sure.
E: Me, too.
Q: You too, what?
E: Want to hear a joke?
Q: Sure.
E: Me, too.
Q: You too what?
E: Why?

Why do we keep them locked up with their own kind? The real question should be – Why would we release them to the world? Let them talk to each other. They understand each other. Just don't let them raise children or be in charge of anything.

I know it sounds harsh, but they *are* a tad different and we aren't really sure what to do with them when they aren't at work with others of their kind.

Interestingly, they don't know what to do with themselves when not in the office, either. The emotional world of elementary and middle school teachers, children, wives, most animals, mothers, girl friends, shrinks, politicians, and management are foreign worlds they try to avoid. But, they do have some good uses for the gene pool.

Engineers of all types bring a certain ... logic and processes, an order if you will, to life; even if they don't fully appreciate the human element. We could certainly do well to have more of this in our legislatures, where they have the opposite problem.

Engineers aren't perfect people, either. They tend to get focused on the little things or small areas of interest at the expense of the bigger picture.

As an example, remember the space craft that was sent to Mars and missed the entire planet? The engineering team was so focused on the design and process that they failed to get the units of some of the numbers matched together with the units in another part of the space craft.

It's a small matter if you're driving across town and get miles and kilometers mixed up. When you're going to Mars and do the same thing – it's not good. You not only miss the block of your planned landing, you miss the entire friggin planet! Bad for the resume.

Another time, on a craft designed to return space materials back to earth, everything worked perfectly. Except for one minor detail. A little sensor was designed such that it could be installed upside down (incorrectly) – which it was. As a result, when the craft came back into the earth's atmosphere, the parachute didn't deploy. The result? Smashola in the desert.

Luckily, some other smart engineers found a way to get useful samples from the now flattened craft. Otherwise, nothing would have been salvaged from it. Details, sometimes you miss just one or two and it messes up your whole day.

Anyway, this book is about the gene pool and our role in it. So what do engineers have to do with the gene pool? The answer: a lot, actually, and not all of it is good.

In the old days of Ferd and Sherman, those with an engineering kind of mind had the basics of survival to think about. As we've seen, their capacity for thinking was far less than what we have these days. (Well, mostly, anyway. I've seen some people who make me wonder if Ferd and Sherman aren't still alive.) Somebody had to figure out that fire might be a good thing, then figure out how to control it and take it places. The first engineer to do that had a warm and dry cave, hot food and lots of friends.

They didn't have to study Newtonian physics, thermo-dynamics or the history of fossils. They had other things to worry about. Besides, soon they would become fossils them-selves. How to kill better – that was high on the list of things to do today and every day.

These intrepid engineers of ancient times also had it made, by today's standards. No time clock to punch. If you weren't hungry, just sleep in a while longer. No meetings. No reports. No computers. No bosses. Life was simple. The big concerns of the day were how to make a better spear or make a cave wall paint that was blue. Or getting some belly-to-belly time with the red haired wench in the next cave over.

But, being the engineering minded people they were, these few thinkers conjured up plenty of things to ponder and solve. Why can't we store summer and use it in the winter? Why don't rocks burn? There are plenty of rocks around and trees are hard cut up. How does one make leather that doesn't stink like a dead rotting animal? (Well, it *is* a dead rotting animal. Duh.) How to cut one's hair and get a good close shave? How to carry fire around without getting burned? How to change the shape of a rock? How to make a rock stay on a stick when it's thrown? What should we call that big round thing in the sky?

There were so many problems for the early engineers. Thankfully, they solved them and we're all better off for it today. They lived when the non-thinking schmuks (the Schmukers) in the other valley died off. The Schmukers had real incest prob-lems in their group. The rumors had it that they were a bunch of mother Schmukers. But, those are just rumors.

Anyway, the smart people tended to live and make new

smart ones. The dumb ones, like the Schmukers, died off and didn't waste the gene pool's time. This is the essence of the gene pool. The smart, the lucky and those who make good decisions will win.

As the centuries passed, the engineering types would also tackle how to make the ugly people look better through paint, tattoos and surgery.

This went over big time in Egypt where the rulers had so much inbreeding that they were turning out uglies by the week. No wonder they took to burying their royalty deep in the hills and under huge stone buildings. They were so ugly, no one wanted to take a chance someone would dig them up. Hide them deep and paint them over – that was the best they could come up with.

Perhaps, if they'd talked to the Vikings or some of the American Indians, they would have seen the wisdom of cremation. It sure would have saved a lot of effort and provided some fertilizer for the crops.

As time crawled on, the engineering talents of the world were used for buildings, and hunting, and the occasional medicine man and voodoo woman. They were also harnessed for fighting. As we've seen time and again, people just can't seem to get along without fighting about something. Throughout history, we seem to always fight about the same 4 or 5 main subjects.

- Women – "Our women are ugly. Let's go steal some good-looking ones from the next village over the hill." Or "She was looking at me, not you. She's mine!"
- Territory – "This is my cave and you can't have it. Get out." Or "I like this cave and want it, so you get out."
- Sex – "You can share my cave, if you do this one little thing for me." Or "I like that cave – honey, would

you please get it for me? Pretty please? I'll be ever so grateful."
- Work share – "You didn't help kill tonight's dinner, so you don't get any." Or "I killed that rabbit, not you. Let go of it, or else."
- Stuff – "That's mine and you can't have it." Or "I want that and I'm going to take it from you."

For some reason, God has not been able to get the competitive gene in us under control. It was good for the monkeys when they were fighting for every banana they could find. Or for the dinosaurs, so only the best would survive. Or when we lived in caves. But, it hasn't died off much in humans after all these many millions of years.

For some reason, we seem to need to fight. We fight with our spouses.

We fight with our neighbors, and our bosses and coworkers.

We fight with strangers on the roads who tell us we're number one in their book.

We fight for no reason, for imaginary reasons, for religion, for no religion, for the wrong religion.

We fight for women, about women, with women, because of women.

We fight for sport, for money, for pride, for medals.

We fight so people will like us and so people will hate us.

We fight with people we love, people we like, people we hate, and people we don't even know.

We fight by rules, with no rules; with weapons, with no weapons.

We fight for space, for stuff, for air, for trees, for spotted owls.

We fight with words, without words, with pictures, with sign language and gestures, and with silence.

We actually do an awful lot of fighting. And over many millions of years, we've gotten very good at it. We aren't as good at it today as at other times in history, but we certainly are a lot more efficient at it – as long as no one gets hurt too much (liberal influence). Very strange, oxymoronic attitude, isn't it?

Anyway, the Romans were VERY good at fighting. So were the Greeks, the Egyptians, the Incas, the Gauls, and those nice tourists Genghis Kahn brought over from the Far East. Yes, there have been many more peoples, tribes, groups and countries that were better at fighting than we are today.

By the way, if I didn't mention you or your group, I didn't mean to slight you. I only have so much room and have to make a point in here somewhere. So don't go looking me up to prove how good you can fight. Just stick your head up your butt and fight for air while recording it. Then, post it on the internet. I'll see it and that will be enough evidence for me. Trust me and I'll trust you. (Yeah, right.)

Moving on. As all societies, groups, tribes, clans and countries convinced themselves that they just *had* to be able to fight, they always turned to the engineering types to help develop better fighting tools and machines. It started simple enough, like the time Ferd defended his woman from being stolen in a true, man-to-man, in your face, fingers in the eye, bite his nose off and smash him in the head with a stone, fight. How proud she had to be of Ferd for fighting like that for her.

These were the good old days when you had to look your enemy in the face and smell his bad breath as you killed him. The gene pool was very proud of these contests, because they truly represented all of the goodness that the gene pool represents. The survival of the fittest at work.

But Sherman, Ferd's friend, was one of those early engineering minded guys. After one such fight, while helping patch up Ferd's wounds, he pondered something to Ferd that neither of them had ever thought of before.

Sherman said "Ferd, you keep getting into all these fights over your woman. Aren't you tired of it?"

"Of course, I am!" replied Ferd. "But the other guys keep trying to take her from me and I can't let that happen. She's mine. I own her fair and square."

Sherman scrunched up his brow (or would have if he knew what scrunching was) and told Ferd "Well, I've got an idea that I think will solve your problems with the fighting."

"Really!? Let's hear it. I'd do just about anything to stop getting beaten and bitten so I can do other things." Ferd declared.

Sherman's eyes brightened a bit hearing his friend say this. "Well, Ferd, why don't you give them belly-to-belly time with your woman, like you do for me? You and I don't fight. That seems to work well. Why don't you do that with those other guys?"

Not being a bright sort of caveman, Ferd had to stop for a moment at the brilliance of the suggestion Sherman had. He let Sherman have belly-to-belly time with his woman and they didn't fight. True enough. In fact, they got along well together. Maybe there was something to this idea of his.

"But, there are so any of them and only one of her." Ferd finally said.

"Oh yea, that's right. When would you get your own belly-to-belly time? Maybe I need to think about this some more." So Sherman thought and thought. After a couple of days, he approached Ferd again. "Ferd, I've got it. The real answer to your fighting problems."

"You do? Great, tell me."

"Think about it," Sherman said, "why do they fight you? Because you have a smoking chick and they don't. If she wasn't so hot – they wouldn't want her and you wouldn't have to fight to keep her!"

"Wow!" Ferd exclaimed after a moment. "That's brilliant, and I don't even know what that means. It would solve all the fighting for sure? That would be great. So, how do we do that?"

Ferd wasn't the sharpest knife in the drawer, but he did have the hottest girl around. So, he had to ask the hard and complicated questions of Sherman. Sherman was like the one-eyed man in the valley of the blind. He wasn't the best, but he saw things no one else saw. And he was smart enough to get a share of Ferd's woman without having to have one of his own – not brilliant, but way ahead of his time.

"Well," Sherman thought out loud "I can think of two ways right off the bat."

"Bat?? Where?" yelled Ferd, who was deathly afraid of the bats that were often in his cave.

"No, not that kind of bat! Calm down. This is more like an idea that hits you in the head in the dark – like the bat that flies, but it's an idea." Sherman said, trying to calm Ferd down. "Now, where was I?"

"An idea that flies in the night? I don't like the sound of that." Ferd responded.

Sherman was starting to get confused by Ferd's logic. He concentrated and tried again. "Your woman. If she wasn't so good-looking, you wouldn't have to fight to keep her, right?"

"Well, yeah, right." Ferd agreed slowly.

"Ok, as I see it, you have two options." Sherman started. "Either you make her as ugly as the other women or you trade with someone to get you a wife who isn't as good-looking. Fighting problem solved!"

This was just the kind of breakthrough thinking that Ferd needed. It was why he kept Sherman around. He always had the right answers. "That is a great idea, Sherman!" Ferd said. Pausing for a few seconds, he added, "But, how do we do it?"

"Hmmm," thought Sherman, who hadn't gotten that far in his solution thinking. "You could make her ugly by just shoving her face in the hot coals. That would do it. You could also wash her hair – no one would want her then."

"But, then she would be ugly for me and I wouldn't want her either!" realized Ferd.

"Right. A minor sticking point in the plan. So, you're saying that you don't want her to be ugly for you, just for the other guys. Right?" clarified Sherman.

"Well, duh! Of course I don't want her ugly for me! What good does that do? Oh, yeah – no more fighting. But, no more good-looking woman, either. That won't work."

"Let me get this straight." Sherman said, trying to clarify things. "You want her ugly for the others, but not for you. I guess it's true what they say down at the river – once you've had good-looking, you can't go back."

Thinking a moment, Sherman realized "I guess that means you won't trade with Bubba for his wife either, huh? I mean, if you can't have ugly, and Bubba's woman is really ugly, then trading down won't do."

"No." Ferd said sadly. "That won't do. Whoever said it down at the river was right. I can't go back to ugly. I guess I'll have to keep on fighting." Sigh.

"There is one more option." Sherman said, tentatively. "I didn't want to bring it up, because it means you'll have to keep fighting, but it may keep you from getting hurt so much and the guys may back off some. You want to hear it?"

"Sure – the other ideas won't work and I have to do something about the situation."

"Ok, here it is." at which point Sherman brought out a big stick he had hidden behind a rock in the cave.

"What's that? It's just a stick!" declared Ferd, always the great observer.

"Oh, it is much more than that." Sherman declared with confidence. "You know how close you have to get when you are fighting? How you get hurt trying to get close enough to clobber the guy using a stone?"

"Sure I do." said Ferd, rubbing his arm where the last fight left him bruised.

"This stick solves all that. Look, Ferd, you don't have to get so close with this stick. You can clobber the other guy and he can't reach you. Watch." And with that, Sherman clubbed Ferd on the head with the stick, friendly like.

"Ow!"

"See what I mean?" asked Sherman. "I got you and you couldn't get me. In your next fight, use this. You'll win without getting all busted up for a change. And you can keep your good-looking woman."

Well, the live demonstration did the trick. Ferd was convinced. In his next fight over his woman, Ferd won, not because he was motivated by his woman's beauty, but because he had "the stick" and the other guy didn't.

Of course, the imbalance of weapons didn't last too long. After a while, others caught on and started using sticks, sometimes bigger ones. Soon, the fighting was no longer about who had the best looking woman, but who had the biggest stick. It's been that way ever since.

The evolution of smarts and weapons helped the gene

pool achieve its goals for survival. And the engineers, like Sherman, helped along the way while also proving the adage that ... bigger is indeed better.

Throughout history, the thinking folks like Sherman were smart enough to develop better and more lethal weapons and methods to kill, and maim and defend themselves.

They were also smart enough to figure out how to stay out of the middle of the battles. They were happy enough making tools of war for others to use. The engineers weren't dumb.

When they developed a nuclear hand grenade in the 1950s, they looked for *someone else* to test it. "Let's see who wants to test this out? See how far you can throw it and we'll see if our calculations for killing radius were right."

"Opps, sorry about that. Slide rule error, but within the margin of acceptability with a really strong arm and a good wind." (True story.)

Engineers have been involved in every facet of warfare since Sherman's great stick discoveries, and they always will be. I have a stick, you find a bigger stick. I throw a rock, you find a way to throw it farther. I find a way to throw a stick and you find a way to shield yourself from it. You find a way to throw a real large rock and I find a way to build a real sturdy building. On and on it goes.

The engineers work for all sides. Why? They're thinkers, not fighters. Those of the engineering mind are driven to solve problems for anybody.

Problem – I can't win a fight. Solution – get a bigger stick.

Problem – the enemy is across the ocean. Solution – build boats or boil the ocean.

Problem – the enemy is dug in. Solution – bulldoze them over or send in sand fleas.

Problem – the enemy won't fight by the rules. Solution – declare victory, make a political pull out, and send in the Peace Corps. Or change the rules. Or cheat.

For every problem there is a solution – it just may not have been found yet or you may not like it.

How does all this fit into the gene pool's plans and goals? Smarts are important for the future of the gene pool. There's no doubt that the engineers are pretty smart folks. They often make good decisions, at least when logic is involved. The gene pool likes those things. Also, engineers are generally not lazy, especially when there is a problem to solve.

Yes, they see things differently than others, but that's part of their charm. Who else would think of things like: seeing in the dark, birth control for women, post-it notes, sewage treatment plants, front snap bras, tampons, computers, heated toilet seats, lightning rods, and Velcro.

Remember the famous NASA motto – "Build Things Faster, Better, and Cheaper"? Engineers and scientists worked for many years trying to do just that. Of course, they all knew in their hearts that you can't have all three at once. The best you can do is to have any two of these three features. It breaks the laws of nature. But, God bless those engineers, they worked so hard to prove nature wrong. They didn't make it, of course, but they tried their hearts out.

Engineers are thinkers. You can't take them to a party like you would normal people. That's why we put them in special companies who have special management techniques to control and focus them. If you doubt this – read Dilbert.

Or look at all the engineering companies and government engineering departments we have. Special places in special companies for special people with special problems. All because we can't let them run amuck with the rest of the people.

We have good reasons for keeping engineers locked up in cubicles and special companies. We don't let them play with others, too much. They rarely run for public office. They don't diddle little kids in the name of religion. They create neat stuff, some of which is useful. They don't cause trouble. They serve a purpose.

All through the ages, engineers have created great things that improved life on earth. Medicines, surgical techniques that save lives, earthquake resistant buildings, ball point pens, air conditioning, plastics, computers, electricity, lights, and much more. Without engineers of all kinds, humans would not have survived, let alone thrived.

The down side? Without engineers, humans would not have nearly destroyed themselves again and again throughout history. Of course, without greed and pretty women, we wouldn't have all this fighting to begin with.

We'd be able to put more engineers to work getting us to the moon, or teeth that don't rot, or food that grows in the desert, or sweat that doesn't stink, or 50 MPG cars, or grass that only grows 2 ½ inches high, or cheap electricity or voting machines that work.

The gene pool needs engineers. Humans need to learn how to get along. And we all need more pretty women. Simple enough, even an engineer can understand it.

Chapter 12 – Draining the Gene Pool

In the end, as it has been since the beginning, the gene pool wins. Why? Because it was created by God! He made the rules and he can change them anytime he wants. He's also motivated for the big picture success, namely his grades. We aren't motivated by such things.

The gene pool contains within itself the "prime directive" for the development and survival of intelligent life on earth. God gave the gene pool rules to manage and control life. Rules to filter out the unwanted characteristics and eliminate them from the gene pool. God created it to promote the characteristics in life forms on earth that were the best of the best. His grades depend on it. His future depends on it. OUR future depends on it.

We've come a long ways since Ferd and Sherman, sitting in a cave trying to figure out how to stay warm and how to get some belly-to-belly time with the gals in the other caves. Hell, we've come a long ways since 1950.

Yet, questions remain. Do we still have a long way to go? Isn't evolution done yet? Is the end in sight? Can this struggle for intelligent life ever actually create any? Is that a light at the end of the tunnel or just another meteor coming to wipe us all out again?

The evolution cycles have been going on since God was a freshman at Universe U and it shows no signs of letting up. Every day, we hear of a new and wonderful species being discovered. We also hear a lot of screaming and crying about the demise of another poor schmuk of a species that some do-gooder, liberal, kum-ba-ya tree hugger wants to save. I wish those folks would just take the unwanted animals and plants into their own homes to love, and leave the rest of us to our own fates. Sorry for the digression. (Not really.)

God is still playing with the gene pool and coming up with new things for us to discover. Who knows what we may find. Maybe grizzly and polar bears will mate producing a big, mean brown bear with white spots, or stripes. A zebra bear!

Maybe television will develop shows with real intelligence and thought behind them (odds are against it).

Maybe we'll finally find out what is really under all that ice in Greenland – after all, someone had to name it Greenland for a reason, other than as a joke, right?

Speaking of Greenland, here is the greatest Greenland story there is. Naming Greenland was the greatest prank of the 400s AD.

Sven the Viking returned from being away from home for three years with his crew. Sven told wondrous stories of a great place just a short ways over the great waters following the afternoon sun. It was warm there, he declared, with trees, and plants and animals … and it was GREEN! So green, in fact, Sven had named it Greenland.

Sven told everyone he'd stayed in Greenland for 2 years after discovering it and claimed to have started a town and colony for everyone in this wonderful, green place. Sven told everyone how to get there and worked hard encouraging all his friends and neighbors to go to this wonderful place.

And they did! By the boatloads. They yearned for a land that was warm and where plants and crops would grow easily. A place where they could all flourish. A happy place to call home. They left behind their villages, their homes, their friends, and relatives for this new place ... this Greenland.

As they left, Sven the Viking, the great explorer, laughed and laughed. Only he and his crew, all sworn to secrecy on a blood and brother oath, knew the truth. Greenland sucked. It was as cold back then as it is now. Colder! There were no trees. There were no animals. There were only the remnants of a couple of tents they'd left behind. Sven the Viking had a great laugh, alright.

Oh yes, they had been to Greenland, but only for a short time. It didn't take Sven the Viking, also known as Sven of the Seven Women, long to leave that frozen, empty, *white* place.

He left Greenland and headed for what is today Northern Scotland and then France. In these places, Sven had some women (seven actually – hence, the nickname) set aside for just this kind of emergency. He knew he couldn't go back home too soon or people would think him a failure or, worse yet, afraid. He couldn't stand the thought of being Sven the Coward Viking. He had to stay away for a while and Greenland was NOT where he planned to do it.

Sven took his crew to Scotland and France and they lived it up with the local women. They supplemented their funds with a tiny bit of raiding, as resources got low. Sven and his men stayed long enough so they could return home as great explorers with no suspicions.

As his fellow neighbor Vikings sailed off into the setting

sun to this Greenland Sven bragged about, Sven and his crew made themselves busy getting reacquainting with the women left behind. Their smiles were not all because of the ladies' pleasures, for they knew the secret.

Slowly, over time, some of those who went off to populate Greenland returned. They claimed that Greenland was nothing like Sven had described. It was cold and white and miserable. They were pissed (to say the least) at being duped by Sven. And all Sven ever said in response was: "It was green when I left it."

How do we know all this about Sven the Viking? The story comes directly from archeological diggings and research in Greenland, Denmark and Scotland. Interestingly, there is no written evidence of Sven from his travels to France. We know he went there from other writings, but not directly from the French. The archeologists think that the French, ever so prim and proper, were adhering to a "Don't Ask, Don't Publish" form of chivalry.

Writings from Scotland, however, confirm Sven's destination upon leaving as France on at least two occasions. Writings from both Greenland and Denmark contain descriptions of this account and the anger people had at being fooled by Sven. After all, they had picked up all their belongings, left their homelands and relatives, and moved to Greenland.

It was a great joke, if you had a sense of humor. However, no one, not even a Viking, had a sense of humor big enough to enjoy Sven's little joke. Or being stuck in Greenland until the ice cleared and they could get back home.

Now, for the twist to the story. The word "gali" is an ancient Danish word for a story, often told by travelers passing thru villages, or by parents to children. Soon after Sven the Viking had his fun, a new term was coined to mean a story that was not true and not to be believed, regardless of how good it sounded. This new term we know as "Svengali" – inspired, of course, by Sven, the greatest Gali of them all. And that is the truth. Honest.

Back to the gene pool.

Is the gene pool overloaded with slime, and waste, and flotsam, and jetsam and all forms of ne'r-do-wells clogging up the genetic search for intelligent life? Do I hear a big DUH?

How do we protect our future? How do we assure our own survival? How can we clean up the gene pool? How do we make sure that only those of us who are worthy to swim in it survive?

Since the gene pool always wins, how can we be sure that WE are on the winning side? How do we keep THEM out of the gene pool and make it safe and pristine once again?

This chapter is where we'll explore that very question. Sit back, relax, read on and take notes, because your survival depends on it. The gene pool of your children and grandchildren depends on it.

There can be no intelligent debate about WHETHER the gene pool needs to be cleaned, to be drained of all the pollutants in it, and given a fighting chance to revive itself. Look around you. The filth is everywhere. The core of the gene pool is corrupted and only the strongest of genetic bleaches will work.

Pay close attention, dear readers. As you should recognize by now, if we don't clean up the gene pool, HE will. Remember all the lessons of the past. Remember the dinosaurs. If we leave it up to God, it will be brutal, merciless and final. The only good thing about it is that it will probably be quick.

We can't let that happen. We have to take action on our own and show some maturity for the bumbling, ignorant species we are. We have to clean up our own mess or else!

In the cleaning process, we'll have to treat the gene pool with considerable respect and care and, yes, some fear. God created it with powers we can never hope to understand. After all, he is at Universe U and we are only the test subjects. Leave the air conditioning in the lab on too much and God gets a cold. We get an ice age.

Of course, we'll be playing with things way beyond our knowledge and ability to understand. But, that never stopped us before. We're fragile, but we're also resilient, stubborn and, hopefully, smart enough to survive in the gene pool. We can do this!

But how? That's the question.

The Low Hanging Fruit

So, how do we get rid of those who pollute the gene pool? How do we create more of us who promote its most cherished characteristics? If you think about this, as I have, you will no doubt come to a similar conclusion: it will not be easy. It will take sacrifice and harsh measures.

The undesirables, those who just have to go, will not want to go. They will fight. They will lobby those with power and money. They will start trouble all over the globe. They will pretend to be something they are not. We have to weed these people out for the sake of humanity's survival. Someone will have to make those hard decisions. I hope they are truly smart and wise.

In the rules of the gene pool, the strong, the healthy, the smart, the good-looking ones live on. Let's consider changing the rules we live by, all over the world. Suppose we encouraged the special people, the "keepers" to thrive and populate the gene pool.

And let's say, we encouraged those who are less, shall we say … desirable, to not thrive or survive and pollute the gene pool? We all know who "they" are, don't we?

What if we made a few simple tweaks to the basic rules and give the gene pool a little room to work its magic? With a lot less human intervention!

We can start with the easy measures, like the low hanging fruit. These are measures we can institute that will help thin out the crud of humanity who are ruining things for the rest of us. It's sort of like skimming the crap off the top of the pond – easy to do and easy to see results quickly.

With these measures, we just have to step back and allow the gene pool to do its work, without intervening or boo-hoo'ing. Let's let those who don't belong, those who aren't deserving, pass away into history the way it was meant to be. The gene pool will do a lot of the work for us and make great strides towards cleaning itself up. We won't have to lift a finger – it will do all the hard work for us.

Let's look at some of these, more benign, measures, shall we?

Motorcyclists are a special breed. There can be no denying that. They challenge fate every time they get on the road. They love the freedom to go anywhere and to feel the wind in their faces. They want, no – they *crave* the freedom to ride where and how they want. Don't try to fence these folks in.

Maybe we shouldn't. Why don't we let them live on the wild side? If they want to ride fast – I say, go for it. If they don't want to wear a helmet – I say, God bless them. There is no real reason to not let them have the full motorcycle experience.

This includes the experience of feeling all the skin being peeled from their bodies and their bones breaking when they hit the asphalt. It's the final high of motorcycle freedom they seek. Let them have it.

I say, in the name of the gene pool, repeal all the laws protecting motorcyclists against themselves and let's see who survives.

Of course, this means eliminating any laws requiring a helmet. Let's see who survives the falls and crashes. In reality, we don't want the ones who need a helmet in the gene pool, anyway. Let them die off from bad luck, poor judgment or inadequate skills. It doesn't matter – we need those people to be gone.

So, let's eliminate motorcycle laws.

This will easily whittle the bikers down to only the ones who deserve to stay. Let those who are capable riders live. Drain the gene pool of the rest. Let them die off from natural selection. Don't let all the do-gooders, who have no good sense or perspective of the big picture, intervene.

Those bikers who survive, those who are good, who are lucky, who have great reflexes – we want them in the gene pool. More than that, we need them in the gene pool. The gene pool needs their luck and skill. It needs their ability to face danger and survive. It needs their daring.

What the gene pool does not need is all the others. The ones who are bad drivers or who are unlucky. These are the ones who have accidents, who ride into trees, who plug up the emergency rooms and require long stays in the hospital as they get their skin re-grown. Save us all the grief and wasted resources.

If they can't ride well – too bad. Let them survive or die on their own merits. If they can't grow their own skin to replace the skin they left on the asphalt, too bad. If they can't stick their own bones back inside their bodies and get them to grow together – what good are they to the future of the gene pool? None! Biker – heal thyself or die.

While we're at it, let motorcycle accident "victims" find their own way to the emergency room. Save the ambulances for those of us who are worthy of the gene pool. This will assist the weeding-out process without costing us a penny.

To further help the process, let's outlaw any insurance for motorcycles or their riders. You can't have it. You can't get it. Now, go and enjoy your freedom! Feel the bugs hit your face. Speed down the road and show us just how fast you can go doing a wheelie. Free entertainment for the rest of us. Have a good time till your genes catch up with you. The rest of us will be waiting.

Still on the automotive subject, let's look at a few additional things we can do to help skim the scum from the gene pool, without having to work at it too hard.

Suppose we gave special driver's licenses to people who desired to drive as fast as they want? Not just motorcycles, but cars and pickups, too. Have them take a special course in high speed driving (at their expense, of course), charge them a bunch of money to have the license ($500 should do it), let the insurance companies charge more for special coverage (but don't require it) and then, let them go at it.

If they're good drivers with good reflexes, and eyesight and health – they'll survive. These are good traits for the gene pool. If they aren't good at it, they die off. They do the hard work for us. Be honest, we didn't want speed demons in the gene pool anyway.

On the good side – this effort is self-funding. These speedos will pay for their special schools and licenses, the insurance companies will charge more for those who pay for it. We can also expect unemployment rates to improve as new people are hired for the driving schools and special license testing. And, of course, people will have to be hired to replace those who don't survive. It's all good for everyone, except those who don't belong in the gene pool. Just like God planned.

When we allow people to drive as fast as they want, there are bound to be a couple of side benefits to help with the gene pool. It's inevitable that, as these speedos kill themselves off, they'll also kill off a few unlucky people in the process. Don't panic. Remember this is how the gene pool works. We can't have the unlucky ones polluting the gene pool, either. They have to go, too.

Some folks will demonstrate their bad judgment and die from riding along with the drivers who don't have what it takes. Oh well. Remember, the gene pool always wins.

Let's not forget about the other people on the roads and the pedestrians who are going to demonstrate their individual bad luck and/or poor judgment, by getting in the way and getting themselves killed, too. While this is sad for some people, it's necessary for the gene pool.

The best part? We don't have to do anything overt. We just let it happen. Natural selection at work. And it isn't like these people are innocent collateral damage. They're genetically guilty! They have to go sometime and now is their time. Rules of the gene pool.

There'll also be those folks driving along minding their own business when some speedo crosses a lane and wipes them and their family out. No fault of theirs, other than being at the wrong place at the wrong time. But, the gene pool can't get cleaned of these bad luck genes if we don't let them die through natural selection. Collateral damage is just part of the gene pool.

From time to time, someone will be sitting at a red light, waiting for it to change, when they get rear-ended by a speedo who lost control or has bad brakes (not a good thing if one is going to drive fast). There will also be the unlucky pedestrian trying to cross a street, or walking the dog, or sitting in their living room as some speedo comes crashing through their house wall at 105 MPH after losing control. So sorry, but that's life.

Think of the bright side – the economy gets a big boost in the funeral business and unemployment rates improve just a little more. And the gene pool is a little bit cleaner. All survivors are winners!

While we're looking at helping the undesirables earn their rightful place outside of the gene pool, maybe we can tweak a couple more laws to help them a little more. An obvious one is to remove seat belt laws. Sure, it may save the lives of the unlucky or unskilled, but we don't want them saved to continue mucking up the gene pool. Rescind all seat belt laws immediately and alert the EMTs.

Remember, good drivers will create good survivors and lucky riders will create lucky survivors – we need them. Bad drivers will kill off not only themselves, but also those with bad judgment and bad luck. If they survive – good for everyone. Otherwise … bye, bye.

A companion element to seat belts is baby and child seats. Let's be honest – if it's good enough for the adults to go without seat belts, it certainly is good enough for the little ones. After all, they're as much, or more, a part of the gene pool as adults. Let's find out early on whether or not the kids are really worthy to belong on the gene pool. Let's find out before we waste a lot of time, and money, and grief, and schooling on them.

Besides, there are plenty of little places to stick kids to keep them from flying through the windshield in an accident. Consider the floor space behind the seat or in the trunk.

Along this line, we could roll back the minimum driving

age to 12 or 13 and see who really has gene pool potential, before we spend a lot of time and money sending them through high school. They'll thin themselves out for us and take a few unlucky innocents along with them. This keeps them from passing on their defective and unwanted genes to a new generation of gene pool scum.

Why this early? Why not? Kids can get married as young as 14 in some states. In some parts of the world, they get married much, much younger. If you can get married before you learn algebra – you can drive.

Besides, I'd be willing to wager that many of these young kids can drive a lot better than the old farts on the highways diving with their hands on the steering wheel in a death grip. You can easily see these drivers on the highway because their hands are above their ears and they're staring out front looking between the steering wheel and the dash.

Also, they're going only 25 MPH and they drive like they don't see anything until it gets within 15 feet of the car. That's because they can't see anything further away than 15 feet!

While we're talking about old farts – maybe we should let old timers drive till they die. If they last, that's ok. They've already created whatever kids they are going to have, so there isn't much, genetically, that they can pass on.

They also add to the fun factor as everyone else tries to navigate around them. And they're so cute sitting at traffic lights holding onto the steering wheel for all they've got with their hands above their ears.

So intent, so serious. So lucky. They have to be to get that old. They have to have some good health genes, too. Otherwise, they'd have died off years ago, preferably before they passed their bad genes on by creating children. Who knows, maybe they'll stroke out on the road or meander into the wrong lane and contribute to cleaning up the gene pool.

Onwards. Speed limits should be just suggestions, as a way to help speed up the weeding out process and improve the unemployment rates.

One other thing we could easily change that would greatly help the gene pool, for free. We should remove the *left* or *right turn on arrow only* lights at intersections and the *no right turn on red* signs. How many times have you been sitting at a light waiting for it to turn and there's no traffic coming from the other direction? What a waste of time and gas! If someone isn't smart enough to figure out that they can't make it across the traffic or to merge into traffic – we don't want them!

Bad judgment. Bad luck. Bad timing. Bad eyes. Bad reflexes. Let them weed themselves out and take a few unlucky ones with them. They're polluting the gene pool and ruining it for the rest of us.

Another idea. Let's remove laws requiring turn signals. Face it, no one really takes these seriously anyway. This is especially true for lane changes, where one is supposed to signal their *intention* to change lanes. Who has time for intentions while driving?

This law means we should be paying attention and thinking ahead. We don't have the time or brain-power to do that while we're trying to talk on the phone, text our friends, eat, change the radio channel, yell at the kids, and put on makeup. A person just doesn't have any extra time for thinking about lane changes, they just do it. No intentions are involved. So, let's accept the obvious, no, let's embrace it. No turn signals!

This would actually help drivers pay better attention to their driving by keeping them guessing at what the others are going to do. It also prevents overloading the majority of drivers by trying to get them to pay attention to their driving. Of course, those who are good at this "loaded driving" concept won't have any problems, because nothing will change for them.

As for the others? Well, again, the unlucky ones and those who aren't good at driving will die off. A few unlucky passengers and pedestrians will also die off. But, as I've already explained, that's just the way of the gene pool.

There are probably a hundred other traffic laws that should be eliminated in this cause. Remember, the gene pool only wants to keep those of us who can drive fast and well, with good luck thrown in. If you can't operate a car on the road with others on the road, without getting in the way or impeding others – get off or die off.

We need to let genetic selection work the way God intended. Remove the laws that do nothing but protect and preserve those who shouldn't be in the gene pool. We won't have to really work at it – the undeserving will do the hard work for us. They'll kill themselves off, hopefully before they have a chance to pass on their lousy genes to children. Maybe they'll take their kids with them! Either way, it's good for the gene pool, good for mankind, good for the rest of us, and good for unemployment.

What other laws uselessly protect idiots from themselves at the expense of the gene pool?

How about suicide? Why is that illegal? If you really don't want to be here – go! Jump. Shoot. Toast bread in the bath tub. Suck the car exhaust. Catch the end of a rope. Do it and get out of here. We'll clean up the mess you leave behind and find someone to do your work for you. Really – if you can't handle the stress of life – you certainly aren't good material for the gene pool and neither are your kids. Life is tough and only the tough should survive. So have at it. Give it your best shot. (shot – get it?)

What do we do about those who try to kill themselves and fail? You'd be surprised at how many thousands of people, in the US alone, try to kill themselves and fail. Not because they chickened out – they just didn't do it right.

There was this one guy who tried to blow his head off with a shotgun and missed. He missed! With a shotgun! He put the barrel of the shotgun under his chin, just like in the movies, and pulled the trigger – and missed! And he lived!

All he succeeded in doing was to blow off the entire front of his face. It was a mess. The medical bills were tremendous, just to restore him to something others could look at without tossing their lunch! What a waste. Especially for someone who didn't want to be here anyway. Maybe he should have had a Do Not Resuscitate (DNR) sign hanging around his neck.

What should we do with someone like that? We shouldn't arrest them and lock them up as crazy. That much I can tell you. I say we should be gentle and understanding with them. We should kindly explain that they have the right to kill them-selves and give them a second chance – but, first, sign this organ donor card and this DNR form, if you please.

Here's another example that gets honorable mention as a prime example of unexpected consequences in a suicide at-tempt. This guy, we'll call him Joe, should get special seating on the beach of the gene pool – but never, NEVER allowed back in. It seems this fellow decided that he was unhappy and the only way out was to kill himself.

Now, Joe didn't like pain or blood and was afraid of heights. That ruled out cutting his wrists (which doesn't really work well, anyway), or shooting (which has a lot of blood, but the pain only lasts a short time – if done right), or jumping from a bridge or hanging himself. No, all his life Joe was a chicken and he wanted the easy way out.

Being a smart kind of guy, one night Joe made sure the family car had a full tank of gas, slipped out after his wife was asleep, and went into the garage and turned the car on. Joe made sure he tuned the radio to a smooth, music-to-die-for channel. Then, Joe went to sleep, with the help of excessive amounts of carbon monoxide and carbon dioxide. Joe died a peaceful death, just like he wanted.

But, what Joe never knew was that there was an air leak from the garage into the house. While Joe was peacefully sleeping to death, so were his wife and three kids. Poor judgment for marrying him? Poor judgment for staying with him? Poor luck for being born to him? Who can say? Regardless, Joe went out big and did all of us an unintended favor by not allowing his genetic frailty to be passed on in the gene pool.

Thank you, Joe, and all the other "Joe's" out there, who are helping clean up the gene pool.

Are you thinking now? Good. Have you found other stupid laws we can eliminate and help the gene pool?

How about any prohibition about owning and carrying guns. If everyone carried a gun, the bad guys would be greatly outnumbered. If they tried to rob a bank, heist a car, or do something else bad, the good people of Gene Poolville would pull out their guns and blast away.

Saves on legal fees and court costs. It would cut down on repeat crime, too. And, if we get the bad guys when they are young – they don't get to pass on their bad genes to the gene pool. Good for everyone, now and in the future.

Let's make it legal to jump off of bridges. It could be fun to see who has the biggest splash, assuming there is water under the bridge. The jumper could win a posthumous award for it. Or maybe they could see if they can hit that boat going under the Golden Gate Bridge. It's a one-way trip, either way, so keep those cameras running – this could be interesting.

We could even make it an Olympic event! I can see it now.

"And now, ladies and gentlemen, our next competitor is Siegfried, from the good US of A, doing a 28 tuck, with a 14 twist, belly flop from the high rails of our bridge, 182 feet above the water. Give him a big hand on the way down, because he won't be hearing anything after he hits the water at 127 miles per hour! With a dive like this, he's a natural for the newest Olympic sport of Really High Bridge One-Way Acrobatic Diving."

And we won't have to worry about those medal ceremonies. We can play a country anthem, but there won't be anyone to accept the medal, unless they assign a stand-in on the application form.

I remember one fella who jumped off a high bridge and went into the water feet first. Evidently, he was afraid of getting hurt. (?!) He survived hitting the water, which is where most people die. He was going so fast, he went straight to the bottom and got stuck in the mud. He drowned there, slowly, stuck in the mud, instead of the quick water splat he'd expected. Good thing he never got a second chance, he'd have screwed that up, too.

Another idea? Why don't we remove all those silly rules about drinking too much and then driving? Include all the rules about drinking *while* driving, while we're at it. Let the bars have drive up windows for a drink on the go, with a free bag of bar peanuts that doubles as a barf bag … on the house. This one action will help clean up millions of bad drinkers, unlucky drivers and pedestrians, and bad drivers in just a few short years.

Just think of the benefits to the gene pool for generations to come. If we can get to the younger ones, those who haven't had the chance yet to create any genetically inferior off-spring, it will be a bonus for the gene pool and the rest of us. Everybody who is deserving, wins!

Allow kids to ride their bikes in the street and the highway. And dump those helmets – they just keep unskilled and unlucky kids around to pass on their inferior genes. Weed out the unlucky and unskilled ones early. Those who can take a knock on the head and keep going may be useful to the gene pool down the road. Give them a second chance. But, the rest? Just more flotsam on the surface of the gene pool. We'll have to be rid of them anyway at some point, might as well do it early.

We should repeal the cigarette smoking ban so those who want to smoke can. Anytime. Anywhere. In California, they could exhale into little activated charcoal bags to collect the smoke, just to appease the liberals (we'll take a closer look at them soon, don't worry).

Of course, we have to disallow any insurance payments for smoking related medical issues. You take your chances when you choose to smoke and you pay for the consequences all by yourself.

The rest of us get to sit around and watch you kill yourself – at your expense. The gene pool gets rid of millions more scum makers who have bad health (if not, they'd live) and the bad judgment to smoke in the first place. Additionally, whatever money they have goes to the community in the form of higher taxes and higher medical bill payments. The insurance companies don't have to pay for it, which should lower the premiums for the rest of us. (Don't hold your breath for that to happen.)

Along this line – actually just a little extrapolation of the smoking thought – we could eliminate all restrictions on drug use. Think about it, maybe the hippies of the 60's had the right idea. Cheap drugs for all who want it. If you want to blow your mind, go ahead. We won't be needing you in our future gene pool and your future won't be so very long. Have a good time as you go.

Don't try to steal the money for the drugs, because everyone is carrying guns to blow you away and prevent your last nirvana. So, be nice and peace loving and trip your way out of the gene pool. We'll get along without you just fine.

You may just make interesting entertainment, as you reconnect your brain's synapses into something never imagined by God or nature. If we do it right, we can make fertilizer out of your body and sell it to the poor people of Sri Lanka, or Somalia or some such place where, for once, something useful can come from your life. Maybe we can turn the deserts of Australia into a druggies plantation. A place where all kinds of great crops can grow. All thanks to the drugged up bodies turned into fertilizer.

Let's sum up the easy-to-implement, low hanging fruit ideas that give us good, quick head start on cleaning up the gene pool.

- You can drive your motorcycle all you want, as fast as you want, without a helmet, if you want. Just don't expect any help from the rest of us when you have an accident and get hurt. You're on your own for covering the costs for accidents, to get yourself to a hospital and for medical treatment. Good luck and happy riding.

- Other drivers – good news! You can drive as fast as you want, too, anywhere you want. No seat belts to get in the way and you can drink while you're on your way to oblivion. No rules! Just like driving in New York or Boston. What fun! What joy! What a mess when you go SPLAT! And you will. Just do it before you have children.

- Those who ride with the others or are unlucky enough to be in their path – sorry about that. But you weren't welcome in the gene pool, anyway.
- All you depressed people – suicide is now an accepted and encouraged option. Go for it. If you screw it up the first time – some nice government person will help you get it right the next time. If you think you are really talented, try out for the Olympic Bridge Diving Team.
- Smokers – light em up. Rot your lungs.
- Druggies – shoot em up and smoke em up. Rot your brain.

Just from these few, simple rule changes, we can clean out tens upon tens of millions of losers from the gene pool. Careful analysis shows that we should be able to get rid of 93% of the surface scum from the gene pool plus 7% to 11% of the rest of the undesirables who pollute the gene pool. It would be a great start at finally getting some genetic rejects filtered out and re-establishing a clean and pure gene pool. The rest of us will finally have a little room to swim a bit, while we work to finish the cleansing job.

Not so low hanging fruit

Let's move on to some other changes we need to make to clean up the gene pool. These ideas will take more work and will be harder to implement. We'll have to take active measures to implement them. But they are necessary, if those of us who are deserving of the gene pool are going to survive!

The undeserving, at least those who catch on, will resist and fight, but this is the way it has to be. The gene pool insists.

Hard measures are required to achieve success. We have to be tough and firm on these rules and keep our eye on the objective. If *we* don't – God will. Remember the dinosaurs. If we don't, God does.

We'll start with a couple of obvious items.

The Uglies

Remember how good looks are important to the gene pool? They're important to continued genetic purity and survival. This next step should be no surprise to many of us. If you're ugly, you must be eliminated from the gene pool! This is a must-do action.

At the very least, this means sterilization! There's simply no other way. Well, there is – death. If you force us to get extreme, we'll just have to go there. But, in the spirit God intended for us and the gene pool, we'll try the easy way first.

If you are ugly, too bad. It's not like we aren't sympathetic, but we just can't have your "ugly" genes in the pool. Sterilization will be mandatory. If you have other talents to offer to the gene pool, we'll be glad to accept whatever of value you have to share. But, the ugly MUST be eliminated. Sorry about that. (Not really.)

On the other hand, if you're good-looking, you get to have all the kids you want and the government will give you money to keep having them. Gals, keep popping them out, we'll cover the costs. Guys, we'll pay cash for good sperm.

If you like doing it the old fashioned way, we'll even set up fertilization resorts. These are quiet places where you can go to relax and do your God-given, belly-to-belly duty for the gene pool and humanity. We'll call them – the Happy Humping Grounds.

Now, I know you're thinking of the one stumbling block to

this plan. Just who decides who is good-looking and who isn't? I have an answer, of course.

We do NOT let the media, the rag magazines, television, the movies, the beauty contest people, or others of their ilk, get involved in this. No. This has to be completely free of favoritism, air brushes and photo manipulation software.

There's a fairly simple solution, if we approach it like pornography and art. I can't tell you what it is, but I can tell it when I see it.

Here is the plan. We find regular ordinary men and women, ages 17 thru 42, and select from them judges to determine good and bad looks. Of course, these people will have to be among those of us who are genetically acceptable, according to the gene pool. We can't have genetic undesirables doing the judging. That would be so unfair to the rest of us who *are* acceptable. Again, no offense (well, maybe a little offense), but God made the rules, not me.

It's also well known that any regular Joe or Jane knows a good-looking woman or man when they see one. It is so much easier than you think. Just go to your local mall, or park or other gathering of lots of people and look around. It's easy to quickly go thru a hundred people and give them a mental thumbs-up or thumbs-down.

In fact, we do it mentally all the time. Think about it. How many times do you look at someone and think "Boy, is she hot!" Or "Love that outfit on her – she makes it work." Or "Yew, ugly dude!" Or "I wouldn't let any young children near him." Or "I wish he would come over and ask me to dance." These are all forms of judging them (or ourselves) on their looks. Maybe the cute guy is really an axe murderer or child molester. You don't know, but you still make that judgment on looks alone.

See how easy it is? You, yes YOU, could be an "ugly" judge for the gene pool. Apply now.

Why limit the age range for judges? Another good question. The ranges were selected from extensive research in the natural selection process of primates and humans and the sub-conscious visual distortion matrix factors unique to the human brain and its electro-chemical inter-stasis evaluative recall algorithms embedded in our DNA genome. Does that help clear it up? Good.

The lower range is optimal for tapping into the instinctual response mechanism of the primitive "herd preservation" gene. At this age, judges are at their peak for detecting good and bad looks and have the least social programming to counter their initial, instinctual responses.

In other words, they are best at a quick, instinctually accurate ugly/not ugly evaluation.

Many studies have shown that the accuracy rate of this lower age group, given only 3 seconds to evaluate a subject, are an outstanding 94.7%. This is significantly faster and more accurate than any other age group.

The upper range was once again determined through many years of in-depth human psychological and physiological studies of reactions to varying factors, including attraction, based solely on looks. The upper range limit was also selected to be just before a distinctive change occurs in both men and women. These changes affect what men and women find attractive and not attractive.

Above this age, men tend to give girls extra points when they shouldn't, especially the younger ones. They also tend to be harsher on the men than is appropriate. Much of this has been blamed on the so-called male mid-life crises, but that conclusion is still not sufficiently proven. So they get cut off at 42.

The women have a similar situation, but for a different reason. It's been scientifically established, for many centuries, that women react to chemical and other factors in their bodies beyond age 42. It seems that the females' sexual peak (at about age 39) is followed by a rapid drop in sexual desires and hormone changes over the next 4 to 6 years.

These changes have shown to also have a profound impact on the females' sense of what is good-looking and bad looking. (They are also affected in several other areas, such as, situational judgment and impetuousness.) Above 42, women start to exhibit a pronounced skewing of their judgment towards the good-looking male and against good-looking female.

The impending onset of menopause is another biological factor that, again, skews their judgment. We really want to stay away from menopause issues if we can, don't we? Besides, if we raise the limit too far, we'd never get the room temperature right, let alone agree on the evaluations. So, 42 is the upper limit for the ladies as well.

Judges could meet in a local pub over drinks or work virtually on the internet. Whatever works for them, as long as they get the job done. The subjects of the evaluation would submit their pictures to the central committee, which would then send selections to different regional group judges for evaluations.

Candid pictures and videos are recommended to get away from the posers and the effects of make-up. Think about it, if it takes a lady an hour of time and a pound of makeup to be good-looking, she would just cause more pollution in the gene pool when all that face crap washed off.

No, like the animals in the herds, we need to insist on natural beauty that won't wash off. As for ugly – well, we know it can't wash off (unfortunately). Burkas and darkness are only temporary solutions. This is a major contribution of Islam to civilized society – burkas to cover ugly. Way to go. Thank you, Allah.

Now, what if you're in between good-looking and ugly? Better pray something good happens in your life to turn you into a swan. What if you're beyond child making capability? Again, you better have something else to offer the gene pool or you won't be in it for long.

Nothing personal. It's just the rules and the way the gene pool works. You have complaints? Talk to God – he made us, the gene pool, and the rules. We're the ones who messed it up.

Think of how pretty the rest of the gene pool will look once we get rid of the uglies of the world.

After close analysis of demographic and social tastes in good and bad looks around the world, we can easily get rid of 6 to 9% of the population with this program. What an improvement that would be! Look at the world around you and think about it – 6 to 9% of the people you see, talk to, and interact with are just too damn ugly to keep around! Don't you feel better knowing that YOU aren't in THAT group? Of course you do.

And don't get all soft-hearted and pity the uglies. Remember, they're just genetic aberrations that are too ugly to remain in the future of the world. The gene pool has spoken. You can thank God for that, he made the rules. And don't forget – remember the dinosaurs.

Bad Parents

On to another addition to the 'sterilize or don't sterilize' equation. We need to sterilize those who are either bad parents or who had bad parents. "What! Sterilize parents? That is so cruel!"

Not really. Cruel is letting bad parents raise kids and the damage it does to those kids and to society. That is cruel. They can't fit in. They can't contribute. They repeat the bad things done to them. None of this is good for the gene pool. We have to stop it.

On the surface of it, this might sound like it would be hard to do. And it would be, if we left it to the government to figure out. They'd have to study it for a decade or so, figure out some test for parenting, and then test the test. After all that, some yahoo would challenge it in court.

No, leaving such things to the government would do nothing but drag it out forever and accomplish nothing. It's what they're good at. We don't have time to waste on such stupidity. We need action – now!

If you give this a little thought, you'll see that this isn't such a difficult problem to solve. We've all had experiences where we've commented to ourselves, or someone else, about the lack of parenting skills of someone we know or we've seen. Some people should never be allowed to have children, let alone raise them. We've all seen them.

This problem is easy to solve. Report these horrible people to the sterilization committee, who will round them up, ask them a few simple questions to verify their status as bad parents, and start the sterilization procedure.

If we really get into the groove on this one, we should be able to send them home within 2 or 3 hours from the time they are brought in for status verification. Snip, snip; tie, tie; a couple of band-aids and aspirin, and off they go – no longer a menace to the gene pool.

What kind of questions could we possibly ask that would verify their status so convincingly? Fair enough of a question, even if it does tag you as a do-gooder liberal, just for asking.

Ok, here are some sample questions to ask:

Good-Bad Parent Questions – choose the best answer from the possible answers listed:

1 – If your child were beat up by a bully, you would?
   a) Ask him/her if the other guy looks worse than your kid does.
   b) Ask what he/she did to get picked on.
   c) Ask if your child is all right.
   d) Go beat up the bully's father.

2 – What are the names of your child's three best friends?
   a) Uh – Joe? And uh, gee, wait, let me thing, Sue? She's one isn't she?
   b) What 3 friends? He has 3 friends? When did he get 3 friends? George, did you know your son has 3 friends?
   c) Joe, Bruce, and Cybil.
   d) He don't need no damn fool friends.

3 – How do you punish your child?
   a) I smacks 'im till the wailin' stops.
   b) I lock him out of the house till he gets clean.
   c) I have a serious talk with him and remove some of his privileges.
   d) I put his picture on a milk carton and set it out on the front stoop.

4 – What does your child want to be when he grows up?
   a) Who cares, so long as he gets out of the house and doesn't come mooching back.
   b) I don't know if he'll ever grow up or even if he'll live that long.

    c) A Marine.

    d) That isn't my problem, but jail offers three meals a day, a roof and a bed.

5 – Is your child allergic to any medicine?

    a) I don't know – isn't that the doctor's job?

    b) What's medicine? What does allergic mean?

    c) Yes, and I keep it listed in my wallet for emergencies.

    d) He's had a few reactions from time to time, but only when he's sick and the doctor gives him medicine stuff, other than that – no.

6 – What time does your child go to bed?

    a) Whenever he wants. Who am I to tell him when he's tired?

    b) What's a bed?

    c) 9:30 on school nights and 11:00 on weekends.

    d) We start the process at 8:00, then he gets out of bed and we take him back in, then he gets out again, and so on till we end up locking his door and turning up the music to cover his crying.

7 – Does your child have a criminal record?

    a) Yes, but he didn't do it, no matter what the others say.

    b) No – 'cause he never got convicted.

    c) Of course not!

    d) The juvenile record doesn't really count, right?

Now, these are just a few ideas for determining who is a bad parent or good parent. You may have other ideas for weeding out the bad ones. Regardless of how we find them, we have to try to get to them before they propagate.

Naturally, some of them will slip through and have kids. We all know, by training and example that the bad traits and actions of parents rub off on children. We also know that these bad habits will resurface when they have children of their own.

We just can't take that chance with the gene pool. Especially after going through so much trouble to rid the pool of the bad parents in the first place. So, we have to also sterilize the children of these bad parents. We just have to. I know it sounds harsh, but we have to make the gene pool clean for the rest of us and for our futures.

If we can enact these measures, we can clean up another 4 to 5% of the gene poll population while giving many others jobs that didn't exist before. This improves unemployment and helps the world economy, in general.

In particular, the medical world will get a boost for a few years from all the sterilizations. Once we've fixed the problem, we'll only have a minor trickle of bad parents and their kids to sterilize each year. You see! There's a bright side to this.

The Weak and Wimps

The weak and the wimps make up another general group of genetically unsuitable and unwanted people we have to deal with. These are the cry babies and those who think the world owes them something. The way the gene pool was designed to work is this: you have the right to starve to death, to freeze to death, to die swimming or just sitting around doing nothing. That's your choice.

No one has any responsibility to help you if you don't try to help yourself. Period, end of transmission.

Get off your ass or die trying. We have to stop being soft on these folks and let the gene pool sort things out.

But how do we do it? Simple. Quit trying to help them. We're wasting our time, money and effort. We might as well try to teach a pig to sing. No matter how hard we try, it won't sound good and it's still going to be a big, noisy pig. So stand back and let nature (the gene pool) take its course.

Here are a few simple ways we can do this, and cut out 3 to 5% of the population we really don't need or want among the rest of us worthy ones.

- Stop hand-outs and freebies for people who won't help themselves. You have the right to starve to death and I don't have the responsibility to help you or save you from yourself. If you won't work for yourself, you sure won't work for the rest of the gene pool. This is a team event and you didn't make the cut, so you're off the team. Goodbye. Don't write. You're too lazy to swim with the rest of us.

- For those who can't work at what they want. Did you always get everything you wanted when you were growing up? If so, read back a couple of pages to the part about bad parents and report to the local parental sterilization center.

If not, get off your ass and do whatever it takes to survive. That's the law of the gene pool. If you can't adapt, you're not gene pool material. Either learn to do something useful for the gene pool or get out of the genetic well.

If you really are that bad off and really can't do anything, we'll leave you alone to die in peace. Good luck, nice knowing you – just kidding, it wasn't all that nice.

- Stop all NICU operations. If preemies or newborns can't make it on their own, take a damn hint. The gene pool doesn't want them and it's trying to tell you this. Listen to a higher power and let things be. We're spending billions of dollars all over the world trying to

save these kids, when all the genetic signs say "DNR".
Let them be!

The gene pool knows they don't have what it takes to be part of the future. We can certainly use the medical talents elsewhere, like helping sterilize the uglies and bad parents, and helping those of us the gene pool actually does want. Save those worth saving.

- Charge $5000 to $10,000 for ambulance service. People will take a little extra time to think about it before calling for help and that extra time will give the gene pool a chance to work its magic. Why rush to the hospital for every little fracture, or car accident or chest pain? Just take a little extra time to see if you are going to die anyway. This saves the rest of us the burden of dealing with them and carrying them along when they add nothing to the gene pool.

Need examples: broken ankle – walk or drive yourself. Brain tumor – an ambulance won't make any difference. Guts are spilling out all over the place – shove them back in as best you can and grab a taxi. Brains spilling out – relax and enjoy the last few moment of your life and don't waste our time.

- Make the emergency room a real emergency room – too much medical and gene pool talent is spent on those wastes of humanity who plug up the emergency rooms. No thanks to the do-gooder, liberal politicians who don't want anyone to hurt. Forget about it.

If you aren't bleeding, and I mean blood spurting, arterial bleeding, it's NOT an emergency. If you don't have bones sticking through your skin, it's NOT an emergency. If you've stopped breathing, wait a few minutes to see if you start up again before calling it an emergency. After all, you have a couple of minutes before brain damage sets in and medical care is really, truly warranted.

If you have a cough, or a bump on the head, or a headache, or a rash, or a fever, or pain when you pee – you do not belong in the emergency room. Go home. Take some aspirin. Sometimes, these things just work themselves out on their own. Stop wasting society's time, and money and talent on your tiny little problems. We have big problems to deal with and you aren't one of them.

ER doctors always rush to save a person at all costs and it often doesn't work. Maybe, if they hadn't rushed in so fast, the situation would have resolved itself without all those unnecessary costs. Next time, Doc, take a good, long coffee break before jumping in and give the gene pool a chance to solve the problem.

- DNR Cards – we have a selection on driver's licenses for organ donors. It's high time we added DNR to drivers' licenses, too. For those who don't drive or can't get a license, give them state issued DNR cards, just like ID cards. Or add it to the current identification cards.

This is simple. Everyone has the chance to get a DNR classification, with the strong encouragement of a gene pool savvy government, of course. This is such a great way to stop wasting time and talent on people who not only don't need the help (in gene pool terms, that is) but, THEY DON'T WANT IT!

Let's get over ourselves and let the gene pool work. Come out of the DNR closet and proudly display your DNR status!

- Take away Novocain for dental work – those with good teeth will create children with good teeth. Those with a high pain tolerance will give us more in the gene pool with high pain tolerance. All good for the gene pool.

Those who can't take it will just have to suffer or eat soft foods. Sorry about that, but bad genes are bad genes. Don't blame us. Blame your parents, and their parents and their parents. Suffer and deal with it.

Either way, these people sure won't feel much like making love, meaning they will have fewer children to muck up the gene pool. It may take a generation or two, but these people will be weeded out of the genetic mix by natural pain selection, leaving a gene pool with good teeth and a high pain tolerance.

- Keep doctors out of the under developed countries – keep them home where they're needed and let the gene pool do its thing. If the people in the less developed countries have what it takes to survive in the gene pool, they'll be there down the road.

Let's leave them to their own genetic destiny and stop trying to play God with them. We aren't good at it anyway.

In the end, the survivors in the underdeveloped countries will be good for the gene pool, creating a better group of genetic survivors to help all mankind. Give them a chance.

- Make education free for anyone who has a 3.5 GPA or above – promote those with a brain, the interest in using it, and who are trying to make something of themselves. We need smart people in the gene pool, so let's help them out a bit. The others? If you think you're smart enough, prove it. The best will succeed and, if you aren't in that group, get smart or get lost.
- Stop funding rocket scientists and astronomers – they aren't helping the gene pool right here on earth. Their

heads and hearts are all somewhere else in the universe or in the past.

Does anyone else really care if the big bang was 13.5 billion years ago or 14 billion years ago? Admit it – does any normal person really give a rat's butt or even comprehend this? Of course not. Only those few with their heads in the intergalactic clouds pretend to understand it.

What does it have to do with survival of the gene pool right here on good old earth? Nada!

Can you imagine these people discovering a new world and deciding to populate it, like in the science fiction movies? Consider a very tiny gene pool made up only of techno, science nerds. That's what they'd have. Mars populated by scientists and others who have no clue about reality. Ykes, that's a scary concept!

Maybe we can use their help solving the problems we have right here on earth helping us get control of the gene pool and get it squared away. Focus, people, focus! We need that vision turned inward. If you can't help us solve our earthbound problems, take a long walk in a short air lock and go into low earth orbit.

- Remove all handicap parking spots – replace them with special parking for pregnant women. We need to take special care of the future of the gene pool. Giving special privileges to the old, the sick and the lame doesn't do anything to achieve that. Besides, most of the "handicapped" people are old. They've already done whatever real damage or benefit they can to the gene pool. They're the past and we have to look forward. Help the mothers.

If you think the above examples are severe, you've just labeled yourself a wimp and you belong in this group. You aren't strong enough for the gene pool. The rest of us will remember you fondly over beer sometime – NOT! Don't pout, or whimper or cry. And put that quivering lip back in your face. It only proves that the gene pool is right. Man up or wimp out.

The Politicians

Professional politicians are a particularly insidious group of genetic misfits. They have no obvious redeeming values to add to the gene pool or society. If they did, they'd have a real job like everyone else. Their only evident claim to fame is that they can lie to your face, steal you blind, renege on every promise they ever made and still make you like them.

Try as hard as I can, I can't find a role for that kind of person in the gene pool God created. Yes, in the corrupted gene pool that we have now, people like this have a home, but they're not needed. Nor are they useful for a productive genetic future.

Where, in God's gene pool, can it productively use someone who will use everyone else's hard earned livelihood, money, energy and freedom for their own advantage? How can we use someone we can't trust? Someone who will sell us down the river tomorrow, if it helps them the day after? How can it be useful to have someone like this make rules and laws, only to change them later at their own whim?

How much good do you think we could accomplish if all the money spent on politicians was put to work for the true benefit of others? All the money spent on getting elected and re-elected, on the ads, on the parties, the girls, the boys, on the trips and golf outings, and all the lobbying money to influence them. Now, expand this around the world and throw in the illegal corruption, bribes and outright theft from the people?

What could we do with these billions and billions of dollars to benefit the deserving members of the gene pool? What a wonderful place that would be.

I might be impressed if politicians and other do-gooders spent all of *their own* money to help others. Then I might be inclined to at least listen to them. But, that isn't going to happen, is it?

Politicians are genetic aberrations programmed to spend everyone else's money while hoarding even more money and power for themselves. They have no concept of lowering themselves to the same level as the rest of us. They don't know HOW to be normal.

Ponder this – from the beginning of recorded history (and indications are, from a lot farther back to the beginning of unrecorded history) all civilizations have segregated those genetic misfits we call politicians. They had special and separate caves, tents and houses from the rest of the people.

Why, you ask? Well, obviously no one wanted politicians living with or near them. They're obnoxious, dysfunctional and freeloading. Those who work hard for their survival certainly don't want some mooching politician around. Have them over for dinner and all they do is tell grand stories about themselves while eating all of your food. Food THEY didn't work hard for.

We don't want them around us and we don't want to be around them. Civilized societies went further. We, all civilized societies, created special cities for the politicians to keep them hemmed in. All civilized societies, great and small, create a special city, a whole city, just to house their politicians and to keep them away from the normal people, their wives, and their children. This has to tell us something.

There's no other group of people in history, other than prisoners, that have been so completely segregated from the rest of society. And prisoners don't have entire cities built for them. Only politicians have entire cities built just for them. That's an indication of how badly we want to keep them away.

We accept them as a necessary evil, but we pay them to go live in that special city, far away. This is appropriate, since they are already predestined to not have a clue about being like the rest of us. At least keeping them together in "the city" lets us know where they are.

Once in a while, we let them out to mingle amongst regular folks, like you and me, but soon their parole is over and they have to go back to the asylum.

We have special elections to choose the worst among us to call a politician and to send them away for a few years to that special city. These elections are great free entertainment. The candidates scrap and fight about the truth, their upbringing, their backgrounds, their morals, their parentage, and their love lives. We even have special reporters who focus on digging up the truth about politicians so we can all have additional laughs.

What a folly all this is. We don't need them. God didn't have a place for them in the gene pool. We haven't found a good use for them in all of human history. If they were a plant, such as poison ivy (appropriate don't you think?), we would create a special weed killer and eradicate them. Instead, we send them as far away from the rest of us as we can and pay them good money to stay there.

So, what good are they? I don't know. Get rid of them. Send them to Mars with the rocket scientists and see what happens. Or let them have the moon and they can negotiate with the rocket scientists on how to get there.

If we have to keep them earth bound, we have to put them somewhere safe and away from us good folks. The South Pole seems like just the place. Anyone want to second that motion?

Regardless of how we do it, we have to get them out of our gene pool, which would reduce the gene pool by another 2 to 3% of useless pond algae.

The Predators

You wouldn't think that this group would be a real menace to the gene pool. After all, the gene pool is made of predators. Preying on the weak is one of the tenants of the gene pool and the reason we have lions and tigers and bears – oh my. They help keep things in balance. Remember how critical balance is to the proper operation and survival of the gene pool?

But, the predatory people I'm talking about are not your regular predators. They are not like a wolf or a hyena, they kill to survive and only kill what they can eat. No, these human predators hurt others for the fun of it. They destroy much, much more than they need. They hurt us all and are ruining the gene pool. It's time we fix this problem and allow the gene pool to self-correct.

It may take a little while, but it can be done. Along with all the other measures we've talked about, the gene pool still has a chance.

Cleaning up this particular problem area will help us get rid of about 8 to 11% of the gene pool. That's a small number, but the damage they cause goes far beyond a measly 8 to 11%. When you consider all the hurt they cause, the many progeny they create, the horrible parents they are, and the truly sociopathic way they ravage society; their impact is equivalent to 20 to 25% of the gene pool.

These individuals clearly have genetic defects, which we haven't yet identified. Defects that are triggered by other factors in our societies. Whatever it is, it's getting worse as we keep mollycoddling them. It's time to stop this. But how?

Again, good question, Suzie. How did we do it in the good old days before things got out of control? People who were caught doing really bad things were punished. There was no question about getting the punishment, only about getting caught. And people who harbored such predatory criminals were also punished. There was no upside to being a predator.

As far back as the caveman days, predators of their fellow cavemen were punished and not tolerated. The survival of everyone depended on it. Those caught stealing, or hording food, or taking a woman who wasn't theirs, was kicked out of the cave or given a couple of raps on the head with a club. Either way – they were in a world of hurt.

In almost all societies, there has been punishment for criminals, up until the twentieth century. Say what you want about Islamic law being harsh, but their rate of criminal behavior amongst their own kind is very, very low and their recidivism rates are smaller still. You steal something, you lose a hand. Simple and direct with no question about what the punishment is or whether you will get it.

A few of you may remember back to your childhood where the biggest threat from mother was "Just wait till your father gets home!" She could holler and scream at you and slam doors and pots and you knew you still had a chance. But, once she uttered those seven magical words, you knew you were in for it. There was no doubt that, once you pissed off the lady of the house, the old man was going to give you what for. Justice was firm and sure.

Nowadays, if there *is* a mother at home and a child is told to wait till their father gets home, he's more than likely to wonder: "Did you finally find him?" or "Really? When did he get out?" or "I thought you didn't know who my father was."

It's all screwed up and there's no sureness to the threat or pain to the punishment. We carry these lessons into adulthood, for those who actually make it that far. They become predators unafraid of punishment, the law or society.

We don't need to hear any more of the liberal crapola about punishing the innocent or how the punishment hurts. Tough noogies. Punishment has no meaning if there is no pain. Pain can be emotional, physical or mental. But there have to be negative consequences for punishment to have meaning.

Unfortunately, most of the predators are also sociopathic and psychopathic. What does this mean to you and me? It means they don't give a shit if they hurt you or kill you. It also means they don't give a shit about the rules, either. It means that you can't "talk" to them or "reason" with them.

There can be no emotional punishment, because there is no emotional part to them to reach and hurt. There can be no mental punishment, because these types of people are mental midgets and Neanderthal rejects. There IS no mental to connect to.

What's left? Physical punishment and keeping them away from the rest of us.

To the predators we're talking about, the threat of "Just wait till your father gets home." has *absolutely no meaning whatsoever!* There's no fear in them for two reasons. The first is that they've got some genetic mutation that makes them dangerously fearless.

Second, the threat of "father" has been a hollow one for too many decades. There is no way we can win by treating predators like real people. They don't care and we don't have the will to make them care. They win and we lose.

For you liberal excusers of all things unpleasant, let me briefly address deterrence. Of course it doesn't work! Read the above. It can't work. Not the way YOU do it! No way – no how.

Society isn't willing to spill the blood of the guilty and to hear their pained cries, while we tolerate the blood and pain of the victims. Under these conditions, the predators will continue their ways, unfettered. We'll build more jails and complain about crime and the number of people in the jails. But, we won't actually DO anything effective to fix the problem.

For "father" to have any deterrence value, "father" has to be real, sure and painful. "Father" has to have a fear factor that even these caveman rejects understand. As unpleasant as this sounds, it certainly has to be better than accepting rape, burglary, murder, assault, drug overdoses, kidnapping, extortion, fraud, and all the other violent crimes as normal parts of society and excusing it away. Especially if it happens to YOU!

So what do we do? Well, we have to do a couple of things. First, we have to streamline the path to execution for the death penalty. Yes, we *need* the death penalty. But, it has to be real. Imagine a society where people are actually afraid to have the death penalty. It used to be that way in the United States and Europe, believe it or not. Read your history books.

Here's what we should do. We take the death penalty and, once pronounced, make it required to be carried out within six months from the date of conviction. As a little concession to the liberals, we could let the soon-to-be-deceased have one quick appeal. But, that still can't change the original six month deadline!

Also, the appeal can ONLY be based on something that's directly applicable to proving that the convicted didn't really do it. No more of this procedure crap to get people off. Either they did it or they didn't. If the evidence says they did it, only other evidence to the contrary can be brought forward.

This brings a screeching halt to this horse manure about the process going on and on for decades. Six months. That's it. Now wait till your "father" gets home!

To make sure that everyone gets the message, and that young kids learn what happens if you do really bad things, all executions should televised live at popular times. Remember Ed Sullivan and Bonanza and Gunsmoke? Everyone with a television watched these shows each week. No one would dare miss them.

This would be the same thing. We'll call it "Prisoner Smoke". Prime time television for you and your children to watch what happens to bad people. Smoke `em Danno. Fry `em to crispy critters.

Finally, let there be examples of bad people getting sure, swift punishment for their crimes! Let children grow up *afraid* to be criminals. Motivate them to do good things and to be nice to others. This is *not* a bad thing.

How we actually DO the executions can use some imagination, too. Instead of having all those hearings about how Smitty was such a good little boy and wouldn't hurt a flea and has found God and all that bullshit. Let the victim or their families have a say in the method of execution. Better yet, let *them* make the decision.

Maybe we can have a viewer call-in for their favorite method. Give them a choice between: suffocation by a plastic bag over the head; a toaster tossed into a tub of water; a firing squad consisting of a bunch of half-blind National Rifle Association members, all with lots of bullets in their guns; buried alive with internet camera in the box; lowered head first into a swimming pool; hanging from a street lamp post; an overdose on heroin; sent to Haiti where their head is shrunken and put on a necklace; a wood chipper feet first; or make them listen to Barry Manilow for hours on end. Maybe you have some other good ideas?

We could even sell sponsorships for the executions. The state could make back some money with advertising from Ruger, Smith & Wesson, Glock, the NRA, the ACLU, lawyers, judges or District Attorneys running for office, psychologists, hospitals, funeral homes, churches, victims organizations, insurance companies, alarm companies, rights groups, and others.

No crying for the prisoner, either. They're getting what they deserve. At least they won't be around to become a repeat offender. Punishment needs to be something they fear and that hurts them, for the good of society, for the victims and for their families. And, it has to set an example for the little gene poolers about rules, responsibility and consequences. Sure and swift, just like family justice in the old days.

The point is, we can't make it easy and painless – where in the punishment in that? "Father" is home!

That takes care of the death-deserving bad guys. What about those who aren't quite that bad, but who still deserve punishment? Obviously, the same concept of visible sure and swift punishment has to apply. Being in jail should be punishment and it shouldn't be fun. People should fear going to jail.

As it is now, the only people who have a reason to fear going to jail are child molesters; little, wimpy guys; ex-cops; and white guys. There has to be more to it.

So, here's what we do. We take away the televisions, radios, CDs and books. Get rid of the basketball hoops, sports fields and weight training equipment. No more game rooms or internet access. No work release or day worker programs. Make jail a prison. Make it hard. Make it hurt. Imprint on the inmates, and everyone they know, that this is NOT a place you EVER want to be.

Eliminate the free college education for prisoners. Did you know that some inmates have gotten free college educations, including Doctoral degrees, from *major* colleges? This is absurd! Good behaving and deserving citizens, people who pay taxes, can't get such educations. They have to actually WORK to pay tuition for an education.

Governments owe support and access to government resources first, to the good behaving people; then, to those who need a lot of help; then, to those who need a little help. Last on the list are the people who hurt and kill and plunder society and other people. Last are those who go around taking from society. Last are those who will not conform. In fact – remove them from the list all together! They haven't earned a place on the list.

I can hear some people saying that these predatory malcontents *can't* conform. That they are sociologically damaged or mentally ill. This is more reason to get them the hell out of the gene pool!

But, stop and think about that argument for a moment. They really aren't sick or damaged. We know they CAN conform and learn. They conform when they want to conform. They join gangs, learn codes, and follow the disciplined requirements of organization crime leaders. They learn how to work their way through the rules of complex video games and government bullshit.

Let there be no doubt that they CAN conform. They just CHOOSE not to conform. According to the gene pool, this choice means they have to live with the consequences. They think they are such bad asses? So, make jail a bad place and put them there. And take them off the list for society's good things.

Another thing – cut this religious crap in jails. Remember separation of church and state? Well, once you enter the state or federal penal system (a *government* system) you're officially separated! If we separate out religion elsewhere in the government, it is natural that we should separate religion out here as well.

This is certainly appropriate, especially since the law-abiding, tax-paying, good citizens can't even have the Ten Commandments in the court-house. If we can't have religion in courts, the halls of justice, then prisoners can't have it in jails, the application of justice. It can be in your head and heart, but that's it. No displays of religion or religious ceremonies. You're in a government world now. You've been separated.

Also, we have to cut out this crap about time off for good behavior. That's just a liberal's way of cutting down on jail populations. If the liberals want to reduce jail population, follow the guidance of this section of the book. Guaranteed to do the job.

If it isn't fast enough for you – here's a deal for the liberals. You can adopt any jail inmates you want and as many as you want. BUT, you have to take *personal responsibility* for them, their care and their actions.

If they rob, or rape, or kill, or shoot someone, or get into trouble in any way with the law, you do, too. You get the same penalty as they get for any offences they commit while they're your responsibility. And, you have to put up a million dollar bond for each of them, just in case.

Let's see how many of the softhearted liberals will put their lives where their mouths are. You really think they're innocent and don't belong in jail? Fine, YOU take responsibility for them, rather than sitting on the sideline bitching about it and doing nothing useful. Now, you have your chance. Put up or shut up!

When an inmate gets released, they should get a GPS tracker implanted under their skin that reports their position 24/7 for the rest of their lives. If it's tinkered with, it explodes and ends the issue for good. *After* sending a final position and status report, that is.

This way, we know where they are at all times, even if they are doing nothing wrong. That's part of the price you pay for your crime and the protections society has to put in place to protect the innocent. Deal with it.

Now, when these fine folks come out of prison, after paying their debt to society (Remember that term? It used to mean something.) we really don't want them running for public office (though some do), or teaching our children, or becoming bank tellers, or doctors, or nurses. No, we can't ever trust them, once they've been in the big house.

So, let's create a jobs agency that hires ex-cons. This agency would take contracts from federal, state and local governments, and from companies that want to have work done that benefits society. They could do jobs like shoveling the snow for all people in the city over age 50. Or jobs cleaning up all the leaves in the fall, or the trash along the highway, or sorting recyclables at the local dump, or building roads, or digging ditches, or cleaning up New Orleans or picking weeds on farms. Something to help them give back some of what they took from society.

They get a wage and supervision, pay taxes and stay out of trouble. Remember, we know where they are at all times.

Maybe we could find other ways to prevent repeat offenders and, at the same time, influence those who have bad things on their minds. Example … rapists. Consider the idea of electronic panties – stops rape dead in its tracks with an 80,000 volt taser charge. Once you get there, you won't walk away, and you will **never** be the same man you were. It also helps dads sleep well at night knowing their daughters are safe from other men. Caution – do not wear around water.

Clearly, some predators have their place in God's gene pool design. Just not senseless predators who add nothing and take far more than they could ever contribute. Even vultures clean up the mess after others have had their fill. No, these predators have no useful place in society and must be eliminated. Clean up the gene pool and – remember the dinosaurs.

The S-T-U-P-I-D

This is another one of those "You know them when you see them." categories. They just seem to point themselves out and yell out "Hey, there! Pay attention to me! Watch me do something s-t-u-p-i-d!" Estimates have this part of the population, worldwide, at between 8 and 14 %.

I know that's a pretty wide spread, for a scientific estimate. A little closer look at the data reveals the reason. Like drunks, s-t-u-p-i-d people stand out like a fart in an elevator. The problem is, as with drunks, some people are more s-t-u-p-i-d than others and the line between *acting* s-t-u-p-i-d and actually *being* s-t-u-p-i-d is often a bit difficult to discern.

Some people appear drunk when they really aren't and others are drunk when they don't act like it. Same thing goes with s-t-u-p-i-d people. Some are really s-t-u-p-i-d, but have developed coping mechanisms that let them live an apparently normal life without anyone finding out. Of course, we always find out, eventually, even if we don't tell them that we know.

Then, there are the s-t-u-p-i-ds who are obviously just

dumb as dirt, have no coping mechanisms for anything, and couldn't save themselves from drowning by lifting their heads out of the toilet.

I'm not sure whether to feel sorry for these folks or to put them in a burlap bag with the cats and throw them off a bridge. I *do* know that they don't have a place in the gene pool, except on the outside looking in.

As with other members of undesirable groups, the gene pool cannot survive, let alone thrive, with the s-t-u-p-i-ds in it. So, what's a struggling, survival-focused society to do about the s-t-u-p-i-d ones in their midst?

We know what we can't do with them. We can't send them to school, because they can't learn and they hold everyone else back. Society can't afford to learn and grow at the pace of the s-t-u-p-i-d ones in class. It's also a huge waste of money.

We also can't elect them to public office because they would fit in too well and we wouldn't be able to tell the s-t-u-p-i-d politicians from the real politicians. Come to think of it, we kind of have that situation now. Maybe some slipped in.

We don't want them driving trains, or planes or buses. We can't have them driving ships. Taxis are questionable, only because it would be so hard to tell the difference between then and now.

Police officers? No, never give a s-t-u-p-i-d person a gun AND bullets.

Doctors or nurses? I don't think that would work out well. EMT's? Same issues as driving and doctoring. They'd run over you as they arrive and then put a tourniquet around your neck to stop the bleeding. Not a good plan.

Fireman? It would never work. Again with the driving, but also giving them sharp axes and hoses that squirt out stuff smarter than they are. Not a good combination.

Lobster fisherman? Same problem with something smarter than them.

The issues go on and on. There just is no place for them. So what CAN we do with them? What to do, what to do?

First, we tackle the obvious s-t-u-p-i-d people. We round them up and give them a test. We put them in round rooms and tell them there is a hundred dollar bill in the corner and they have five minutes to find it.

Those who fail this test get a one-way trip to the South Pole to join the politicians. We all know how much politicians like to talk and think they are being listened to. The politicians can talk to them all day long and the s-t-u-p-i-d people won't care or understand.

Those who pass the first test then get to take a second, more advanced test. They're put into a room painted white and told to find the white cow eating grass in a snowstorm. That'll take care of the rest of the obvious s-t-u-p-i-ds. They get to join their friends at the South Pole, too, but at least they get appropriate due process. No harm, no foul.

This process would probably weed out about one-third of the s-t-u-p-i-d people. Now comes the tough part, finding and dealing with those who are borderline s-t-u-p-i-d and those who are covering it up, your so-called, functionally s-t-u-p-i-d. They can be found everywhere. Your boss, my boss, the neighbor, the cop on the corner, the grocery store clerk. Every walk of life.

They teach our children and then get on the computer and look for naked pictures of them.

They're the lifeguard at the beach with a hard-on 'cause he's paying far too much attention to the cute girl in the tiny top and thong to see if anyone is drowning.

He's the bank robber who writes a robbery note on his

own deposit slip or shows his driver's license when the clerk asks for ID before she can give him the money (true story).

She's the gal who married a pedophile and gave him seven kids because she was a good Catholic.

The remaining s-t-u-p-i-ds have invaded every walk of life and all parts of society. We've all seen them, married them, divorced them, worked with them, been related to them, read about them in the news, talked about them with others, watched them on television shows, seen them on the movie screen, and tolerated them as neighbors. So how do we rid ourselves and the gene pool of them?

For starters, we need to collect DNA for every person on earth. We also have to determine the characteristics in the DNA that relate to the people we're talking about. This has added benefits of putting some of those rocket scientists to work on something of real value.

For those people who are obviously genetically too s-t-u-p-i-d to have around, we put them to work at special jobs. Jobs like:

- testing parachutes at the parachute re-cycling plant,
- testing dynamite,
- catching bombs,
- testing shark repellent,
- testing lightning rods,
- being a crash dummy,
- bungee cord tester,
- suicide bomber negotiator,
- coal miner for China,
- high-voltage fuse tester,
- sperm collector for animals; such as moose, wolverine, coyote, hyenas, elephants, electric eels or sharks,

- breast milk collector for animals; such as moose, wolverine, coyote, hyenas, elephants, raccoons, whales, camels,
- toxicity tester for bio-weapons, or
- land mine detector.

Jobs like these are sure to thin the ranks of the s-t-u-p-i-d people, without us having to do anything *really* overt or obvious. Of course, we'll offer them life insurance, but at a really high rate.

We stop hiring them when they start asking less s-t-u-p-i-d questions, like "Why would anyone want to catch a bomb?" We'll tell them they are dummy bombs and we don't want them damaged.

At some point we'll run low of the profoundly s-t-u-p-i-d people. That's when we'll resort to the DNA tests to sort out the rest.

We know that some s-t-u-p-i-d people, who live under the radar, are sometimes difficult to ferret out. So, we'll set up a national and world-wide internet site where you can report, no, you are *encouraged* to report, people you run across who are s-t-u-p-i-d. You don't have to tell us who YOU are, but you do need to tell us about your "s-t-u-p-i-d nominee" and what they did to qualify for being declared s-t-u-p-i-d. Even better, make a video of them and send it in with your s-t-u-p-i-d application.

Naturally, you are allowed to nominate yourself, if you think you qualify, and want people to know about you. (Self nomination is an automatic s-t-u-p-i-d qualifier, but we won't tell "them", will we?)

If we do this right, we can even make a lot of money on this. Consider the Top Ten S-t-u-p-i-d People Show each week, right after the executions show, "Prisoner Smoke". We could film them getting rounded up and hauled away to the S-t-u-p-i-d Bin (similar to the old Looney Bin, but more practical). What an entertainment hottie that would be!

We can sell advertising time from such great folks as your local university, Democrats, the local comedy club, manure delivery services, the Get Lost One-way Travel Agency, Pull My Finger Jokes Company, and doctors who ask "Does it hurt when you do this?"

We'll round up the rest of the s-t-u-p-i-d people through analysis of their DNA. Not as exciting as watching s-t-u-p-i-d nominations, though it would give some of the current slate of shows a good run for their money.

But, we have to be rid of them. So we hire a bunch of s-t-u-p-i-d finders and send them out with a camera man to round up the s-t-u-p-i-ds. It may be as easy as tossing a candy into the van and watching them go in after it. Or going to a park and asking who wants to go watch s-t-u-p-i-d people?

Of course, we'll have a list of who needs to be picked up, but it's so much more fun when you can have a little free entertainment at their expense. Consider it a little perk of the job.

We still have to get rid of those we collect up. That would be the secret of the S-t-u-p-i-d Bin. People go in and no one ever comes out. Turn them into fish food, or fertilizer or charcoal. Just don't let them back out to swim in the gene pool. Without the rest of us to keep them afloat, they'll just drown anyway.

The gene pool can't support intelligent life with s-t-u-p-i-d people all mixed up in it. So, fertilizer they are. Done deal. Now onto bigger fish and don't forget – remember the dinosaurs.

The Liberals

We've covered a lot of different groups and types of people who are obviously destructive to the gene pool and the development of intelligent life here on earth. I've shown you scientific evidence of these truths, as well as shown you how to identify those who can't hack it in the gene pool, and what to do with them.

I've even gone further than anyone else in the history of print by explaining precisely how we have to deal with these genetic undesirables. How we can get rid of them and save the gene pool for the rest of us.

However, we're only now going to address the largest group of unwanted, unnecessary and destructive people in all the world's societies. This is no exaggeration. This group is also the most insidious and sneaky of all the groups. They are the easiest to like and most destructive of all the groups in the world. They are: the liberals.

This group of malcontents can be found in every society on earth. If you look into this, as I have, you'll find that liberals have many traits in common, no matter where you find them. Traits that are worse than useless – they're destructive!

Liberals are like crows, they feed on the hard work of others to satisfy themselves, all the while contributing nothing but bird shit and guano to the situation. They cry and bitch and moan to be given what others have. They want this and they want that. It doesn't matter what it is – they want it all.

Liberals believe in the concept of self-righteousness, which teaches: you are a valuable person, no matter what kind of a shit bird you are; your feelings are valuable, no matter how s-t-u-p-i-d or unfounded they are; your opinions are just as good as anyone else's, regardless of how s-t-u-p-i-d they are; and no one is better than you. Therefore, you deserve what everyone else has.

Oh, yes – one more thing big liberals teach little liberals – if you want it, take it, because you deserve it and the world really owes it to you just for being born.

Extensive worldwide research into the historical developments of societies and liberals has revealed a common practice by liberals to get their own way. The liberals did not actually invent this technique. They stole it from little brat kids throughout history and claimed credit for it; but, they called it something else – justice.

Just like little brat kids, this is what they do. Liberals make such a fuss and a stink about whatever topic is itching their armpits at the moment, that societies the world over (and throughout history, I might add) will do ANYTHING to shut them up and make them go away.

Sadly, they never really go away, and their message attracts more brat people. The world suffers terribly from these narcissist, infantile, spoiled brats. They suck the life out of others, give back nothing, and lower the standards for achievement everywhere they live.

It's like feeding mice. The more you feed them the more of them come out of the woodwork looking for the handouts. How did the mice all find out about the food? Word of mouse, of course.

This tactic has worked from the earliest days of recorded history. Nothing civilized societies have done has ever been able to appease liberals or keep them in check. Heaven knows they've tried.

Note the word "civilized". These are societies that developed a set of morals and values by which to live and get along together. They have rules, and bounds and rewards for hard work.

This is one big area of difference between civilized societies and liberals. Liberals have no morals that involve others, except to get what others have. Their morals and interests are those which are convenient for the moment and don't require effort on their part. They're self-righteous and self-justified in their actions and words.

They're the kind of people who made up children's stories that always ended with "… and they lived happily ever after." Hogwash! No one ever lived happily for long, except the s-t-u-p-i-ds, and they don't know any better. Besides, we already took care of them.

The only times in history that the liberals have been suppressed were in times of extremes. Times when the rules of the gene pool overruled man's rules. Times when staying alive depended on working for yourself.

Times when society was just not that well developed, or just wasn't around, to help out. Times when social rules were strict and punishments for offenses were severe and sure. (Does this sound familiar?)

In such times, liberals had no one else to mooch from. They had to morph into socially compliant citizens to survive the times. But they always looked forward to the day when they, or their children, could revert to their true nature.

It's easy to see the appeal being liberal has on those of weak mind, weak character, low morals and low self-expectation. They teach that you can have what others have and not have to work for it. Goodness! Who wouldn't want to have that? The only work you have to do is to work the system!

This is why liberals are such insidious threats to the gene pool and why they are so difficult to eradicate. They thrive when societies are soft and caring. They go dormant when life is hard and cruel.

For some unknown reason, the rest of us haven't yet

figured out that we have to stop giving in to these brat people. The rules of the gene pool have it right. If you can't hack it – you lose. You don't get a chance to stay around and suck the life out of everyone else.

What should we do when people flock to an ideology that teaches: you have a divine right, as a human being, to have whatever you want, especially if others have it first. How do we say "No" to people who have never before heard the word "No"?

Can we truly go back to the 1700's and 1800's, a time when you died of starvation if you didn't plant your crops or couldn't hunt worth a damn? To the days when you got shot if you tried to take what wasn't yours? That was the gene pool at work. Checks and balances against extremes.

Yes, of course we had liberals way back then. But, we had them in check, thanks to the workings of the gene pool – survive or die off. Unfortunately, they had children who spread their crazy ideas across the U.S. and throughout the world. Millions and millions of little, liberal brat people. More guano makers.

Now, you might think that I'm being too harsh on liberals. You might even think that they are people, too. That they must have some positive things they've done which we can celebrate. That's the liberal in you crying out at the injustice of the truth.

Ok, just for grins and giggles, let's try your way (see how appeasing I am) and think about this a moment. The only positive thing that the liberals brought to society, to any society, in the last 800 years or so, was the "Burn the bra" movement of the 60s & 70s. Those were some exciting days. Not much else compares. It still brings occasional smiles to the faces of the rest of us.

That's it. That's the full extent of their positive contributions to the world.

If you don't agree, can you think of some true, positive contribution to the world that liberals have given us? Something that would make the gene pool, and thus God, proud? Something that would contribute to the survival and continuation of the gene pool? You can't, because there isn't anything.

Examples? Sure. I can back up my statements with facts. Can you?

The spotted owl, a cause created and forced on us by liberals. Their efforts haven't saved these birds. They were always smart enough to fly to another tree when they didn't like the one they were in. The results? The cost of lumber, thus homes, skyrocketed because of senseless rules. Thousands of loggers and wood factory workers lost their jobs.

The spotted owls? They moved on to better trees on their own. If the spotted owls are so s-t-u-p-i-d that they can't move on – let them die off. Maybe the striped owls are smarter.

Another one? We have farmers out west going out of business because the liberals made a huge brat-stink about some little two-inch fish. Evidently, the liberals care a lot more about these little brat fish than about humans and food. Maybe someone will get smart and learn how to farm the fish and grow them to 4, or even, 5 inches. There's no good reason to even cook a fish only two inches long. Just swallow it whole – save on the greenhouse gases.

In the meantime, we have chaos. The result? No water for the farmers; the brat fish live, love, birth new little brat fish, and then die normally, as if nothing's wrong. Farms are sold off in bankruptcy, food prices across the U.S. go ever higher, and unemployment goes up even more.

All this disruption and suffering over a made up issue about these stupid little brat fish. A message directly to you from the gene pool: eat the damn fish, give the farmers the water and feed the people.

Here are some more short examples to further make my case. Actually, it is not MY case – they're making their own case and they're proud of it. Go figure. Remember, only a real dummy is proud of doing s-t-u-p-i-d things.

In the old days, prisoners were executed and it hurt. People didn't have much pity because the prisoner did things that really hurt others. With the flourishing of the modern liberals around the world, we now have to consider the feelings of the soon-to-be-dead person. The liberals have made it almost impossible to execute someone, except in societies that still have their senses intact.

We can't hang them, because it hurts. We can't shoot them, because it's "cruel". We can't electrocute them, because some idiot actually went and caught fire briefly and scared the witnesses.

We can't shoot them full of drugs, because the "doctors" giving the drugs messed up finding the vein and botched a couple of executions. We can put our favorite old pet down painlessly, but we can't kill some bastard who deserves it.

The liberals have been crying and howling about this and tying up the courts with law suits, after getting the courts stacked with liberal judges, and forcing these changes upon us. They completely lack logic or morality, even though morality is one of the main concepts behind their message.

"We can't stoop to their level!" they cry. Oh yeah? Watch us! It is the only level they understand!

"We are civilized and can't let them suffer. It's inhumane!" they say. Bullshit – they gave up their moral rights when they did the crime. Let them suffer a little. It would be a good example to others of what happens to the bad guys.

"Executions do not have any effect on the crime rate. It does no good, so we shouldn't do it!" they cry. More bullshit – the rate of repeat offenders goes to ZERO! Also, knowing *for sure* that they will be executed does have an impact on the vast majority of death penalty criminals.

As you can see, the liberals have brought us no end of trouble with people who just refuse to not get along well with others. People who cause nothing but hurt and grief wherever they go. Let it go, libs. Just like children, they need to respect the boundaries of society or face the punishment. The gene pool requires this if intelligent human life is to survive.

We now have schools with no grades and no failures. What the hell is up with that? The liberals insist that we have to be kind to the children and not hurt their feelings. Children should not have to hurt, or fear, or suffer or worry about competition. (Remember one of the tenants of liberalism? You are just as good as everyone else.)

All children should get rewards just for being a person. What a bunch of ka-ka. Maybe it's ok for the 3 or 4 year-olds on the mini-peewee soccer field to not keep score – they don't have a clue yet. But this crap has no place in the real world.

What do we have because of these liberal pipe dreams imposed on us?

We have 12 year-old 3rd graders.

We have college students who can't read, or write, or do math, or find Afghanistan without buying a plane ticket to Kabul or enlisting in the Army.

We have generations of people who actually believe they DESERVE the minimum wage, just because they are an employee. They actually believe that all workers are equal and should get the same pay and raises, regardless of how hard and effective they each worked. It's their fair right!

These people believe that someone else (you and me) should give them what they want, especially if it's too hard to work for it on their own. In fact, they believe it's ok to steal from their neighbors during storms, because the owners weren't around to guard it.

They can't even consider the fact that some people will be better, and some worse, than them. That some will get more in life and others will get less. They believe everyone should get equal rewards, regardless of their work or contribution.

Where did they get this notion? In the 1st grade? In the 2nd grade? In the 3rd grade? No, they got it in all grades and from the treatment they got from social governments.

These concepts, and their tragic consequences, are not the way of the gene pool. They destroy the gene pool. Everyone is *not* equal and they're not *treated* equally. That's life. Somebody, please publish Animal Farm for Dummies.

Heterogeneous student groupings are another educational wet dream foisted on society by the liberals. This concept builds on their theory that all kids are equal and should learn equally and be treated equally.

How does this work? Simply put – it doesn't.

The theory put forth is that all children can learn from other children and should be able to share with each other. They should learn early-on to accept their differences.

Also, they believe that children should all learn the same things all at the same speed. We shouldn't hurt their feelings by putting some in an "advanced" class and others in a "regular" class, and still others in a "remedial" class. This supposedly stereotypes them and causes irreparable harm to their egos and psyche for the rest of their lives, resulting in continued poor performance as adults.

Of course, reality has shown for decades that this concept is just foolish victim mentality run amuck, and plainly s-t-u-p-i-d. Every learned person with any common sense knows what happens when we put a mix of kids in a class. Two of the kids will learn a little. The rest will learn nothing and sit around bored to death.

Worse yet, the bored kids (not the two limiting factors) learn to actually resent the ones holding them back and causing the boredom. The real lesson they learn is that working hard doesn't get you anywhere and being lazy and s-t-u-p-i-d gets you just as much in life as being smart.

Is that really what we want our children to learn from school? Why learn at all? It doesn't get you anywhere.

Can't we teach responsibility and the work-reward relationship? How will their love relationships work if they have high expectations and low work ethics? How can they hold a job? How can they raise children? How can they prepare for their retirement? How can they think on their own?

Competition has to happen. There will be some losers and the survivors are the ultimate winners. This idiotic social experiment gave us generations of brat liberals who want to be treated as if they are smart (like in school) and governmental social weenies who don't have the heart (or the balls) to tell them that they are just too dumb to be smart.

Look out gene pool, there are liberals on the shore. They can't swim, but are planning to jump in anyway. They expect to get saved when they get into trouble. Prepare to shuffle the floaters off to the shallow waters.

Another example of liberal idiocy and "have pity on the s-t-u-p-i-d" type of thinking, includes the changes they've pushed through (with help from their friendly judges in the courts) on tort laws. These laws help protect you and me, and everyone else, from dangerous designs and poorly manufactured products. They provide a legal opportunity for a "victim" to be paid for damages from injuries caused by the product.

The changes the liberals made in these laws have made a mockery of them. All you have to do, to get millions in damages, is to spill hot coffee on yourself while driving. YOU spill it on YOURSELF and THEY have to pay? How s-t-u-p-i-d is that? It happened before and it will happen again.

Remember the case where a man injured himself when he picked up the running mower in his hands and trimmed his hedges with it? In the process, he trimmed some of himself as well and couldn't face his own responsibility. He sued the mower maker and won damages for his injuries. One conclusion of the courts was that there were insufficient safety devices on the mower to prevent this guy from getting hurt, just in case he was to pick up the running mower and trim his hedges.

Why do the liberals insist on protecting people from everything s-t-u-p-i-d they could do? We need only one new warning: *"This product is covered by the gene pool. Any consequences of your use of this product are yours and yours alone."*

One of the consequences we now live with is that almost anything you buy has to protect you (and the manufacturer) against your own s-t-u-p-i-d-ity! Check out the owner's manual of your car, your mower, your blender, your toaster, your vibrator, your electric shaver or your hedge trimmer. You'll find page after page after page of warnings and cautions about everything the lawyers can think up ... generally in three or four different languages.

Thank the liberals, who are here to help you, whether you want it or not, and to protect you from yourself. More precisely, they are protecting you from the dumbest people on earth by making everything idiot proof and more expensive. Let the gene pool rule. Let the s-t-u-p-i-ds mess up and die off. Let the smart ones live without carrying the burden of the gene pool's rejects.

Seatbelts in cars is another example of the liberals messing with your life and the gene pool. Why are we trying to save the people who aren't good drivers, or those who ride with them or are unlucky? Let them take their genetic consequences.

Seatbelts were brought into law by our liberal brethren, supposedly to keep the driver behind the wheel in an accident after the initial impact, so they could steer away from hitting something else. This is still the official reason on the government's books for starting the seatbelts craze.

It's a pretty silly concept (excuse) on the face of it. Once you get hit in an accident, who has the wits to do anything other than crap in their pants and hold on?

Also, why do we have seatbelts (and now shoulder harnesses and air bags) for every single passenger? Are they going to jump into the driver's seat in an accident and steer out of trouble for the driver? Nope!

This is just more of the liberals protecting those who don't ask for it and don't want it. It's their mission in life to stick their noses in the lives of others and tell them how to live! Like it or not, they're everywhere and sticking their noses in your life.

Other examples for your consideration

Liberals keep harping away at achieving religious sterility in anything supported by the government. Schools, libraries, court houses, national parks, even some cemeteries! Somehow the concept of not establishing a government religion evolved into a totally religiously-sterile world. Should we thus extend this to jails, the military, our money, Congress, the presidential oath of office, the Declaration of Independence, and the Constitution?

We now have a society fearful of saying anything that might offend someone. This is because the liberals taught us, in their government schools, that children should not have fear and should never have their tender little feelings hurt. These kids grew up and complained about every little thing that offended their itty-bitty, tender feelings.

"Don't look at me like that!" was common. So now we have a *legal definition* of just how long looking at someone is before it is "staring" (15 seconds).

"I don't like that calendar." translated into cute puppies and mountain scenes, replacing the husky guys and bodacious babes in calendars of old.

We live in constant fear of saying the wrong word that could possibly, maybe accidently, be overheard by some super-sensitive idiot who can't mind their own damn business. Enough already! If you don't like what is said, forget it and consider the source. Grow up already.

Try this saying to help you: "Ignore the ignorant".

We have societies all around the world, nurtured and fed by liberals, in which the predominant, and most accurate, descriptor would be – victim mentality. If you are offended, you are the victim. If you steal and go to jail, it is not your fault, you are the victim. If you didn't get the job you wanted, you were victimized. If you were fired, you were victimized. If you are hungry, you are a victim of the government.

The liberals have taught this concept to everyone they could get to listen. It sounds so good to so many people. "Nothing is your fault." "You are the victim." "Others are oppressing you and doing you wrong." "Rise up and demand what is rightfully yours!"

We need to stop coddling the little cry babies.

Liberals gave us a new definition of sex, during the Bill

Clinton years, that's still causing trouble for parents of teens. Thanks to the word-splitting defiance of Mr. Clinton, tens of millions of teens and adults now believe that oral sex is not sex.

First of all – think about this – it's called oral SEX, because it IS sex. It's only "not sex" when someone doesn't want to get caught doing something wrong, like having sex when and where they shouldn't.

Along the same line, liberals have given us countless examples of getting caught doing the belly-to-belly with the wrong person and trying to play word games to get out of it. Apparently, according to the examples of liberals, if you don't get caught, or if it isn't proven in court, it didn't happen.

Many a young man has been horse-whipped, or shot or forced into a marriage for doing the same things our liberal friends hold so dear. Were they as innocent as Mr. Clinton claimed to be? Can they plead that it wasn't really sex? Explain it to her father.

One last item, which recurs consistently in liberal thinking, projects, plans, ideas, problems, words, and actions when things don't go as they want. Perhaps you've heard something like it from a child. "My intentions were good."

Another escape ploy when things don't turn out right, or they get caught doing something wrong or they hurt someone. They didn't "intend" to cause harm.

Seems to me that this excuse wears out for the rest of us somewhere in the 6 to 9 age group. About this age, we start being held to increasing levels of responsibility for our actions. People, especially mom and dad, stop cutting us slack for bad actions and good intentions. We can't survive on good intentions and bad performance.

If the liberals were at the Alamo, they would have

negotiated a fire-free zone with General Santa Anna, then sat down to smoke some good Mexican grass and munch on chocolate chip cookies to discuss the blueness of the sky. Then, they would've declared the Alamo a religious site, where there should be no fighting, and left the rest of Texas to Santa Anna.

The preceding list is long, I know. Liberals have provided so many good examples of how dangerous they are to the gene pool. I shortened if up over and over to get to a few good examples that make the point. A fair review of these examples would easily lead a reasonable person to not want people like this in the neighborhood, the schools or influencing their children.

We consistently do all the wrong things in dealing with liberals. We try to ignore them, which just makes them kick, and cry, and scream and act out all the more.

We give them a little power and they steal more and force their ideas on the rest of us.

We let them have the lead and they fight among themselves, resulting in worse versions of their ideas forced on us.

We try to put them into places where they can't do much harm and they screw that up worse than we can imagine.

We keep doing all the wrong things with them.

The liberals represent the largest portion of humanity in the gene pool. They're also the biggest threat to its very existence. Liberals are an anathema to the gene pool. The gene pool was created to develop and perpetuate intelligent life. Liberals pollute it to its deepest parts and at all points along its shore. They must be eradicated from the gene pool.

I cannot think of any easy way out of this. Forced retraining camps, like those used in China and North Korea, are effective only on a small scale. Their effectiveness also has to be questioned. If they really worked, those inmates would be seen returning to the regular world as "right-thinking" contributing citizens. We haven't seen that happen, so we have to assume that the retraining isn't going according to plan.

Anyway, our problem is world-wide and massive. Such camps won't work on that scale.

We could mark them with a big red "L" on their foreheads. That would at least give others fair warning of what they are dealing with when meeting them.

We could ban them from public office so they, at least, couldn't continue to do as much harm as they do in a position of power.

Sterilizing them is not a bad idea, but there are so many of them that it would take forever and cost more than a NASA trip to the moon.

We could send them to Antarctica with the s-t-u-p-i-ds and politicians.

The gene pool has the real answer. God saw to that when he created it. Intelligent life cannot survive with more than a small smattering of liberals and these should be limited to a few caring mothers, so they can care for small kids. But, that's not where we've ended up. Across the world, the liberals have single handedly softened up the gene pool to the point where even God doesn't recognize it.

No, we have to get back to the methods that the gene pool gave us that worked. If you don't earn your way, you die off. No bad on anyone's part. It's just life and the gene pool. No more handouts and no government giveaways. If you don't help yourself, no one else will either.

If we don't want to do that, then we have to just dump them in the ocean and feed the sharks and whales and tuna fish. At least they can contribute to the environment this way and help reduce their carbon footprint.

The gene pool is a harsh hole filled with water and crap. The liberals like it that way. But, they don't remember the dinosaurs.

The Conservatives

We've made great progress, so far, cleaning up the gene pool. I'm sure those of you left are gloating at your success and survival in the gene pool clean-up. It's always easy to see the wrongness in others. Easy to see how *they* are causing all sorts of trouble. It's easier still to find ways to get rid of *them*, the unwanted. History is full of examples where this has been done. These include purges, holocausts, killing fields, ethnic cleansings, wars, and hanging chads.

Whatever you call them, they're the same thing. Unbidden power applied to the unwanted and undesirable in a society. It should be easy, by now, for you to apply these thoughts and historical examples to liberals and the rest of the gene pool undesirables.

Hold off on your enthusiasm for a bit, however. Let's examine the situation just a little further, before you set about cleansing the gene pool all on your own.

You might have missed it up till now, but it's worth pointing out in case you did. The gene pool operates differently for humans than it does for all other animals. As God was progressing through his curriculum to create intelligent life, the animals and their societies became increasingly complex. Of course, this is what one would expect as one moves through a university program – things get harder and more complex as you progress.

God made it through the one-cell animals, the multi-cell ones, those who propagate on their own and those who need another of their species to create more of themselves. Animals that swim, those that breathe air, ones that fly. Then, on to warm-blooded animals with complex heat management systems requiring ever more complex brains and programming.

Walking upright was a separate two-term class of its own because of the complexity involved. Walking upright includes balance, sensing and movement in three dimensions, body and muscle movement designed for upright motions and strengths, and brain processing upgrades to manage all these things at the same time.

Walking and running are so complex, to program and achieve these took up 35% of the class time, by themselves.

Upright animals also had to be able to learn new skills, like new hunting methods, and running, and lightning avoidance (because they were now higher). These, in turn, required new, specialized programming and brain capacity increases.

Upright animals didn't have the same natural weapons of other non-bipedal animals. What kind of weapons? Just the usual – things like claws, long sharp teeth, great eyesight, great hearing, extra sensitive smell, fast running, aggressive attitude, flying, large bodies, thick leathery skin, poison, stink spray, night vision, hole digging, camouflage, or the ability to change skin colors and patterns. Certainly, other animals had the advantage over the bipeds.

Because God recognized these disadvantages, bipeds had to be able to develop, learn, and communicate new skills, such as: hunting, herd management, housing, what plants to eat and which ones to give to your brother, what to do in the water, tree navigation, using hands to feed themselves, and more.

He wanted these new animals to be the beginning of a totally new type of life form. Bipeds were to be the foundation for his final thesis before graduation. To achieve this, he had to build in additional survival and learning abilities to ensure that the bipeds survived, above all the other animals. Nothing could be allowed to ruin his thesis project.

God also knew that the gene pool and its rules had to remain at the core of the life systems he created. This is the only experimental control he really had for everything he created. Life forms came and went. They evolved and died off. They flourished and changed. Some were dependant on others for survival, like the pilot fish and the shark or the gazelle and the lion. Some were content to live together in peace, like sparrows and crows. Others were interdependent, like honey bees and flowers.

The biped animals, however, were a different matter. To resolve this issue, God decided to accept their differences and to make allowances for them in their own special gene pool. He modified some of the gene pool rules slightly and relaxed the parameters of others to allow bipeds to survive when others might not.

He had to accept different behaviors in bipeds as they evolved. Societies of bipeds developed and learned how to survive (or not). The complexities of all the new movements, skills and thinking created increasingly complex evolutions of the bipeds.

It's a fact of life that, as things get more and more complex, there are increasing opportunities for mistakes and for the occasional "unintended consequences". God's bipeds are not immune from such situations. Mistakes happened – the first kangaroo without the pouch, early humanoids with no fur and the ostrich. One of the most serious issues, actually an unintended consequence of good intentions, was the development of a strong sense of self that evolved into what we call ego and pride.

Ego and pride were okay early on. It's obvious that God was playing with these characteristics in the E-den when he gave those two everything they needed, except one tiny item – his lunch. Would they be satisfied with it all? Would they succumb to their evolved programming? Would their egos drive them to disregard God's admonition and seek out that which was denied them? Unfortunately, according to God's lab notes, they acted as predicted. They failed.

As we've evolved, we developed bigger egos and pride. We created reasons to celebrate them and activities to implement them. Societies across the world, and throughout history, have celebrated events where they prove how special they are, more special than others.

They've also sought out ways to get rid of others who threaten their specialness. Tribal raids to kill the men and grab some women, is an old example of this ego run amuck. Wars over religion are another form, as are gay bashing and picking on the "different" kid in junior high school.

For some reason, only humans exhibited these characteristics and only human development took it to the extremes we read about in the history books. It's a ponderment that has frustrated God and humans alike. God, being a lot smarter than we humans, finally gave in to the nature of the beast.

Of course, we responded as predicted and with fervor. We acted, and continue to act, like the immature little galactic human brats we are. "My father can beat up your father!" was morphed into "My God is better than your God!" and "I can do what I want because MY God is more powerful than your God." and "I must kill you and take over your territory to save you from your insufficient God."

More recently, this has further evolved into "My God is the only right God and if you don't believe as I do, I must kill you." Well, progress is not always positive. There are bound to be some setbacks.

God made adjustments to the gene pool to accommodate the human propensity for killing others for no really good reason, like survival. Survival was the basis and foundation of the gene pool rules. Survival is not the reason why humans kill each other and other animals. At least, not since the lunch incident in the garden. Unintended consequence or not, we are a special case requiring special rules.

Why go through this long diatribe about bipeds and egos? What's this have to do with the gene pool and our future? What does it have to do with you? When will we talk about the damned conservatives? See how impatient you are. Settle your ego a moment and we'll get right to them.

As I just demonstrated, we all have egos, thus answering question one. We all have times when our egos get us in trouble or cause pain to someone else. It's part of our nature. It's how we are wired. Therefore, it's part of how we will, or will not, survive. Because of these and many other factors, it's also part of the gene pool to which we belong. Our ego is integral to our lives, our actions and our survival.

Without egos, humans are no different than complex biped animals. Sadly, this comes with a few negative side effects, as we've discussed several times throughout this book. It also sets us apart. While individual humans are all a bit different, we are also all somewhat alike. And we're very different from all the other animal and plant life forms on this planet, this little laboratory at Universe U.

I think I answered the second questions sufficiently. If you don't agree, go back a few paragraphs and re-read the material and pay attention this time.

The third question is a good one. Thanks to whoever asked.

Ego has to do with you because you're part of the rest of us. You've proven this by reading this far and cheering for the bad guys to get voted off the planet. Thank you for voting.

Now we can talk about the conservatives.

Conservatives are the second most populous group of human gene pool undesirables on the planet. Their percentage of the population changes over time in relation to the percentage of liberals in the population. It is a symbiotic relationship, similar to two pendulums swinging back and forth trying to balance each other, but each always out of sync with the other.

Conservatives develop as the reactionary Ying to the liberal Yang, striving for balance.

Conservatives are often seen as the rocks of civilizations. This is, indeed, an accurate representation, as they are the rocks. They are bedrocks and the stones upon which are built the foundations of societies and great civilizations. Unfortunately, this is also their downfall.

One of the strongest characteristics of conservatives is that they are rooted in the past. They strongly resist change, just for change's sake. They can't quite get a grip on the notion of the gene pool or our evolutionary past, regardless of the evidence staring them in the face every day.

But they, God bless them, help us maintain social stability, especially in time of turmoil. The more turmoil societies experience, the more conservatives develop to counter the change.

Now, why would the gene pool allow this to happen? As I said, it's a matter of checks and balances. The more liberals, and other genetic malcontents, stir up trouble and try to change things, the more conservatives blossom, keeping things in balance and preventing change from happening too fast.

This is one of the reasons it took humans so long to go

from the cave to the tent. Consider this exchange captured on a cave wall.

A young one has seen things while hunting that fascinate him. Things that are very different from what he knows from his life as a cave dweller. He approaches one of the elders to talk about them.

"Why change?" asked the big conservative leader, Rufus. "We have a big strong cave here. No water leaks. It is strong in storms. It keeps us safe from animals. It is easy to defend from the others across the valley."

"But, we've been in this same old, crummy cave for years now. We need a change. Maybe some of us want separate caves of our own." exclaimed the young liberal, eager to try something new.

"What is so wrong with this cave? If you'd help clean it up a little, it wouldn't be so dusty. It is strong and we can all keep a watch on each other for safety." retorted Rufus.

"But, the others across the valley have a new cave. They have one they can move. Their families each have their own cave. And look at them. They are safe. They are happy. Their women are strong and bear good, strong children."

"Ah-ha!" exclaimed Rufus. "You want this change because the others have it. Would you do everything they do? Would you eat the little red berries on the death bush if they did?"

"No, of course I wouldn't eat that berry, no matter who else ate it." answered the eager one. "But, they have fresh air and can move to where there is food. They don't have to carry food far to a cave that will not move. They can be near water. And when their bathroom is filled and smells, they move on. They don't have to get in it and clean it out. And their women are strong and healthy."

"Carrying fresh meat is good exercise and builds strong

muscles. It also helps you remember the way back to the cave. Do you remember how you keep getting lost, even though you've been here all your life? How would you ever find your way home from hunting if the cave was moved? You'd be lost forever." Rufus said.

"I can understand the bathroom issue." Rufus continued "That is a problem for us. But we are a strong and proud tribe and it never hurt your father, or his father, to clean out the bathroom when it was their turn."

"Yes, but ..." tried the liberal again "their women are strong and healthy. And they know how to carry fire. And they can make a cave from animal skins."

"Animal skins! Boulder crapola!" Rufus cried. "You want to live in animal skins? Are you crazy, like old Burt? Will animal skins protect you from the bear? Or from the falling trees? Or block the winds? Or protect you in the snows? Of course not! Impossible!"

"And who needs to carry fire? We don't. We just keep it going, like we have since before you were born. If you carry it, you'll get burned. Or you might lose your way and take it somewhere else. Or you may get rained on and have it put out. Where would you be then? Huh? Trust me – no good can ever come from carrying fire. I'm telling you. Stay away from such foolishness."

"But, they don't lose the fire. And only one bear has gotten into their caves. And their women are strong and healthy." responded the little lib, running out of ideas.

"Ah, now you bring up something of interest that we should think about. Their women." said the old conservative, thoughtfully. "Now we know that their caves are weak and their women strong. Our women are old and covered in that black smoke from the fire. Perhaps it is time that we go and get us some new women. Yes, tomorrow we go and get new women."

"I'm glad we had this chat." said stay-the-course Rufus to the trouble-making young liberal. "We should do this less often."

This old story from long ago just illustrates the point – you can't refute Rufus.

And so it has been from the beginning of time. Whether it's the coming ice age that indicates the tribe should think about moving to warmer places; or the rising creek that never, ever floods; or the herds of food that moved away from the happy hunting grounds. Conservatives have consistently missed the clues and hints and held back the rate of progress from day one.

If conservatives were to build a boat, they would have their anchor full out all the time, just in case an unfriendly wind or tide came upon them. Noah was a conservative, which would explain why God's instructions for the Ark didn't include an anchor. He was certainly focused and sure of his mission. I can only imagine the ridicule and abuse he took from his friends and neighbors, let alone his in-laws.

One thing you can count on about conservatives is – their predictability. This is because they live in a world of the past where they don't have to worry about the future. Why? Because, the future is supposed to be just like the past! Simple and straight forward! No "What-ifs" or "Maybe's". What was will always be. No worries. Amen.

No worries, that is, until they run smack into reality and it conflicts with the past. Then, they can be counted on to go into their primary defense mechanism. They keep nitpicking back at whomever brought the bad news and wants to make a change. They keep throwing back reasons things won't work;

because of this or that.

Just as liberals keep crying like spoiled brats till you give them what they want, just to shut them up, conservatives keep tossing back excuses why something won't work till you give up. Why something is just not possible. Why this just isn't the right time. They tried that years back and it didn't work then and it won't work now.

Then, their challenge changes to … "What is so wrong with the way things are?"

After this, they challenge and nitpick every little example you provide about what is wrong with the way things are.

Finally, they throw in how it was good enough for Rufus, your Aunt Sally and others. Just like our caveman friends, they keep resisting until you finally give up and quit.

The tactics of the conservatives to prevent change are just as energetic and intense as those used by the liberals to create change. They are also just as maddeningly resistant as liberals to rational people trying to make a point that doesn't agree with them.

Reviews of news reports covering the past 53 years shows that conservatives are responsible for 44% of the "person gone crazy" killings. You do the math and you connect the dots.

One question we keep running into regarding conservatives is "Are they really all that dangerous? After all, they're so nice and so caring." Simply put – yes.

They are disarming in their demeanor which lulls people into believing that they really care. In fact, the only thing conservatives really care about is keeping things the way they are and keeping you from changing that. Yes, they are caring, as long as you don't try to change anything.

Conservatives are not a small group. In years of research and studies of people and societies, it's been documented that conservatives represent about 22 to 24% of the world's population. This is the second largest group, by percentage, in the gene pool. (Remember that the liberal group is about one third larger than the conservative group.)

To be sure, the conservatives are a formidable, extremist group that unreasonably impacts the gene pool and prevents reasonable genetic evolutionary progress. They certainly have a role in the gene pool, but it should not be this large and not this extreme.

How extreme are we talking about? Let's review some examples of conservative extremes.

They can't change when change is indicated – sometimes change is indicated and people just miss the message and the hints. I'm sure you've known someone like that, especially in your teen years. They just can't get with what's going on in the world. They have stories of the past, but haven't done anything new in 30 years.

They always go on vacation at the same time to the same place. They have traditions for holidays that go back to the Pilgrims.

If Catholic, they yearn for the good old days when mass was held in Latin.

They haven't changed their hair-style in 25 years. They still believe that Columbus discovered America and that children should be seen and not heard.

They know only one way to get to work, to the store and to Aunt Mabel's house.

They're still waiting for Eisenhower to make a comeback.

They are inflexible – this kind of goes with the first item. They can't help it. To them, progress is painting the living room another shade of beige. The alarm clock has been set for the same time for 28 years. Dinner is always at the same time.

When they eat, they always eat each of their foods on their plate separately and completely before moving on to the next food on the plate.

Being flexible, to them, means *not* having meatloaf on Thursday night or going to bed *before* the designated bedtime. They can always be counted on to do what they've always done, but sometimes they're as boring as watching beige paint dry.

Because they're stuck in the past and because they don't change fast, conservatives tend to have the morals of the 1700s (or maybe the early 1800s for real progressive ones). Judging from some of the crimes they commit, and stories we learn about them after the fact, many conservatives obviously have another side to them. A dark side that wishes they could do the things they only dream about.

It's like they have a little liberal inside of them fighting to get out and do what others do. Of course, this emotional turmoil just adds to the disaster that awaits any little liberals who escape conservative captivity.

Conservatives are big on religion. Big God followers, they are. Funny thing about Godly conservatives is that each and every one of them knows, for certain, that *their* particular form of religious worship is THE correct method, form, procedure, dress code and path to heavenly salvation. No doubts. No questions.

It's interesting that so many of these same conservatives are the very ones who are ruining the gene pool. They can't accept evolution, even though their God invented it and it's the basis of how they got here themselves. Go figure.

Lastly – as you may have already noticed, conservatives, like their liberal brethren, are driven by their genetically evolved and misguided makeup. They have to tell others what to do and how to live.

- You have the wrong God. You must have MY God.
- You can't say *those* words. To gain salvation you must say *these* words.
- You *must* believe this. You *can't* believe that.
- You are going to hell unless you do as I say and only as I say.
- You must love all people. You can't love THAT kind of person.
- You must procreate and do your heavenly duty.
- You can't have sex until marriage.
- You can't have THAT kind of sex – ever.
- You can't have a child out of wedlock.
- You can't have an abortion.
- You shall not kill. War is not killing. God's wars are holy.
- All life is precious. The death penalty is valid.
- You need to dress this way or that way.
- You can't have a drink, unless it's in church.
- You *must* read these books. You *can't* read those books.
- You can't watch *these* shows. We can't broadcast *those* shows.

The ability to change when change is indicated is a trait cherished by the gene pool. To keeps the pool alive, and thriving, and growing and adapting. It's obvious that the conservatives do not fit this paradigm. We can tolerate a few conservatives – but we are waaaayyy overloaded now and it needs to be corrected.

One aspect of fixing this situation is to rid the gene pool of the liberals. The gene pool will create fewer conservatives to counter them. Fewer liberals – fewer conservatives – the gene pool wins both ways.

The issues and problems of having the conservatives in the gene pool are obvious to someone in a coma. The rest of us see the problems, too. We're primed and ready to fix it. We just have to change a couple of things.

Unfortunately, a few minor tweaks here and there will not be sufficient, nor will it be quick enough. More drastic measures are needed and are needed now.

One measure that will have an immediate and dramatic impact on conservatives is fairly simple. All governments around the world need to start taxing church assets. Tax their income, bank accounts, inheritances, property, buildings, cars, stock portfolios, statues, etc. This includes no more tax deductions for church donations.

If we can eliminate, or reduce, the money motive, a large number of so-called conservatives will show their true colors and abandon the cash cow.

Another tactic we need to adopt is to make them live as they profess. To actually live in accordance with the rules of their claimed religion. Then, we make those rules into criminal laws and hold their feet to the legal fire. Live as you preach or go to jail!

Get caught coveting – 30 days in the clinker. Take the Lord's name in vain and its 3 days and a $500 fine.

Adultery? That has to be a big one because it is so very popular among conservatives. For adultery, the punishment is a $20,000 fine, 90 days in jail plus 10 days in a seedy motel room locked up with the adulterous partner. No sex allowed, of course. You just have to stay cooped up in a single motel room for 10 days.

If that doesn't cure you, the next offense will be that much harsher. For example, spending 10 days in the motel room with your adulterous partner AND your spouse. It might even make interesting entertainment for reality television.

Walk the talk, or pay up or give up extreme conservatism.

No matter how we solve this problem, and it has to be sooner rather than later, it has to be decisive. The gene pool deserves better than we've given it and the conservative element of the pollution has to go. Natural evolution must be returned to the gene pool and those holding it back must be filtered out and beached.

Summary

That about does it. If we follow all the guidelines outlined in this chapter, we can finally clean up the gene pool. I know it was long, tough slogging to get through all the issues. After all, it is a messy gene pool and it requires a LOT of cleansing!

Some measures are harsh, but all of them are effective and needed, especially for those of us *not* included in any of those groups. It sure makes life better and happier for us, right?

Humans have thoroughly messed up God's gene pool. It is up to US to make it right, again. If we don't take these measures and clean things up, God will … with the bleach. Remember the dinosaurs!

Chapter 13 – The Gene Pool's Future

Now we know just how messed up the gene pool of today is. We also know what specific actions are needed to clean it up. It may take some time to accomplish, but it IS worthwhile. The really good news is that the gene pool is salvageable. Good news indeed, especially for those of us not caught up in the cleaning process.

Let's review the makeup of all the trash and rubbish that clogged up the gene pool. We owe it to ourselves to briefly examine just how polluted it was and rejoice in the good job we've done cleaning it up.

What was the make-up of God's gene pool after we screwed it up? What did it devolved into? Let's look at the numbers from the previous chapter:

- Low hanging fruit: 7 – 11%
- Uglies: 6 – 9%
- Bad parents: 7 – 10%
- The weak and wimps: 3 – 5%
- Politicians: 2 – 3%
- Predators: 8 – 11%

- S-t-u-p-i-ds: 8 – 14%
- Liberals: 30 – 35%
- Conservatives: 22 – 24%

Obviously, two groups dominate the gene pool. But, it is also overwhelmed by a variety of lesser ash and trash groups who screw up the entire operation. Together, they've totally destroyed the gene pool. They're the ones who have to be eliminated, as I've described, and for the reasons I explained, ad nauseam.

There is one tiny bright point in the data, however. When all the data is analyzed, there is one group missing – the Worthy Ones. The Worthy Ones are the salvation for the gene pool, for humanity and for God's grade.

Unfortunately, however, the Worthy Ones are a veeerry small group, representing only 0.001% of the population! That's all that's left of the gene pool once we clean it up! Did you realize we were THAT screwed up? I did.

This demonstrates just how badly we've messed up a good thing and how far God let us take things off course. It should also be a warning about just how close we are to joining the dinosaurs!

We've overwhelmed the gene pool. We've ruined God's lab experiment. We've ruined his chances of getting an "A". We're on the verge of really pissing God off and getting the old lab heave-ho, a-la the dinosaurs.

If these facts don't get your attention and spur you into immediate action, then I know two or three categories of un-desirables you fit into. It's time for action! Lead, follow – or get out of the gene pool!

Looking again at the numbers, it doesn't take a math ge-nius, or a fourth grader for that matter, to see that things are pretty dire. When we're done cleaning out the gene pool, we've pretty much emptied the damn thing. We're scraping bottom!

But, we'll have accomplished what God wanted – we saved the gene pool! We cleaned out the trash and got the gene pool down to the pure few who can bring it back to its full, former glory! The special few who can save the gene pool.

I wondered, as you might, just who are these genetically chosen few? Who are these survivors worthy of remaining in the gene pool with me? Who are these few who will resurrect it in the manner, and to the standards, God intended when he created it?

I wanted to identify and meet these other individuals who join me as the only hope for the future of mankind and God's graduation. Who are these genetically anointed "Worthy Ones"? Good question, I thought.

After including myself, naturally, I set out to find them, the "Worthy Ones". In the process, I wondered about how they could be identified when I found them. Do I use DNA? Do I look for the mark of God on them? What would the mark of God look like?

Should I look in churches? In scholastic institutions? In homeless shelters? In the leper colonies? In hospitals? I tried to take a logical approach to this dilemma, but I had to act fast – the gene pool is in critically fragile condition.

To solve this problem, I established a huge scientific expedition of one to travel the world, virtually, and find the rest of the "Worthy Ones". I wanted to know their secrets and to find out how I, with their help, was going to rejuvenate the gene pool. After we finish draining it, that is.

The investigation started by identifying the ones we knew are not welcome or wanted in the gene pool and those who are destructive to it (refer to the previous chapter). I applied the information and observations gained in my research to identify them and to eliminate them from consideration.

It should be obvious that, after eliminating all the dead-wood, it didn't leave a lot of options for further investigation. It isn't exactly what fighter pilots would call a "target rich environment".

I searched high. I searched low. I searched for months taking up tens of hours in labor and several dollars in research costs. I created page upon page of documentation.

But I did it! I found the "Worthy Ones"!

Rather I found the "Worthy ONE"!

I was shocked! I was saddened! I was also left out!

As it turns out, the gene pool is damaged far, far beyond the most pessimistic expectations. It is in far worse shape than any worst-case scientific models predicted. The gene pool is on the verge of drying up and dying. It sits one car accident away from annihilation. Why do I say this?

The "Worthy Ones" is ONLY ONE!

There is only ONE "Worthy One"!

Should I say it again – **THERE IS ONLY ONE "WORTHY ONE"!**

The "Worthy One" turns out to be a nice enough young, single fellow living alone in East Freehold, New Jersey, USA! Of all the people in the world, and all the research, this one man is the only hope for humanity, for the gene pool and for God's grade!

He will not let me use his full name, or any other identifying information, for obvious reasons. His first name is Levi.

Levi is the only human on the planet who has the right genes for the survival of the gene pool. He is the only one who has – **THE LEVI GENES!**

One might wonder, how can the gene pool regenerate

itself with only one man in it? Don't worry, I'm on the case. Obviously, Levi cannot allow his genes to get mixed up with anyone else's, otherwise, the entire gene pool is history and God flunks.

I'm keeping close tabs on Levi to see if he develops any mutations towards self-impregnation and self-regeneration. Some animals actually have this ability when their own gene pool is skewed off track. Some even change sexes and make themselves pregnant and have their own babies. We'll just have to wait and see if Levi starts to exhibit any "changes" in this direction.

Maybe cloning will be the answer. Unfortunately, that will take longer to get perfect than Levi has left to live, won't it? We could freeze him and his sperm until cloning is perfected and then create a female version of Levi – call her Levette – and impregnate her with herself, or himself, or however that works.

No matter which way this turns out, I'm on it and will keep the world informed of new developments in the story of **THE LEVI GENES** – God's only hope for the gene pool.

Chapter 14 – Levi – The Beginning

I've kept in touch with Levi since I discovered him. He's taking the status as the gene pool's last hope very seriously. Since the original research, Levi moved to be closer to a large city and has re-discovered the pleasures of masturbation. He collects and stores his sperm in case it's needed later. He donated a little of it for scientific study, but prohibited any use for cloning.

He's cooperating with several top international scientific genetic institutes, hoping to add to the better understanding of the gene pool. He's also helping new DNA searches, in hopes of finding someone else with the genes close to The Levi Genes, preferable a female. So far, no such luck.

Levi is also on anti-depressants as he deals with his new reality – humanity's only genetic hope. Ladies no longer hold any interest for him because there is no hope or future in it. No matter who he would mate with, she would not only be genetically inferior, but, by definition, she'd be a gene pool reject. Any resulting children would also be gene pool rejects. Just the opposite of what Levi, and Levi alone, represents.

Sometimes, Levi walks around like a man with a sad secret

that he can't tell anyone, which is exactly the situation he's in. He also has bouts of superiority, knowing he is the only human good enough for the gene pool. Then, he swings into depression from the very same thought. Will he be the salvation of mankind or the end of it?

He's alone in the midst of billions of people with no hope for help or change, or for a better solution. And no way to escape. The human race is doomed and he can't fix it, alone; yet he is the only one who *can* save it. Talk about being between a rock and a hard place!

Being humanity's salvation was definitely *not* in his list of future occupations when he talked with the high school guidance counselor.

Levi has also been studying ancient societies and religions for some clues from the past to help him deal with the situation. He thought he'd rediscovered God for a while, but got disillusioned when he didn't get any answers to his questions. He decided that this gene pool thing can't really be from God. How would God let things get so screwed up?

He's also studied animal genetics and their separate gene pool for clues and insight. This has proven to be more depressing, because the animal gene pool is much more severe and much less forgiving than the human gene pool. Not even cross-species genetic reproduction is viable.

Levi can't have a woman and he can't have anything else either. He's destined to remain alone in a world full of people with no hope for children. The Levi lineage is over! The human lineage is over!

As you can tell, Levi is not doing all that well. He, and he alone, represents the best of all humanity and, at the same time, the end of its future. He's struggling with being the only one with – **THE LEVI GENES**.

Acknowledgment

Writing *The Levi Genes* was an interesting trip down the genetic memory lane, researching and reviewing all the wonderful examples of gene pool successes and failures. History is replete with wondrous examples of God's toils in this planetary Petri dish. The variety of God's experiments are clearly seen in a brief view through a microscope at normal pond water, a visit to any zoo, or a trip to any large mall. Without these, and many other, examples of genetic mistakes and mischief, *The Levi Genes* would not have been possible.

Thank you, God, for your variety in your imagination, your tolerance and patience, and the many great stories you continue to give us.

I want to thank Levi for his inspiration, his wonderful genes, and for putting up with what happens to him in the sequel, *The Mark of Levi*.

I would like also thank my dear mother for her genetic hand-me-downs and for not helping in writing *The Levi Genes*. With her help, this book, and its sequels, would not have been possible.

Finally, my editor insisted that I thank her for finding my mistakes and for making *The Levi Genes* a better book. (Does that make you happy, Irene? Did it work?)

The Mark Of Levi

The Mark of Levi picks up where *The Levi Genes* left off.

In the first book of the Levi Trilogy, we discovered just how badly humans have messed up God's gene pool, starting from day one. We also learned about who the worst gene pool offenders are and how to get rid of them. While we were doing all this, we also discovered that the *only* person on earth who had the genes necessary to survive the gene pool is Levi. He is the only one with *The Levi Genes*.

Levi is alone, despondent and scared. He has discovered that he is the only human on earth who has The Levi Genes, the genes needed to allow God to replenish the gene pool. The pressure of this reality causes great struggles in Levi. He struggles to hold a job. He struggles to sleep. He struggles with the impending end of his lineage. He struggles with the expected bleaching of earth. He struggles with his sanity.

In a mysterious disappearance, Levi finds himself face to face with God at Universe U. God is under tremendous pressure as the end of his school term nears.

He has to produce self-adapting intelligent life in his lab and things have not worked out well at all. He can't start over – he has no time for that. He can't just use the humans on earth – the gene pool is horribly ruined leaving him no good breeding stock. Levi is his last and only hope.

The conundrum God faces is simple, to a Universe U grad student. But, in the short time available to God, it is a difficult assignment. To us – it is impossible. How does God re-create intelligent human life on earth with only one man to work with?

He tried that before with Alpha and Beta in the E-den. We all know how that worked out. He can't afford to try that borrowed-rib trick again.

No, this time, God is smarter and more experienced. He has some new plans and he isn't going to make the same mistakes again. This time, God is going to make humans perfect. (We've heard that one before too, haven't we?)

As God puts his plans to work, Levi finds himself in a strange new place. Levi learns about God first hand as no other human ever has. He discovers the full powers, and weaknesses, of God. He also discovers God's plan to regenerate the human gene pool on earth, using only Levi as the starting point. After he gives it a good bleaching job, that is. Always remember the dinosaurs!

Levi finds that he is the center of this plan. At first, he isn't very confident in this Universe U student. After some time, Levi realizes the dilemma God is in. He also begins to understand the predicament the earth, its inhabitants and the gene pool are facing. The reality isn't pretty. The plan to salvation isn't easy. Levi isn't sure how he can survive it all, let alone take any pride in it.

As the plan is put in motion, Levi becomes the center of earth's salvation and resurrection. He is the genetic cornerstone for the new gene pool and all who follow him. He is the beginning of the future of mankind, with the help of God and *The Mark of Levi*.

About The Author

O.E. Vey is an observer of life and visionary who has been writing for many years, mostly for his day job. For fun, he is writing a list of things he doesn't know and writes grocery lists. *The Levi Genes* is his first novel, to be followed soon by its sequels; *The Mark of Levi* and *The Return of Levi*.

Always fascinated by the free entertainment provided by his fellow humans, O.E. Vey has been collecting historical anecdotes and stories from his imagination for many years.

In The Levi Trilogy, O.E. (as he is known to his friend) focuses his engineering background and out of the box thinking to provide us with new perspectives, insights and possibilities about human life. His main goals are to make readers laugh and perhaps think, but only a little because it hurts too much.

O.E. lives with his two cats that are often seen rolling on the floor in laughter at his stories.

If you have questions or suggestions about Levi, or just need someone to listen sympathetically, you can contact O.E. at TheLeviGenes@aol.com.